Hostage

Lucas Martin wanted to stretch Bridie to the limits of her sexuality. She was not only beautiful, she was wholly sexual. The only other woman he had known who could take two men at once and enjoy the experience was a roughly spoken tavern slut.

The eagerness with which she had accepted both him and Seamus convinced Lucas that she would be a willing participant in anything he suggested. He would come back for her one day.

Hostage to Fantasy

LOUISA FRANCIS

Black Lace novels are sexual fantasies.
In real life, make sure you practise safe sex.

First published in 1998 by
Black Lace
Thames Wharf Studios,
Rainville Road, London W6 9HT

Copyright © Louisa Francis 1998

Reprinted 1998

The right of Louisa Francis to be identified as the
Author of this Work has been asserted by her in
accordance with the Copyright, Designs and Patents Act
1988

Typeset by SetSystems Ltd, Saffron Walden, Essex
Printed and bound by Mackays of Chatham PLC

ISBN 0 352 33305 7

Chapter One

*B*ridie heard the horsemen approaching just as she was lifting the cast-iron stew pot to return it to its hook over the fire. Curiosity rather than concern had her hurrying to finish what she was doing. Their farm being some ten miles from Barkers Ridge, and the township itself being little more than a pathetic gathering of poor dwellings with a handful of business establishments, visitors were rare. Anyone who came to relieve the monotony of her days was welcome indeed. Smoothing her hands down the faded homespun of her skirt, Bridie went eagerly to greet whoever it might be.

Before she was halfway across the room the door of the hut was flung open with a force which threatened to tear it from its hinges. Three men appeared in the aperture. One strode into the room, one halted just inside the door and the third stayed within the doorway, facing outward. All three carried rifles.

A combination of surprise, fear, indignation and anger accelerated Bridie's heartbeat. But Bridie was far too feisty to succumb to fear. Knuckles on her hips, arms akimbo, she glared at the intruders. With defiance in her stance and a challenge in her eyes she was every inch the wild Irishman's daughter.

'What do you think you might be doing to come barging in here without asking?' she demanded.

The tall man, who had been giving the impoverished interior of the hut a casual scrutiny which, Bridie felt certain, missed no detail, brought his gaze to her flushed face. 'Where's Flannagan?'

From the harsh, clipped way he voiced the question it was obvious that, for whatever reason the man wanted her father, it was not one of friendship. Being familiar with her father's penchant for engaging in less than honest activities, Bridie rather suspected the stranger might be after some form of retribution for a misdeed perpetrated by Flannagan. And she was beginning to have an uncomfortable suspicion as to the nature of the crime and the identity of the stranger. Her Irish blood would not, however, allow her to cower before what was plainly intended to be intimidation. Her chin went a little higher.

'And why would you be wanting to know?'

Her response brought a gleam of interest to his eyes and a lilt of amusement to his voice. 'A woman of spirit, eh? You answer my question with a question instead of telling me what I want to know.' Then his expression became harsh again, his tone indicating he would not brook opposition. 'I will ask you just one more time. Where is Flannagan?'

Bridie's gaze darted to the other two men before coming back to the one who was obviously in charge. Despite the way all three held their rifles, ready to raise and fire in a moment, she did not feel they meant her any harm. Her suspicion as to what they wanted with her father had developed into a certainty. This man was no struggling, cocky farmer. His garb was that of a wealthy landowner, his manner one of extreme arrogance. Bridie remained defiant.

'I'll not be telling you where my Pa is until you tell me who you are and what it is you are wanting with him.'

For a long moment he looked at her. In fact, he looked

her up and down, his lips curled slightly at the corners. 'I believe you know quite well the answer to both questions. Eyes of such a clear blue as yours are not very good for hiding secrets. I have been watching the thoughts go around in that pretty head.' Once again his tone changed in an instant from one of mockery to harshness. 'I am Nat Durrant and you know exactly what I want with Flannagan.'

She did that, not that she was about to admit any such thing to this cold, arrogant man. Nor did she intend to tell him her father was probably on his way back from Barkers Ridge. This determination stemmed from her resentment of the man's arrogance and the unfamiliar effect his constant appraisal was having on her. She was in no way concerned with protecting her father from whatever retribution Nat Durrant might be planning to eke from the poddy-dodging old bastard. Bridie knew Flannagan had gone too far the day he 'borrowed' the valuable stud bull to service their own ill-bred herd of cows.

'Did you have anything to do with the bull?' Nat Durrant fired the question so rapidly Bridie instinctively jerked back. He was staring so hard at her she felt compelled to lower her eyes in case they were every bit as expressive as he had declared. Suddenly she wanted him to be gone, out of the hut and off the farm.

'My Pa's not here. He's gone to town.'

'When will he be back?'

'Not till tomorrow,' Bridie lied, thinking only to make the men leave.

Only when Nat Durrant drawled, 'Is that so?' did she suspect the lie might achieve a very different result. On lifting her gaze back to the landowner's face, she realised her queer, tingling fear was not unfounded. His eyes, which were far too dark to ever betray his thoughts, were making an insulting assessment of her feminine shape. When his gaze rested on the swell of her breasts they

3

seemed to grow taut and press against the faded fabric of her blouse in a manner that was surely visible.

A lecherous smile curved the thin line of Durrant's mouth. 'I did have a particular punishment in mind for Flannagan but, since he is not here, I have thought of something far better. If Flannagan thinks he can use my prize bull to service his scrawny cows then I think it only fair I should be able to service his daughter.' While Bridie was absorbing the shock of his meaning he turned his head a fraction to address his next remark to his men. 'What do you think, boys? Would that be fair payment?'

The one standing just within the hut responded with a lascivious chortle. The other turned to leer at her with a display of broken, yellowed teeth. Bridie's stomach churned. The defiant tilt of her chin strengthened. She was not going to beg, cry or scream. She had far too much pride. When all was said and done, Nat Durrant was a fine figure of a man in the prime of life. But the notion that he might intend to allow his less than appealing companions to 'service' her as well was decidedly unpleasant. With renewed defiance she gazed directly into Nat Durrant's eyes.

'Being only a woman I cannot stop you but I'm asking you not to do it in front of your men.'

To her intense chagrin his smile only became more lascivious. 'Now that is an idea. You might find yourself enjoying an audience.'

Appalled at having put the idea into his mind and being positive she would not enjoy any such thing, Bridie clamped her lips mutinously together and glared at Durrant. His leering smile quirked into one which could have been amusement. This time when he addressed his men he did not turn his head. Instead he held Bridie's proud gaze with his own dark unfathomable one.

'All right, men. You know what you have to do. Shut the door when you go out, Jas.'

'Sure, Boss.' The way he leered at Bridie left her feeling

relieved when the door shut behind him to leave her alone with Nat Durrant.

'Undress,' he commanded.

Bridie sucked in her breath then began to slowly release the buttons of her blouse. Her hesitancy came from an uncertainty as to what was going to happen. Oh, she knew well enough why there were bulls and cows and men and women. She had seen a number of animals mating. Only she had never done any such thing herself. Nor had anyone ever explained to her what it was like between a man and a woman. Pride prevented her from disclosing these facts. Nor would wild horses drag from her the admission that for some time her curiosity over such matters had been growing ever stronger. The great problem was that she had always imagined it would be another man for whom she first undressed.

About to release the last button, her fingers were halted by disturbing noises from outside the hut. Her eyes widened in shock and with a swift movement she darted to the window to stare in horror at the spectacle of the other two men wrecking everything they possibly could.

In a blaze of fury she turned on Nat Durrant. 'You bastard. Tell them to stop.'

'No.'

The cool refusal was too much for Bridie who flew at him, beating at him with clenched fists. To her chagrin he caught her wrists to hold her off with ease.

'My men need to be kept amused. If I stop them now I will have to let them come back in here.'

It was threat enough to shock Bridie into submission. The moment she ceased to struggle, the hands which held her wrists released them to grip instead the gaping front of her blouse. In one swift action it was ripped from her body. 'Very nice,' he declared, his gaze on the firm, full breasts he had exposed.

Bridie thought it must be the coolness of the air on her naked flesh that made her breasts feel so tight and caused her nipples to rise to hard peaks.

5

'Take off the rest. I want to see you entirely naked.'

A few seconds later she was. Bridie wore no undergarments under her skirt, those articles being kept for good wear. Bold and defiant, she stood very still, allowing Nat Durrant's appraising gaze to rove over her body. For some reason she was finding it difficult to breathe and wherever his gaze paused for more than a moment her skin tingled as if from a touch. Her breasts were so tight they were aching. Then when his gaze rested at the apex of her thighs she experienced the queerest sensation in the hidden places of her sex. Even while she struggled to cope with her body's unfamiliar reactions she noted how the front of Nat Durrant's trousers had become stretched. Bridie felt an overwhelming curiosity to see what a man's organ looked like when he was ready to take a woman. Not that she knew what one looked like at any time.

'Aren't you going to undress, too?' she asked through suddenly dry lips.

Her question was ignored, his concentration remaining on her mound. 'Your hair is darker there than on your head. Almost black.'

And wet too. Bridie could feel the dampness curling the lower hairs.

'Turn around,' he commanded. 'Bend over the table.'

Bridie's eyes widened once more. In a pointed gesture she turned her head towards the curtained cubicle which contained her narrow bed. He apparently had no trouble interpreting her movement. His lips curled in derision. 'Beds are for mistresses and nights of prolonged pleasure. I merely intend to service you. Now do as you are told and bend over the table.'

There was nothing Bridie could do except obey. In that position, head pillowed on her arms, bare bottom jutting outward, Bridie experienced a heightening of the sensations that had started when he gazed so long at her mound. Then it had been almost as if he had been able to see what lay underneath. Now he would have no trouble looking upon her intimate parts because when he commanded that she spread her legs Bridie again obeyed.

The touch she felt this time was real, not imagined and not at all unpleasant. Most definitely not unpleasant. But Bridie did wonder what he thought of the wetness his fingers were encountering. She had no idea whether or not he would find it odd. The grunt he gave seemed to indicate approval. His finger ceased stroking externally to probe a little way into her.

Bridie could not prevent a small 'Oh' of surprise escaping, only the exclamation was not entirely induced by shock alone. There was a wondrous degree of pleasure as well, then an equal degree of disappointment as the finger which was doing such fascinating things moved away. There was a pause of a few moments and some movement behind her before she was touched once more. Bridie knew that this time it was the end of his cock which pressed against her soft, moist opening. He pushed in a little and she felt her sex lips open to allow him entry, then close around him, almost as if she was embracing him and welcoming him into her body. She could think of no reason to object to what he was doing.

That was until he thrust swiftly to his depth. Pain seared her body and tore a scream from her mouth. Tears sprang to her eyes and she clenched them shut, clamping her lips together at the same time. If this pain, this tearing of something inside her, was what he meant by 'servicing' her she would not give him the satisfaction of knowing how much it had hurt. No matter what else he did she would not scream again, nor cry.

He was embedded deeply, not moving and she heard him give a low, triumphant chuckle. 'Well, well. I not only service Flannagan's daughter, I take her maidenhead as well. What better revenge could I have?'

On that declaration he pulled out a little then pushed back in again. Teeth clenched against the anticipated pain, Bridie discovered it hardly hurt at all. For perhaps a half dozen times he did the same thing, slowly pulling back then pushing in. With each penetration Bridie relaxed a little more. The pain had abated to be replaced by a far more pleasurable sensation.

'What is your name?' Nat Durrant suddenly asked.

'Bridie.'

'You feel good to me, Bridie Flannagan. Warm and moist and silky. And tight. God, how tight. You grip me like you don't want to let me go.'

As he spoke he increased the speed and rhythm of his thrusts, his words heightening the unfamiliar yet enjoyable friction of his cock moving within her. And she was tight around him, gripping him. He was right.

'Tell me how I feel inside you, Bridie.'

'I – ooh,' Bridie moaned. How could she find words to describe something that was beyond her most vivid imaginings?

'Do I fill you?' he asked, driving himself deep within then pushing harder and farther until she felt he must become permanently embedded.

'Yes!'

'Do you like the feel of me moving inside you? Do you like it when I go fast, like this?'

'Yes,' cried Bridie, her body jerking along the table from the force of his thrusts.

'Or when I do it slowly like this?'

'Oooh, yes.'

He was pulling almost completely out of her before sliding slowly, deliciously, all the way back in.

'Do you know, Bridie Flannagan, I think I would like to make you come.'

Bridie had no idea what he meant, her confusion, created by the plethora of new feelings and an awareness of her body, increasing when he withdrew completely. A surprising, and intense, bereftness was alleviated when she felt him rub the head of his penis along her crease. A multitude of reactions tingled where he stroked. Having him do this was almost as delightful as having him stroke her internally.

8

Suddenly he brushed against a small protuberance of exceptional sensitivity. Bridie's body convulsed. Having located that spot, Nat was giving it extra attention. He proceeded to stimulate it even more by rubbing it rapidly with the head of his cock until Bridie was shivering, uncontrollably, all over.

Even though Nat was outside her, she was becoming all tense and tight inside. She felt as though she was about to explode.

Tiny whimpers issued from her lips and her body began to twitch. Her thoughts were subjugated to her flesh yet not able to define if she was being subjected to some kind of exquisite torture or devilish pleasure.

Then, suddenly, urgently, there came his deep, rapid entry. Bridie felt herself explode; heard someone cry out. Was that her voice? She had no idea. All her awareness was centred deep within her sex which was burning and flooding and being pounded by that strong male shaft. Those thrusts became harder, more forceful, until one supremely deep thrust after which he became still. His hands kneaded her buttocks and he began a slow leisurely stroking, as if there was no longer any urgency.

'I am glad I was your first, Bridie Flannagan,' he said. 'Even though I know I won't be the last. Not for a woman like you.'

He pulled free and Bridie felt herself deprived. For several moments she remained as she was before, pushing herself up then turning to face him. His trousers were already fastened, giving her no opportunity to view the instrument of her pain and pleasure. His last words were imprinted in her mind.

'What do you mean – a woman like me?'

He was gazing at her, in a way that was quite different from any of the ways he had looked at her before. No longer was his expression arrogant or vengeful. 'You are made for sex. Now that you have tried it I warrant you will want it all the time.'

'And are you thinking to be giving it to me?' she asked, defiant again. And secretly hopeful.

To her intense chagrin he shrugged his shoulders in a gesture of indifference. 'Who can tell? If it suits me I will, if it doesn't then I won't.' While he was speaking he moved over to the door to open it on the devastation outside. 'I think your father will get the message but just in case he doesn't, tell him that next time it will be more than his outhouses that are destroyed.'

With one last salacious glance at her nakedness he left the hut with the same arrogance of stride that had brought him in. A very short time later Bridie heard the horses galloping away. By then her body was aching all over.

Moving cautiously, Bridie dressed once more in her skirt and blouse before going outside to see for herself just how much damage had been done. The scene that confronted her erased from her mind every memory of carnal pleasure. The fowl house, the bough shelter where she milked the house cow, the barn, the fences – all were in ruins and the pigs were rooting happily in what was left of the vegetable garden. A black rage curled itself around Bridie's heart. What Nat Durrant had done to her was nothing compared with the devastation wrought by his men. Years of back-breaking work destroyed without a care for how long it might take the two of them to repair the damage. Surely the punishment far exceeded the crime.

Bridie's blood boiled. Was this always to be her life? Had they traded the green fields of Ireland for brown earth merely to get persecuting colonial pastoralists in place of avaricious English landlords who cared not for the failure of the potato crop year after year? In the distance were the receding figures of the horsemen. Bridie glared after them, her vow audible. 'You'll pay for this day's work, Nat Durrant. If it takes me the rest of my life I'll find a way to make you suffer.'

'Bridie! You've not been hurt, have you?' The unexpected query of concern from a familiar, well-loved voice brought Bridie spinning around from her vengeful regard of the departing horsemen. With surprise and relief she greeted the young man who came walking around from the rear of the hut. Seamus O'Flynn was as typically a red-headed Irishman as she was a dark colleen. And she had loved him for many a year.

'It's glad I am to see you, Seamus. Have you seen what they've done?'

'A little.' He appeared to be discomfited by the admission though Bridie could not imagine why.

'Then you'll know it was Nat Durrant.'

'I've heard he's a bad man to cross. Your pa should have had more sense.'

'Sense and my father are not companions, as well you know, Seamus. He'll not be saying anything about this either. He'll not want his activities looked at too closely. But I'll not let Nat Durrant get away so easily. He'll rue the day he ever decided to cross Bridie Flannagan.'

The final declaration was made over her shoulder, the aroma of overcooked stew having drawn her back inside the hut. Seamus followed and watched in silence while she removed the pot, gave the stew a stir, then placed it at the cooler side of the fire to keep warm.

'Is what they did outside the only reason you have for wanting to be avenged on Nat Durrant?' There was such a sulky tone to the question that Bridie gave Seamus a close stare. His cheeks were flushed to a shade of red which clashed woefully with his carrot-coloured hair. His eyes, which were a shade of blue lighter than her own, held resentment – and something else.

'What exactly would you mean by that, Seamus?'

The pink in his cheeks deepened to crimson. 'I'd mean what he did to you,' he blurted.

Bridie's heart lurched. 'You know?'

'Aye.' There was sullen defensiveness in the admission which made Bridie's eyes round with shock.

'You watched!'

11

Seamus had the grace to look shamefaced. 'I've always wanted you, Bridie. I was forcing myself to wait until we were married. Now he's taken what should have been mine. And I'm thinking you were enjoying it.'

The pained accusation passed completely by Bridie. Her mind had grasped one thing. 'Marry? Whenever have you asked me to marry you, Seamus O'Flynn?'

'The asking wasn't necessary. We know how we feel about each other. At least that was so until today.'

'Nothing between us has changed.'

'Hah! 'Tis easy the words come. I could see your face, Bridie. You were enjoying every minute.' Silence hung heavy with hurt between them until Seamus burst out with passion, 'It should have been me, Bridie. It will be me. Now.'

He stepped up to her to pull her into his arms. His mouth closed over hers in what was less of a kiss than an act of anguished possession. Crushed close against his body Bridie could feel the hardness of his arousal. To her own amazement the pressure of his maleness against her abdomen revived memories of the new and wondrous sensations Nat Durrant had created within her body. There came an overwhelming desire to experience them again. With not inconsiderable effort she dragged her mouth free of Seamus's plundering kiss.

'I'm willing to do it now, if that's what you want.'

'Aye. As willing as you were with him, no doubt.' Despite the ill-concealed bitterness of the words, he pulled her towards the cubicle and her bed. Unlike Nat Durrant he had no need to command her to undress. She did so swiftly, pleased to see that he was not wasting time in removing his boots and clothing.

Seamus was not as tall as the pastoralist. In fact, he was only about an inch taller than Bridie's own five feet five inches. He had the stocky, muscular build of a labourer. He also had a stiff, thick shaft jutting out in front of his body.

Not having been given the opportunity to view Nat

12

Durrant's organ but with a vivid recollection of how it had felt to have it shafting her, Bridie gazed at Seamus's nakedness in fascination. The shape of him was unlike anything she had imagined. Curving slightly outward and upward, the column was dark hued, almost purplish in colour, with heavy veins standing out along its length. What intrigued her most was the shape at the extremity. The smooth-skinned head made her think of the helmets Oliver Cromwell's soldiers had worn.

Bridie's patchy education had included a great deal of history, Mr Brown, her teacher, having had a penchant for that subject. Her quixotic fantasy made her wonder if Mr Brown's organ had looked much the same the day Seamus and she had caught him kissing the parson's daughter behind the schoolhouse. The couple's bodies had been pressed very close and they had both become red in the face when they sprang apart with Mr Brown turning hastily away from the two curious children.

'What are you staring at?' Seamus's words brought Bridie's gaze from her fascinated study of his manhood to his face. To her surprise it was every bit as red as Mr Brown's had been. Was he embarrassed by her scrutiny?

'I've not seen a man naked before. Have you seen a woman naked?'

On discovering that she felt not the least degree self-conscious standing naked in front of Seamus, Bridie smoothed her hands over her breasts and down her hips. Her eyes held his with a gaze she hoped was provocative. The memory of how Nat Durrant's shaft had filled her was so very real, her body was beginning to respond in the way it had responded to his rhythmic thrusts. There was the same sharp tingling, the moistness, the pulsing. She was about to beg Seamus to delay no longer when he emitted a kind of strangled cry and bore her backward down on to the narrow bed.

He was quickly inside her; so quickly that Bridie's breath became caught in a gasp. Then she discovered that Seamus's cock did not feel exactly the same as Nat

13

Durrant's. For one thing, it did not seem to stretch her so much or to fill her so tightly. But oh! The action of him thrusting in and out did feel so very good.

Whether Seamus found it equally so was uncertain. He had begun to pant and groan, then to cry in tortured tones, 'Oh Lord! Oh Bridie! Oh God!'

With each exclamation his thrusts became harder, more frantic, so that she was jerked backward along the bed. That wonderful thing that had happened before, like she was all burning up and melting inside, was beginning to happen again. Then all of a sudden Seamus ceased his pounding to collapse heavily on top of her. A strangled sob startled her. Seamus was mumbling into her shoulder.

'God, Bridie, 'tis beautiful you are. Why wasn't I first? Why him?' With a shudder and another sob he rose to pull away from her. 'I'm sorry. I'm sorry. I should not have taken you like that.'

The motion of his cock withdrawing from her body was sufficient to make Bridie aware she had not yet experienced that which Nat Durrant had termed 'making her come'. The delicious, molten feeling which had been building inside had dulled to an ache. An ache she badly needed to assuage.

'No!' she cried, digging her fingers into Seamus's buttocks to prevent him from pulling free.

He gave her a startled look. 'But Bridie, I've finished.'

'I haven't,' she declared while thrusting her pelvis upward to drive herself back over his shaft. Instinctively taking the initiative, she pushed upward again and again until the ache was dispersed under a warm feeling. Not even caring that it was Seamus whose buttocks she gripped and upon whose organ she thrust herself, Bridie closed her eyes to give all her concentration to the part of her that lay between her thighs.

Now she was the one whose pelvic thrusts were frenzied. She discovered that a simultaneous gyration of her hips stimulated the nub Nat Durrant had rubbed to extreme sensitivity with the head of his cock. Oh yes! It was happening again. She was burning, flooding. Then Seamus was pounding into her with a force which forestalled any cessation of her climax. Bridie was hardly aware her lusty cries equalled his until at last the burning flood diminished. Their frenzied coupling slowed then finally ceased.

Motionless and still inside her, Seamus supported himself on his hands to gaze down into Bridie's face. Both wonderment and hurt were in his eyes. Bridie lifted a hand to lay the palm gently against his cheek. He was so right. He should have been her first. Had they not loved each other since they were children together in Ireland? Had they not always been together, Seamus and she? Had he not eased her grief when her mother died during the early years of the potato famine? Had he not been the one to persuade her father to migrate to Australia in the first year of the new decade?

She told him these things now and was surprised to see the hurt in his eyes deepen. He abruptly pulled free from her and turned to sit on the edge of the bed, elbows on knees, head in his hands. His voice was ragged.

'Why say those things to me now, Bridie, when you have not said them before? I have always thought you so pure and good even if you were high spirited. I have long dreamed of being with you, of lying with you in my arms. Yet this is not what I was wanting, you giving yourself to me like a whore.' He raised his head to glare at her with resentment. 'I'm thinking Durrant was not the first either. I was blinded by jealousy before but now I realise you were eager for sex with him. How many men have you given yourself to, Bridie?'

'None!' The very tone of her disclaimer should have told him how shocked and hurt she was by his accusation.

When there was no lightening of his expression she knelt up to wrap her arms around his shoulders. Her breasts pressed against the sweaty muscles of his back.

15

Desire was quickly rekindled by the contact. She brushed her lips against the side of his neck, her voice soft and coaxing. 'There was only Nat Durrant – and I do love you, Seamus – and I want to do it again.'

She began to rub her nipples against his shoulder blades, the friction of skin against skin incredibly arousing. Seamus made some kind of unintelligible sound. Greatly daring, Bridie allowed one hand to slide down over his chest and abdomen until it reached his manhood. Her fingers curled around the soft, sticky shaft. It twitched in her hand and Seamus groaned.

Bridie was encouraged by his response to caress him more actively. While she continued to rub her nipples against his back, she held his manhood and stroked his flat male nipples with her other hand. With a louder groan Seamus gripped her wrist, making her slide her hand up and down his shaft. She soon realised why when it began to stiffen and rise. Her own sex was tingling again and she suddenly recalled Nat Durrant declaring that, having experienced sex, she would want it all the time. Perhaps he was right because she did want it again, so very much.

Seamus's cock having become quite stiff, she moved herself around and lifted one leg across his lap. She was then kneeling on the bed, astride him, their genitals almost touching. They did not stay apart for long. Bridie initiated their coupling by sliding down over him. She took control, grinding herself up and down with such gusto that Seamus toppled backward on the bed, carrying her over on top of him.

Bridie paused only to readjust the position of her legs before continuing to ride him. Seamus was now able to thrust upward to complement her actions and they were both fast approaching climaxes when Bridie heard the unmistakable snort of a horse. Fear vivid on her face, she froze halfway through a downward movement.

'It's Pa.' She would have scrambled off Seamus except

that this time his fingers clawed into her hips to hold her fast.

'I can't stop now.' He jerked rapidly upward to bring himself quickly to his climax. But for Bridie, the fear of discovery and her father's certain anger had ruined her pleasure.

The moment Seamus relaxed Bridie scrambled off him to begin pulling on her clothes. 'Get dressed,' she hissed at him. 'Before Pa comes in and finds us here.'

Realisation of the danger they were in galvanised him into action. Bridie slipped out of the cubicle first with the intention of somehow stalling her father until Seamus was able to disappear out the back door of the hut. In truth she was surprised Flannagan had not already come barging in, bellowing his usual drunken demand to be fed. The moment she opened the door she discovered why.

She did not scream, her only reaction being to recoil with a gasp of horror before she called to Seamus, 'Come quickly.'

He was beside her in an instant to stare in equal horror at the thing the horse dragged behind. 'Oh my God. He must have been thrown.' The animal was jittery, made nervous by its burden. Seamus stepped quietly up to it, speaking soft words to soothe it. Bridie had not moved.

'Can you hold her head, Bridie? Keep her calm while I free your father.'

Bridie did so, watching with a strange indifference while Seamus carefully extricated Flannagan's foot from the stirrup. Only when he rolled her father's body over did she close her eyes in sickened revulsion. He had obviously been dragged for many miles.

They buried him down by the creek, with a simple prayer for his soul, wherever it might have gone. Seamus crafted a crude cross from a sapling. 'I'll make a proper one, with his name carved on it,' he promised.

'Thank you, Seamus.' Her calm voice brought concerned blue eyes to search her face.

'I'll have to go to town to report the accident to the police. Will you be all right on your own or do you want to come back with me?'

'I will be fine here.' She gazed at the freshly turned mound of earth with its crude cross then lifted her face to look straight at Seamus. 'He's dead and I feel nothing. Not grief, not regret. Nothing. I could not even say I'm glad he's gone. He might have been my pa but he didn't mean a thing to me at all.'

Chapter Two

'*H*ave you decided what you will be doing with the farm, Bridie?'

Mrs O'Flynn had asked the question. The four of them, Mr and Mrs O'Flynn, Seamus and Bridie, were seated around the table in the O'Flynns' small cottage behind the blacksmith's shop, eating Sunday dinner. Eight days had passed since Flannagan's horse dragged his body home. Despite her assertion that she would be perfectly all right on her own, Bridie had called Seamus back before he had gone twenty yards. Since then she had been staying with the O'Flynns.

Bridie had no need to give any great thought to her answer, her decision having been made almost before Flannagan's body was decently covered with earth. 'I'll be selling, Mrs O'Flynn.'

'Aye.' Mrs O'Flynn nodded her head in recognition of the anticipated answer. 'But you've oft enough complained the soil's too poor for farming. Who will you find to buy?'

'Nat Durrant.'

Three pairs of eyes turned to gaze at her with a different degree of surprise in each. The older couple knew the man only by name. The wealthy grazier had little to do with the battlers of Barkers Ridge. To Seamus, Bridie's calm voicing of that name held a deeper meaning.

'Nat Durrant?' He echoed the name. 'You've spoken with him, then?'

'How could I have done?' The look she gave Seamus was mildly reproachful. 'Have I not been here all week?' She turned her gaze back to include the others. 'We've not had decent rain for months. Cattle need water and there's good permanent water on the land. I'm thinking Nat Durrant will give me a fair price.'

'Aye, 'tis right you are, Bridie,' declared Mr O'Flynn. 'Good water would be like gold to Durrant. But he'd probably not be wanting to deal with a slip of a girl. Would you be after having me or Seamus talk to him for you?'

''Tis kind you are, Mr O'Flynn, but I'll be speaking to him myself. I'm thinking it's time I went back anyway. There's things to be done.'

'Do you mean now? Today?' asked Seamus.

'No. Tomorrow.'

Bridie knew why Seamus was so put out. Living in the cramped cottage there had been no opportunity for them to be alone together. Not that it would have availed them of a chance, her bleeding having commenced regular to the day, setting Bridie's mind at rest. It had prompted her to make discreet enquiries, of a woman with knowledge of such things, how a woman might share pleasure with a man without any unwanted results.

The day Flannagan died held greater importance in Bridie's life as the day when she realised the cause of her restlessness of body and spirit and was shown how it could be appeased. It had been Nat Durrant who had taught her about herself and Seamus who had enhanced the knowledge. Bridie knew there was a lot more she wanted to learn about the things a man and woman did together. Instinct told her there were ways of enhancing pleasure, of taking it beyond the frantic coupling of bodies.

Rose Galway, who was far more accustomed to having men knock at her door than young lasses, was at first amused by Bridie's roundabout manner of asking her question, then speculative. She formed a cunning suspicion the girl was not really concerned with bearing her husband-to-be more children than could be properly clothed or fed.

'A girl like you could do better than tying herself down to a man who can't keep her properly. You're a pretty lass. You've got the looks men go for.'

'What looks?' Bridie had turned to stare curiously at herself in Rose's large mirror. All she could see was the same as she ever saw. Blue eyes, high cheek bones, wide mouth, and dark hair pulled untidily back from her face.

Behind her Rose gave a chuckle. ' 'Tis nothing you can see, dearie, but mark my words, men can. They'll look at you and want to take you to bed and if you're smart you'll make them pay handsomely for the privilege.'

'I could not do that,' Bridie exclaimed, then caught herself up with an apology. 'I'm sorry, Rose. I wasn't meaning –'

'I know that.' Rose forestalled the explanation. 'I didn't mean you should be like me. I enjoy what I do and the men like me 'cause I enjoy it. But I ain't no beauty and my customers ain't rich neither. Now you, Bridie. You're real pretty. All dolled up in nice clothes I reckon you'd be beautiful. And I reckon you'd soon learn how to act like a lady, too. If men want your body, Bridie, don't give it away for nothing. If a man really desires a woman he'll give her almost anything.'

The lifestyle at which Rose had hinted held a degree of appeal, it not being dissimilar to the shadowy images that had been floating about in Bridie's own mind. However there were two major obstacles. To create such a lifestyle for herself she would need to move to Melbourne, purchase an entire wardrobe, find somewhere suitable to live and learn to become a lady. All of which would take money she did not have.

Then there was Seamus who had declared at least three times over the past week that they should marry as quickly as possible. Love him though she did, Bridie did not feel herself yet ready to become his wife. In truth, she doubted if she would ever be ready. Not now. Not since that fateful afternoon. Life with Seamus would not be far different from the life she had always led. A tiny cottage, a constant struggle to make ends meet, baby after baby until she was aged beyond her years and too tired and worn out to enjoy sex.

Her enjoyment of sex was something about which she thought a great deal. Even while she was declaring her intention of returning to the farm she was thinking that Seamus would surely insist on accompanying her. She hoped he would, though, for certain it would be a long time before they got started on the sorting out. She would be keeping Seamus busy with other things.

As it happened, she rode out to the farm alone, Mr O'Flynn being so busy in his blacksmith's shop he was unable to spare his son. So Bridie made the short journey filled with regret that she would not soon be lying naked on her bed with Seamus pounding into her for as long as they both had the energy to keep going. The trouble was that such thoughts only served to make her want that thing even more. The horse knew its own way along the track and there was nothing to prevent her mind from wandering off at an erotic tangent.

She saw nothing of the trees beneath which they passed, the birds which flew across their path or the grey kangaroos which slept in the shade. Bridie was visualising herself bent over the table with Nat Durrant's hard thrusts jerking her body forward and then later of having Seamus's thrusts pushing her backward on the bed. By the time she reached the hut the task of clearing it out was the least of her concerns.

* * *

The homestead stood on a rise at the head of the valley. From the front verandah one had sweeping views of the normally green and lush valley, the distant scattered buildings of Barkers Ridge and the rocky spur from which the town had taken its name. Standing on the verandah, hands resting on the railing, Nat Durrant watched the approaching rider. He recognised her when she was still some distance away. With the recognition there came an unmistakable tightening in his groin.

On the day he had gone to the Flannagans' farm he had been coldly, vindictively, angry. The stud bull Flannagan had taken to service his ill-bred cows had cost him a small fortune. It was a crime for which the man might have expected to serve a lengthy gaol sentence. If Flannagan had been at his farm Nat would have had him thoroughly horsewhipped. Denied that satisfaction and faced with the spirited Bridie, he quickly saw how else he could be compensated for the criminal use of the bull.

He had thought she would plead with him to spare her. Instead she had faced him in provocative defiance, making no coy attempt to hide her naked curves from his gaze. What he later realised was pride he mistook for sexual experience. It had seemed logical to assume a scoundrel like Flannagan would have a harlot for a daughter.

Yet his desire had risen so strongly as to almost drive him beyond control. How warm and wet she had been when he touched her softness, how silken and welcoming she had felt when he began to slide into her. An overwhelming need to have her encase him completely compelled him to plunge himself to his depth with a force that barely felt the resistance. Her cry of pain and the knowledge she was a virgin had startled him. He had experienced a moment of inexplicable regret before he buried it beneath gloating contempt.

Then, when her pain faded and she began to make little sounds of pleasure he had wanted to give her the ultimate pleasure instead of just taking his own. She would not have realised that the act of teasing her and stroking her with the head of his cock had thrilled him to the same degree as she was being thrilled. Nor would she have known how difficult it had been for him to hold back until he knew she was trembling on the brink of her climax. He had rammed into her then, relishing the hot flow of her orgasm over his shaft and coming far too quickly to his own.

The violent spasms of his climax and the supremacy of pleasure had been totally unexpected. After all, she was only one of a great number of women from all walks of life with whom he had taken his pleasure at one time or another. True, she was the first whose maidenhead he had taken but that in itself would hardly have accounted for such intensity of feeling. Then, when she had asked him if he would do it to her again, he had been hard put not to carry her to her bed, to strip off his own clothes so that he could feel the full length of her naked body pressed against his own.

Since that afternoon he had been unable to put her out of his mind. He thought almost constantly of what it would be like to have her in his bed with all the time in the world to teach her every sensual pleasure. That she would be a quick and willing pupil he had no doubt. If ever a woman was made to enjoy sex, Bridie Flannagan was the one.

When he heard about Flannagan's death Nat decided he must bide his time. He could console himself with vividly erotic anticipation. All things considered, he did not think Bridie would welcome his attentions while she grieved for her father. He had been wondering how much longer he could give her, had been thinking that very day that he must see her soon, or go out of his mind with this consuming desire to savour anew the delights of her body.

Now she was coming to him. Nat had no idea why. Whatever the reason he vowed to himself that she would not leave until he had fulfilled every one of the fantasies that had tormented him for the past week.

The housekeeper left Bridie standing in the hallway, feeling decidedly uncomfortable in the unfamiliar luxury. A thick, richly patterned strip of carpet ran the length of the highly polished floor. The cabinets placed at intervals along the walls were of the best quality furniture, the porcelain and other objects they contained looked as if they cost as much as would keep the Flannagans and others like them in food and clothing for several years. About halfway down its length the hall widened with each wall curving outward before narrowing to the same grand width as the entrance. A magnificent chandelier hung directly above the central point.

What, Bridie wondered, must the rest of the house be like when the hallway was so grand? She was soon to find out. The housekeeper reappeared from a door on the left. 'If you will come this way, miss, the master will see you now,' she stated with no more of a welcome in her expression than before.

As she walked forward under that disapproving stare Bridie had to resist the urge to look back to see if her boots were leaving dusty footprints on the carpet. For this visit she had dressed in her best dress, a plainly made blue linen that matched the colour of her eyes. Now she had the uncomfortable feeling that her best was something Nat Durrant's housekeeper would relegate to the rag bag. Her confidence, which had started to crumble when she was close enough to the homestead to see its size and grandeur, had all but disappeared completely. She had so desperately wanted to make a good impression on Nat Durrant. For more reasons than one.

The room into which she stepped appeared to be a library. The walls were lined with bookcases. Two high-backed chairs were ranged either side of the hearth and a large desk was angled across one corner of the room with a drinks cabinet in the opposite corner. A pair of tall arched windows gave a view out to the tree-cloaked, hilly side of the valley where the afternoon sun painted the tops of the eucalypts with gold.

Bridie noticed all of these things. She looked at them very closely because suddenly she felt too shy to look directly at the man who stood near one of the bookcases leafing through a leather-bound volume. When she set out from the farm it had been in a mood of almost wicked anticipation. Now she was wishing she had sent Seamus or Mr O'Flynn to conduct her business. Given the housekeeper's attitude, Bridie felt certain Nat Durrant would treat her with contempt.

The book was closed with a snap which made Bridie jump and brought her gaze to his face. There was nothing in his expression to give her any clue as to his thoughts. Her own were chaotic. He was more handsome, more masculine, had far more sexual magnetism than she remembered.

'Miss Flannagan.' He acknowledged her presence with a slight nod. 'My condolences on the death of your father.'

'Thank you.' The brief acknowledgement was all Bridie could manage. Her throat felt dry, her lips barely able to move. She did not bother to wonder if the expressed sentiment was genuine. Nat Durrant had moved closer to her. Close enough for her to smell the musky male scent of him, to want to reach out to touch him, to want to feel his skin beneath her hand, to want his hardness embedded between her thighs. She swallowed with difficulty and ran her tongue over her parched lips.

Nat's eyes seemed to flame from within and Bridie wondered why she had thought them cold. They were dark; dark enough to shield his thoughts. Could he read her thoughts? Was that why he was staring at her so intently?

'You must be thirsty from your ride. Can I pour you a sherry or would you prefer me to ring for some tea or cordial?'

'I do not want to put you to any trouble, Mr Durrant.'

'A sherry, then?'

Bridie nodded and sipped cautiously at the thick golden wine when he handed her the glass. Not having tasted it before, she did not want to make a fool of herself and endeavoured to portray a sophistication she was far from feeling. The drink was sweet on her tongue and warm in her belly.

Nat Durrant saw her seated in one of the chairs and settled himself comfortably in the other before he asked the reason for her visit. The sherry had restored a great deal of Bridie's confidence.

'I want to sell the farm.'

'I see. Do I take it that you are offering me first choice?' His relaxed pose and apparent indifference unnerved her all over again.

'Yes.'

'I own almost the entire valley, Miss Flannagan. Why would I want to buy your few acres?'

This time the condescension was sufficient to stiffen Bridie's resolve. 'Water. The creek that runs through your property is close to drying up.'

'It's the same everywhere.'

'Ah, now. It's there you're mistaken, Mr Durrant. There is a spring feeds our creek. It'll not be drying out in any drought.'

His eyes flickered with keen interest before the mien of indifference was resumed. 'Is there indeed? If that is the case I might be interested. How do I know you are telling the truth? Your father was less than honest.'

Bridie looked across at him, relaxed in his chair, long legs outstretched, seemingly intent on baiting her and obviously nowhere near as sexually aware of her as she was of him. Irish temper swept away the last remnants of her trepidation. She put her glass aside and rose to her feet.

'You know quite well that I'm speaking the truth. I was thinking you'd be glad of the water but I'm not about to do business with a man who thinks me dishonest. There's no doubt others willl be willing to pay the price.'

'Sit down.' Nat spoke mildly, apparently unperturbed by her outburst. Bridie glared at him. 'Please sit down,' he said. 'I am interested. Very interested.' The tone of his voice lowered on the last two words, as did his gaze which levelled at her skirt, some distance below her waist.

Bridie sat hurriedly, pressing her thighs together to hold back the uncontrollable sensation beginning to flicker. Her heart beat accelerated and she retrieved her glass to take a longer sip of her sherry. This time the warmth spread beyond her belly to deep between her thighs to ignite an ache of longing. Barely able to sit still, she wondered if she should be bold enough to tell Nat Durrant what she was feeling, to disclose the real reason she had ridden out to the homestead so late in the afternoon. He seemed to be watching her closely yet his eyes gave nothing away.

'I believe it might take some time for us to negotiate a mutually satisfactory price, Miss Flannagan. Would you stay and have dinner with me this evening?'

The invitation was totally unexpected. 'I – er,' she stammered. A ghost of a smile was playing across his mouth. It was a firm mouth, the lower lip slightly fuller, sensual. Bridie wanted to be kissed by that mouth, wanted those lips trailing over her naked flesh. Dear Lord! She wanted this man. 'What would we be doing until then?'

'We could ride to the head of the valley to watch the sunset.'

The suggestion was not at all the one Bridie had hoped to hear, unless ... Perhaps he did not want to have sex with her in the house where the housekeeper would surely know what was going on. Maybe he had suggested the ride so they could be alone together.

'I'd like that,' she said.

* * *

Bridie's anticipation was high as they rode through the trees to climb high up to the head of the valley. Neither of them spoke more than a few words. Even when they reached the summit and dismounted Nat merely led her to a rock where she could sit and look back down over the valley. The sun was close to setting. On the western side of the valley the sky was turning an ever deeper orange, streaked with vermilion, while on the eastern side soft mauves and pinks painted the sky in more delicate hues. Rising through them was the enormous pearly orb of the full moon.

Nature's spectacle held Bridie entranced. She had never given much thought to such things nor taken any notice of the brilliant colours of the sunsets. There had always been the cows to milk or a meal to cook or any number of other chores. Absorbed though she was in the ever-changing colours around her, she could still wonder that a man like Nat Durrant could appreciate the beauty of a sunset.

She turned her head to look up to where he stood, one foot on the rock, leaning slightly forward with his arm resting on his thigh. He was watching her, not the sunset. For a long moment their gazes held. A moment in which Bridie knew for certain that his desires matched hers, that he wanted the same thing she wanted.

'It will be dark by the time we get back,' he said. 'It will be far too late for you to ride home alone, even if you did not stay for dinner.'

'You could ride with me,' Bridie suggested, holding her breath in her throat, hoping he would agree.

'I have a far better idea. You could stay with me for the night.'

The very thought of spending the night with this man was sufficient to set every one of Bridie's nerves tingling with anticipation. Until she remembered the disapproving housekeeper.

'What would your housekeeper think if I did?'

'Mrs Roberts is not paid to question my activities, she

is paid to run my house properly. But if it will ease your mind she does not live in the house. Mr Roberts is also in my employ. They live in that cottage you can see over there.'

'I see.' Bridie thought for a moment. 'I'll not have a chaperone, then?'

Nat's lips quirked. 'Do you need one?'

'No.'

'That's settled then. Come. We should go back before it becomes too dark.'

Dinner, to Bridie's surprise, was of plain, simple fare – not the sumptuous meal she half expected. True, there was plenty of it and all was superbly cooked. The wines served with each course were new to Bridie's experience. She enjoyed their tastes, enjoyed the relaxed warm feeling they gave her, the heightened appreciation of the food and her surroundings and the pulsing awareness of the man seated opposite.

He encouraged her to talk about herself, of the mother whose death she had mourned so deeply, of the father whose passing caused no grief.

'What will you do now, Bridie?'

The question held genuine interest and Bridie thought for a few moments before she answered. 'I've not yet made up my mind.'

'You need a husband. A man could do far worse than take you for a wife. Your husband would have no need to look beyond the marriage bed for his pleasure.' His regard became quizzical. 'Is there no young man in your life?'

Bridie, thinking of Seamus before she answered in the negative then immediately putting him from her mind, felt guilty colour rise in her cheeks.

'Really?' Nat's eyebrows arched upward. 'I find that hard to believe. A woman like you.'

'Why do you keep saying that?'

'Saying what?'

'"A woman like you", like I was different from other women.'

'Ah, but you are different, Bridie Flannagan. You are unique. Special, desirable, made to give pleasure and to take pleasure.' His voice deepened to a sensual huskiness. 'I want to pleasure you, Bridie. I want to teach you all the ways there are for a man and woman to enjoy each other.'

His words were melting her inside, his eyes holding hers with sexual promise. Bridie swallowed and moistened her dry lips with her tongue, not knowing that the action sent a stab of longing through his groin. She wanted so very much to learn all the things he offered to teach her. Was that not the real reason she had made this visit? Yet she did not want him to think her a brazen hussy. Therefore she lowered her gaze before she responded.

'I thought there was only one way a man and woman could be together.'

He smiled at her coyness. 'Ah, Bridie. I think I had better start your education very quickly.'

Nat led her from the dining room and down the hall to a bedroom which was dominated by a massive canopied bed. The bed was draped with deep-red velvet curtains. Matching curtains framed windows through which moonlight spilled. A small fire blazed in the hearth, in front of which was a sheepskin rug. The room was brightly lit by several lamps and Bridie wondered if he would turn them down before they went to bed. On that thought her gaze returned to the bed. Nat had made no move to touch her and she wondered if she should start undressing.

Now he moved past her to open another door. 'Come here, Bridie.'

On walking over to the door Bridie saw that it opened into a smaller room in which was built a large copper bath tub. The tub was filled with steaming, rose-scented water.

'I want you thoroughly clean for me,' he said.

Her immediate resentment of the unspoken suggestion that he considered her unclean was swiftly swept aside by the declaration of his intention to wash her himself. Bridie's ablutions normally consisted of wiping her skin with a damp flannel and a weekly bath in a tub so small there was barely room to sit with her knees bent to her chest. The prospect of stripping naked and stretching out in that huge tub of water was both enticing and intimidating. This was a luxury of which she had never dreamed and never before had she bathed in water which was perfumed.

'Do you need help to undress?' Nat's query broke the spell of her bemusement. She shook her head and told him she could manage. Did she not do so every day of her life? Hers was no elaborate gown which required the ministrations of a maid. Those thoughts, though, were not voiced.

'I'll leave you to undress, then,' Nat said. 'I will return shortly.'

Garments as simple as Bridie's took little time to remove. Very cautiously she stepped into the bath and lowered herself until she was seated, legs outstretched and hands clasping the rim. The moment she disturbed the water the scent of roses became stronger. Bridie inhaled deeply. She sank lower until her chin was just above the surface of the water then leant back against the sloping end of the tub without thought for her hair becoming wet.

The door opened and Nat returned. He, too, had undressed, and was now clad in a long brocade robe. The knowledge that he was all but naked and that her own nakedness was visible beneath the water created a delicious ache in Bridie's belly. Once again she had a need to moisten her lips with her tongue.

His eyes were gleaming as he took the few paces to the tub. 'I promised to wash you,' he said as he knelt beside it.

He started with her nearest arm, lathering a rose-scented soap in his hands, working the suds between her fingers and up the inside of her arm to her armpit, then down again to her wrist. With a soft flannel he rinsed away the soap then repeated the entire procedure with her other arm. With that arm finished, he bade her bend forward so that he could wash her back.

The movement of his hands over her shoulders was deliciously sensuous. He trailed a finger down the ridges of her spine to make her shiver. Then both hands were washing her buttocks until one returned to her shoulder blades to push her farther forward and the fingers of the other pressed between the mounds to move over her rear opening and turn the shiver into a shudder of surprised reaction.

'The front now.'

Bridie leant back. Her entire body already tingled with arousal. If he could induce so much sexual awareness by washing her back what would happen when he touched her taut, aching breasts? With lips parted she lifted her gaze to his face, unaware that in her eyes he could see all that she was feeling and that what he saw pleased him immensely.

Breathless was how she felt. Nat used both hands to soap both breasts at the same time. He circled his palms over them, cupped them in his hands, washed away the lather and grazed her nipples lightly with his thumbs to coax them into sensitised peaks.

Bridie gazed down at her breasts in wonder. They appeared so changed. Her nipples were so hard, the areolae seemed to have become larger and darker, the fine skin of the mounds stretched so tight there was a marbling of faint blue veins on the milky flesh.

'Beautiful,' he murmured.

Then she forgot all about her breasts because his hands were on her abdomen and a finger was tracing the indentation of her navel. Bridie had not realised there were so many responsive places on her body. If only his hands would move lower. They had touched every part of her body except the one place that ached to be touched. She slid deeper in the water and pushed her hips upward.

He smiled in acknowledgement of her silent plea for a more intimate touch. Bridie held her breath in anticipation. Instead he turned his attention to her legs, starting with her toes and moving slowly upward. Too slowly. Achingly slowly, so that Bridie's body became tense with wanting. By the time his hands reached her thigh she was trembling. His fingers were so near, so temptingly close, the lips of her sex ached to reach out and suck them into her pulsing opening. A tiny sob of frustration broke from her when his hands moved to her other foot.

At the sound of her distress he glanced up at her with a half smile. The realisation he was deliberately taunting her fired her anger yet did nothing to diminish the almost painful ache in her vulva. Her eyes pleaded for what she would not ask. Nat returned his attention to her foot to begin the torturous washing of her other leg.

Nor did he give her satisfaction this time. After holding his fingers tantalisingly near for so long that she was ready to scream, he told her he wanted to wash her hair. He made her move forward in the tub so that he could release the pins which held her hair. When it tumbled free he lathered it well, using his fingers to massage her scalp in a manner that eased some of her pent-up sexual tension but none of her sensual desire. Only when her hair had been thoroughly rinsed and her face gently washed did he speak again.

'There is only one part of you left to wash now. To do that properly I need you to kneel up.'

He gave her the support of his hands while she manoeuvred herself on to her knees. In that position her genitals were level with the surface of the water. Nat moved his hands back and forth, one in front, one behind

34

her body to create gentle waves which swilled against her delicate flesh.

Needle darts of pleasure tingled between her thighs. Bridie emitted an 'Oh' of disbelief followed immediately by another of delight. Nat continued to swill the water until she thought she could bear the tease no longer. Without being aware she was doing it, she began to circle her hips to magnify the stimulation.

The hand he held in front of her swept forward to touch her, to wash her external folds. The other slid between her buttocks to wash around her anus. The intensity of sensation created by being fondled simultaneously from in front and behind was almost unbearable. Bridie knew so great an ache could be eased only by penetration. She wanted him to press his fingers deep inside and moved her hips in an attempt to capture them in her warmth. Her eyes were closed, the urgency of her need transmuted to a series of tiny moans.

The abruptness with which he took his hands away brought her eyes open and a cry of protest from her lips. He smiled at the anguished gaze she turned upon him. 'Not yet, my dear. We have all night.'

With those words he drew her to her feet and out of the tub to envelop her body in a soft towel. He rubbed her down, drying her body with a thoroughness which only served to inflame her senses even more. When her body was dry he towelled her hair, then he tossed the towel aside and loosened the belt of his robe. 'Now it is your turn to wash me.'

He's beautiful, thought Bridie, her gaze hungry on his naked torso. Dark skin stretched over taut muscles. Not bulky muscle like Seamus's. There was no brawn here, only finely toned, sculptured perfection. A smattering of dark hairs on his chest tapered in a thin line to his navel then lower to cluster in tight curls around the base of his manhood.

That organ was in itself a cause for wonder. Nat's long straight legs were braced slightly apart with his penis jutting proudly erect. No wonder he had filled her so tightly. While it looked a great deal like Seamus's it was also quite unlike the only other male appendage she had ever seen. Bridie realised that men differed in this physical attribute as in all others. He was allowing her a long gaze and Bridie swallowed deeply. How could he find her attractive when he was so beautiful, so perfect?

He stepped into the bath. 'Wash me, Bridie. The way I washed you.'

She started with his arms as he had done, her fingers learning the strength and shape of his muscles while she washed. They explored his back, though she was not quite game enough to slide them between his buttocks. When she came to his chest she had no hesitation in rubbing her thumbs over his nipples. Surprised to see them harden as hers had done, she was exhilarated and excited when he sucked in his breath. The knowledge that her touch affected him gave her a heady thrill.

Her washing of his body was an exploration of discovery, her palms and fingers learning his shape. They assessed the strength of his calves and the more developed muscles of his thighs. At his inner thighs her hands paused, hesitant to touch either the dark sacs with their sprinkling of fine black hairs or the hard erection.

'Wash all of me,' he commanded in a voice far less controlled than normal.

He knelt and she did then what he had done to her, using one hand to wash the heavy sacs and the other to wash along the ridge of muscle behind them and up to his anus. His breathing was becoming ragged and the more ragged it became the more daring was Bridie's caress. She ignored the moisture pooling between her own thighs to concentrate on what she was doing with her hands. From the varying depths of his groans she quickly discovered that stroking her finger along the ridge to his anus affected him far more dramatically than rolling the sacs in the palm of her hand.

'You haven't finished,' he said, gasping, taking her hand to place it on his shaft.

Iron could not have felt so hard. Certainly it would not have felt so heated. Bridie washed the column thoroughly, even sluicing away the drop of moisture at its tip, surprised at the great shudder which racked his body.

'Enough.' Nat stepped from the bath, picked up the towel and handed it to her for her to dry him. She had to stretch up to reach his head and he caught her to him, crushing her breasts against his chest, kissing her hard and briefly before releasing her without a word.

Bridie continued to wipe his body, finding it necessary to kneel to attend to the drying of his legs. Her face was on a level with his groin and she noticed there was another droplet of moisture seeping from the tiny hole at the tip of his cock. She felt a sudden desire to lick it, taste it. Her tongue moistened her lips.

'Take it.' The husky words were more of a plea than a command. He curved a hand around the column to tilt it downward towards her mouth.

Bridie's tongue snaked out to lick the drop of moisture. Nat groaned and pressed the silken textured head of his organ against her lips. They opened, embraced it. He pushed a little and she parted her teeth to enable him to penetrate her mouth. The taste of him excited her senses.

Strong fingers were entwined in her hair at the back of her head to hold it steady. He began to thrust into her mouth and Bridie closed her lips around him, revelling in the wanton pleasure of feeling male hardness slide between them. Suddenly he pulled out of her mouth and reached down to draw her to her feet. His eyes were smouldering dark, his breathing heavy.

'Bridie Flannagan, you are a woman without equal. How I am going to enjoy this night!'

He led her back to the bedroom, both of them still naked, and drew her to sit on the rug with her back to the fire. The lambswool was soft under her feet and against her knees. When she lowered herself to sit with her knees to one side the fibres caressed intimate places. Such was the thickness of the wool it probed every fold and crease to tease her to such sensual awareness she closed her eyes to savour more fully her body's response. She was very tempted to magnify that response by rubbing her sex against the rug.

On opening her eyes she discovered Nat was watching her with intense interest. 'Are you enjoying all that you are learning about sensual pleasure, Bridie?'

'Yes.' The word came with a sigh and she did move on the rug so that the wool fibres tickled her most sensitive point to cause a quickening of desire. Because she was expecting Nat to begin making love to her she was surprised when he picked up a silver-handled hairbrush. With it in his hand he came to kneel behind her to lift her hair and fan out the damp tresses.

'You need to dry your hair,' was all he said.

He began to brush with long, even strokes, occasionally lifting her hair with his other hand to allow the warmth from the fire to dry the individual strands.

Bridie wondered when and where he had learnt to perform such a task and with such expertise. The way he handled her hair was so indescribably erotic she gave herself up to the sybaritic luxury. Several strands fell over her shoulder and she saw they had the sheen of silk. The shine he was brushing into her hair reflected the warm glow which encompassed her entire body, both without and within.

While her sexual awareness remained undiminished, there was also a feeling of warmth, of well-being, of a closeness to Nat that had nothing to do with the physical union which would come later.

He lifted her hair and she felt the warm pressure of his lips on the nape of her neck. The kiss sent shivers racing down her spine causing a sensation near her tail bone. Bridie opened her eyes, turning her head quickly to look up at Nat. His expression was somewhat bemused, as if he too was experiencing new and totally unexpected sensations. Their gazes locked, held. Something indefinable, more pure than sexual desire, hovered between them. Then Nat moved and the spell was broken.

'The hair on your head is dry,' he said. 'What about the other?'

He coaxed her to lie back on the rug with her legs spread slightly apart. Taking up the brush once more, he began, with the utmost seriousness, to brush the dark curls of her mound. Bridie gasped, astonished by what he was doing, astounded by the effect it was having on her body. The bristles of the brush grazed lightly on her skin to render her nerve endings unbearably sensitive.

When he murmured, 'Very nice,' in the husky tone that did such wonderful things to her, she pushed herself up on her elbows to look down at the glistening curls. They were a feature of her body to which she had never given any thought. Now she could see how different they looked. The sight of her pubic curls brushed to shining neatness was yet another intensely erotic aid to her arousal. Judging by the way Nat's shaft remained stiff and erect, the effect on him was equal.

'You approve?' he asked.

'Oh yes.' Bridie's breathy agreement was not referring solely to her gleaming curls.

Nat's lips quirked in that not-quite smile. 'Lie back. I've not yet finished.'

When she relaxed back on the rug he spread her legs wider apart and stroked the brush against the soft folds of her sex. An incredulous cry burst from her lips. She had thought the touch of the bristles on the skin of her mound exciting. That was as nothing compared with the vibrant reactions those bristles were arousing on her more sensitive flesh.

The nerves that were being stimulated were connected to others, deeper within her. And in that deep secret place they also tingled and flared in response to the stroke of the brush. Bridie felt the warm moisture spreading downward and sensed the flowering and opening of her sex in readiness for when Nat would penetrate her. She hoped he would do so soon for she did not know how long she could bear the delicious erotic stimulation. Eyes closed, her breath coming in little moans, she wriggled against the brush, speechlessly begging Nat to give her that which she now desired with aching intensity.

However, it was not a warm column of flesh which slid between her moist and ready sex-lips, it was the cool silver handle of the hairbrush.

Bridie opened her eyes with a gasp of shock, unable to believe what she was feeling. Pushing herself back up on her elbows, she watched wide-eyed as Nat pulled the handle out then pushed it back in. He was manipulating it in an action imitative of coupling and her surprise that he would do such a thing to her was joined by her even greater astonishment at the pleasure it imparted. The internal stroking of the brush handle was creating sensations she thought could only be experienced in intimate union with a man.

Dear Lord! Not only did it feel so very good to have that rounded silver handle moving rhythmically in her, it was doubly arousing to watch it disappear then reappear between her thighs. Nat was absorbed in the action too, his attention entirely on his manipulation of the brush.

And then Bridie realised it was going to happen. The pool of warmth within was building, spreading, soon to flood out. Her body trembled with the excitement of anticipation. Nat pulled the brush away.

'No!' Bridie's cry was tormented. She felt as though part of her, inside, had been cut off with a knife. Her lips trembled, her eyes pleaded. Nat was unmoved.

'Not yet. The longer your pleasure is delayed the greater it will be when it happens.'

When tears began to swim in her eyes he put the brush aside and lay beside her to take her in his arms. He held her gently until her body ceased its trembling and the terrible ache between her thighs eased to a dull awareness.

'That's better,' Nat whispered, brushing his lips against her hair.

'Why did you stop?' Bridie's question was plaintive. 'You knew what was happening to me.'

'I did not want you to come then. I want you to have the greatest orgasm you could possibly imagine.'

'Why?'

'I don't regret that day at your hut, Bridie, but will you believe me when I tell you I wish it had been different? The truth is I wanted you from the moment you stood glaring at me with your hands on your hips, all fiery temper. My determination to extract retribution from your father governed my actions. I knew I would enjoy taking you, the way a man can enjoy any woman. I neither expected you to be a virgin nor to enjoy what I did to you. But you did enjoy it and ever since I rode away from you I have thought about doing what I am doing tonight. Of teaching you all the ways a man and a woman can enjoy each other's bodies.'

He was kissing her as he spoke. Light feathery kisses which touched her forehead, her eyelids, her nose, her chin, the lobes of her ears, the corners of her mouth. By the time he finished speaking his lips were moving down the column of her neck to the hollow at the base of her throat and Bridie was again all atremble.

His lips moved from the base of her throat down the line of her breastbone until they reached the valley between her breasts. Remembrance of how her nipples had reacted to the caress of his hands had Bridie hoping for his lips to touch them now. She shivered with delight when they did. Kisses spotted the insides of her breasts then the underside of one and around its outer slope to the top then down to the nipple. The kisses changed to a gentle sucking which drew her nipple to a wondrous tautness against which he flicked with his tongue. Sweet fire spread from her chest to down between her thighs.

41

Slowly, thoroughly, deliciously, he subjected her other breast to the same treatment. Bridie was discovering that having her breasts sucked by a man's firm mouth created an intense sexual response in more than the top part of her body. By the time his lips moved to her navel she was a mass of quivering nerves. His tongue made a teasing circle of the indentation. When the tip pushed into the hollow she found herself tensing and arched her pelvis upward. She wanted his lips to move lower to kiss the most sensitive place on her body. They never did. Kisses which feathered over her abdomen came to a stop when they reached the upper edge of the dark curls.

Without speaking he rolled her on to her front. The wool which had felt so soft against her back now sensitised her nipples and the apex of her cleft. Head pillowed on her arms, Bridie willingly surrendered herself to the combined sensual stimuli of soft lambswool and firm male lips. Nat was trailing kisses across her shoulder blades and down her spine with the same exquisite thoroughness he had given to the front of her body. Every inch of her skin was being sensitised, her flesh made aware. As her skin sensitivity increased so, too, did that within her core.

Bridie's body was quickly returning to the state where it had been twice already this night; when he swilled water on her in the bath and when he pleasured her with the brush. She was heating up inside, burning, wanting, waiting. Nat's lips were on her buttocks, kissing them, adoring them, hovering where the twin mounds met.

Almost subconsciously Bridie pushed her buttocks upward and spread her legs a little. Nat's hands on her hips encouraged her to lift higher and draw in her knees until she was kneeling face down, buttocks and sex lifted, opened. Then opened more, held apart by Nat's hands to enable his tongue to sweep down between her buttocks until it reached her moist crease.

Her convulsive response to the touch of his tongue against her anus was mild compared with the one that

42

shook her when the tip of his tongue slid the length of her crease to stab against her hardened button. Too quickly it moved away again to tease instead between her folds. It delved into the secret recess to push inside, to move as the brush handle had been used. This time Bridie experienced yet another difference of sensation. Nat's tongue imparted greater excitement. Trembling, she tilted her pelvis higher, enticing more.

Nat seemed to understand what she wanted. The probing tongue returned to the tight nub. There it tickled and teased to inflame her with almost painful stabs of ecstasy. She was moaning, gasping, sobbing, the internal tension almost unbearable. Eyes closed, she threshed her head from side to side. Then it happened. She felt her hips lifted higher and her knees come off the rug. That was the last she knew of reality. She was broken, burning up, her life seeping between her legs, drawn out by Nat's hard mouth, his tongue coaxing more and more when there seemed to be no more left to give.

Slowly, shudderingly, the exquisite agony began to ease. Bridie became aware of the rug, the fire, the walls of the room. There was a degree of surprise in discovering her body was whole and that Nat continued to muzzle her pulsing sex. Until he gently lowered her legs, pulled himself alongside her, rolled her on to her back and kissed her lingeringly on her mouth.

The realisation that the salty tang on his lips was the taste of herself renewed the burning ache in Bridie's sex. The hot flood of her ecstasy had left a void which needed to be filled. The hard length of Nat's cock rested against her hip. She wanted it between her thighs. Moaning beneath his kiss she twisted her lower body to bring them closer.

Nat raised his head to gaze down at her, his eyes even darker than normal. There was a blaze in them that might have been passion or perhaps it was just a reflection of the fire. Certainly there was a burning intensity in his gaze. 'Did you enjoy that?'

43

'Yes, but I want –.'

'I know.' His lips touched hers briefly before he moved to position himself over her, his legs between hers, his manhood poised ready to swoop. As swiftly as a hawk diving for its prey, it came down, straight and true, to ram deep into her burning void. Bridie's cry was one of unparalleled delight. She was complete, whole, filled with perfection. When he began to pump she slipped her hands beneath her hips to give herself leverage, matching thrust for wonderful thrust.

Reality quickly faded again. All her being was concentrated in her sex and the powerful pounding of Nat's organ. Never did she want him to stop. She wanted to go on like this for ever and ever. Pleasure. Ecstasy. Fire. Flood. Falling, falling. Coming together again, to clench around Nat's shaft, to feel him convulse. Long forceful thrusts. Then he was lying heavily, panting on top of her, his organ bedded deep and hard within her body.

Sated, exhilarated, Bridie stroked her hands across Nat's shoulders. With him embedded so firmly she doubted they could ever be parted. Nor did she want them to be. Unified with him, she felt complete.

How long they lay like that she did not know. Gradually she realised that Nat's organ was relaxing, no longer filling her so completely. His breathing had returned to normal and he pushed himself up on his hands to gaze down at her.

'Bridie Flannagan, you are even more wonderful than I remembered.' He lifted away from her then and rose to his feet, reaching down a hand to pull her to hers. Strong arms caught her in an embrace, held her. Warm lips claimed hers in a kiss of infinite tenderness. He was smiling when he raised his head.

Bridie's eyes widened. Something caught in her chest making it difficult for her to breathe. It was the first time she had seen him smile properly and it changed his entire appearance. This man, who smiled so, who held her in his arms, who had pleasured her body so well was

44

not the cold hard man against whom she had sworn vengeance. This man was one she loved.

Suddenly his smile was gone to be replaced by a frown which drew his brows together and the Nat Durrant she first knew was back. Her bewilderment was like a physical blow, then as quickly his features relaxed again.

'The night is still young, Bridie, and our pleasure only begun. Would you like some wine to refresh yourself before we continue?'

'Please,' said Bridie, her mouth inexplicably dry.

'Don't go away.'

'I won't,' Bridie promised. As if she would.

Watching him walk from the room to fetch the wine, proud and magnificent in his nakedness, she acknowledged anew that she had fallen in love with him. Not the way she loved Seamus. This was a deeper, more intensely sexual emotion. Had he seen love in her eyes? Was that why he had frowned? Bridie remembered him telling her she had expressive eyes.

That had been the first time. Her body had welcomed him then. It adored him now. Surely he could not have done such wonderful things to her if he did not feel at least a little love. Bridie walked over to the bed and sank down into its softness with a satisfied smile curving her lips. She had all the hours of the night to show Nat just how much her body enjoyed the pleasure only his could impart.

Chapter Three

*T*he chill mist which shrouded the valley in white could not dampen Bridie's happiness. Even now, three hours after she had woken at Nat's side, she felt as close to him as when their limbs were entwined and their bodies joined in matchless harmony. As they had been for the greater part of the night until the passion had eased to languorous pleasuring from which they had drifted into sleep.

Bridie's first stirring to the grey light of morning had brought Nat's body hungrily over hers in proprietary union. She had welcomed his possessiveness, eager to give him every pleasure his powerful shaft demanded for in that way she too soared the heights of sexual hedonism. Later they had dressed, then breakfasted together in the fire-warmed dining room under the disapproving scowl of the housekeeper. During the course of breakfast Nat had given her the money for the farm. Almost double the amount for which she had asked. Her protests had been swept aside by his declaration that he could well afford to pay her handsomely though she was given cause to wonder why he spoke with such a glint in his dark eyes.

'Surely there are papers I need to sign,' she had said,

her fingers curling unfamiliarly over the bundle of bank-notes. Never before having seen more than one or two bank notes at the same time, she marvelled at the manner in which Nat had been able to casually produce such a vast sum. On lifting her bemused gaze from the wad of money, Bridie discovered he was observing her with an amused indulgence.

'I trust you, Bridie. Take the money now. My lawyer will sort out the legalities later. Now I see Jim's bringing your horse.'

Bridie turned to the window to see the man leading the saddled mare towards the front of the house. The imminence of her parting from Nat deflated her happiness in a way the bleakness of the day could not. Her gaze returned to her lover's face. The face she would know blindfolded if her fingers and lips were able to trace its contours. Not only his face was indelibly etched in her sensory memory. After all the hours of passion, tenderness, exhilaration, gentle coupling and agonising orgasms, she knew his body as well as she knew her own and her own she knew far more intimately than before.

Obviously sensing something of her feelings, Nat drew her into an embrace to kiss her with an ardency which made her tremble with wanting that they could be united again. When his lips released hers he held her slightly away, the gleam in his eyes witness to his own arousal. His voice, when he spoke, was deep with feeling.

'Bridie Flannagan, why do you have to go? What we shared last night was too good to come to this end. Stay with me, Bridie. I want you always in my bed.'

The passion, the promise, of his words kindled the fire in Bridie's belly and set her heart singing. Nat cared about her. He felt the same as she felt. Oh, she had known it must be so from all the tender endearments which had punctuated their passion. If her eyes now sparkled with the love she felt she did not care. Her entire self was bubbling with joy.

47

'Oh, Nat. Yes. Yes. I want nothing more than to be your wife.'

'What?' He stared at her as if he had not heard correctly, shock and incredulity plain in his expression.

The bubble of Bridie's happiness fizzled to flatness. 'You were after asking me to marry you, were you not?'

'Good heavens, no.' Then he laughed. He actually laughed at her. 'Bridie Flannagan, you're full of surprises. You don't really think a man in my position could marry a dishonest Irishman's daughter, do you? What would a person of your background, raised in poverty, know of the type of life I lead? Ah no, Bridie. I have chosen the woman who will make me a suitable wife. I only want you in my bed.'

The pain started when he laughed. By the time he finished speaking it had been joined by humiliation and anger. At the final pejorative 'you' anger got the upper hand and Bridie's hand swung a stinging blow to the side of his face. Before he could recover from the unexpectedness of her action she ran from the house. By the time he strode after her, she was swinging herself into the saddle, not needing Jim's assistance. When Nat called her name, demanding she wait, she urged her horse forward and was at full gallop before she reached the open gate.

Bridie soon realised her fear, or was it hope, that Nat would come after her was unfounded. With her panting mount eased to a walk, she reviewed, realistically and painfully, her brief relationship with Nat Durrant. Self-denigration was the most painful of all. How naive she had proved herself to be by her assumption his interest in her was anything other than purely sexual. Without doubt he was a man well experienced in the art of pleasing a woman. How many women had he pleased? They were probably without number. Was she the only one to have been foolish enough to interpret his adoration of her body as an expression of love?

In an endeavour to assuage the hurt, Bridie tried to convince herself it was only her naivety which led her to believe herself in love with Nat. He had taught her all the delights he had promised to teach her, tutored her in the many ways a man and woman could give each other pleasure. Was she confusing love with sexual euphoria? When all was said and done she had enjoyed sex with Seamus, too. Surely, with the knowledge she now possessed she could make sex with Seamus, or any other man, as exciting as it had been with Nat. Ah yes, thought Bridie. She had the knowledge and the money Nat had given her and she would use them both to her advantage.

On that resolution Bridie thrust the pain in her heart aside and told herself she was not in love with Nat Durrant. There was one hurt, however, which had cut too deep to be ignored. She might be Irish and she might be poor but she was every bit as worthy as Nat Durrant with all his money, his education, his upper-class English background and his suitable fiancée.

One day, Bridie vowed, she was going to show him that she was his equal. Nat Durrant would never again share her bed but he would, by all the saints in Ireland, regret he had ever laughed at her or declared her unworthy of becoming his wife.

Compared with the luxury of the homestead high in the valley, the small hut appeared even more shabby and mean. Bridie looked about her with distaste, glad she need never return to this place. Yet she had no idea where she would go. The O'Flynns had offered to take her in, undoubtedly in the belief it would only be a matter of time before Seamus and she were married. Bridie knew he waited only to have enough money to build a house of their own before demanding she name the day.

The money Nat had paid her for the farm would be more than enough to set them up, and yet ... Bridie wondered whether she was being foolish in wanting more from life than a good husband and a handful of babies. Why should she be so apathetic about marrying Seamus when she would gladly have married Nat? The answer was not one she wanted to hear so she reminded herself instead of her vow to make Nat Durrant regret he ever laughed at her. And that she could never do married to Seamus.

Delicious fantasies of revenge occupied Bridie's mind while she gathered the things she wanted to keep, sorted the items which would be of use to the other battlers of Barkers Ridge, and put aside everything which was fit only to throw away. While the scenarios she envisaged, of having Nat Durrant at her mercy, were highly improbable, they were equally satisfying. ''Tis a pleasant dream you're having, Bridie Flannagan,' she told herself, 'but it's not likely to come true.'

She was bundling her father's few decent clothes together, ready to be given away, and dragged from beneath his bed the wooden box where he kept his personal belongings. Not expecting it to contain more than a few bits and pieces, Bridie was surprised by its heaviness. Neither had she expected the box to be locked and was forced to spend a good thirty minutes searching for the key. By the time she located it hidden high in a crack in the wall her curiosity about what was in the box had driven all other thoughts from her head. Not in a dozen lifetimes would she have expected it to be filled with money, coins, banknotes, even gold and jewellery. And an ancient heavy pistol.

For a long time Bridie simply stared at the box's contents, too stunned for coherent thought. 'The old bastard,' she muttered. 'He's been doing more than stealing a cow or two.' How many robberies had there been? And when? Had Flannagan been involved in that hold-up on the Melbourne road six months earlier? Not having any way of knowing, Bridie stared at the bounty and thought.

Flannagan's name had never been mentioned in connection with any robbery. No one had ever come to the hut asking questions. With her father dead, she was very likely the only person who knew about the hoard. Bridie decided she was more her father's daughter than she had believed. She was going to keep it all.

'I'll not be letting you go, Bridie,' Seamus declared. 'I want to marry you.'

'I'm not ready to marry.' Bridie sighed, upset that Seamus was taking her decision so badly.

'You were acting like you were more than ready last week.'

Feeling the colour rise in her cheeks, Bridie hoped Seamus took it to be from coyness at the wantonness of her intimacy with him. In truth it was from recollection of how much more wantonly she had acted with Nat.

'You said you loved me,' Seamus continued.

'I do love you, Seamus, but I'm wanting to experience more of life before I marry. You could be coming to Melbourne with me,' she added with the impish smile which had always made him agree to anything she wanted. She had told Seamus nothing of the small fortune which was even now secreted in her bag among her clothes. Nor had he any knowledge of her ultimate goal – to bring Nat Durrant to his knees.

Seamus looked sullen. 'Would you marry me, then?'

'My mind's made up, Seamus, but we could see a lot of each other.'

'I could be seeing a lot of you now.' He stared hard at her, the sullenness of his expression only partly replaced by desire. 'I could make you change your mind.'

'Try then, Seamus O'Flynn,' Bridie challenged him, knowing he would never make her change her mind. She also knew that her body was aching to be invaded by a hard male organ; was always aching because most of her waking moments and even her dreams were filled with erotic remembrances of that night with Nat. Not that she allowed herself to think much about the man. Only about the things he had done to her body, the delicious sensations he had aroused, the ecstatic heights of sexual euphoria to which he had taken her flesh.

Bridie well knew, having now experienced those licentious delights, she would not be able to deny herself any opportunity for repeating those pleasures. Nor did she intend to try. A man was a man when all was said and done, whether it was Seamus or any other.

In the moments it took those thoughts to pass through her mind she stepped up to Seamus to place her arms around his neck and kiss him on the mouth. She moved her lips seductively over his in the manner she had learnt from Nat. The effect was dramatic. Seamus pulled her tightly against his body so that her breasts were crushed against his chest and she could feel the stirring of his cock against her abdomen. His hands clawed at her buttocks through the material of her skirt, the stirring against her abdomen now a rigid column, caught between their bodies in promise of imminent pleasure.

The rapidity with which Seamus had been fully aroused gave Bridie a heady feeling of power. She cast aside the niggling fear she had entertained that he would find some other woman to take her place. She had wanted to keep his love and loyalty and knew now that nothing was going to change. Seamus would always be hers. Only she did not want to marry him. Not yet, maybe never. What she did want was that hard organ which pressed against her belly to be thrust deep between her thighs.

Seamus's urgency was becoming greater. While he continued to claw at her buttocks to press her closer he was moving his hips to thrust against her and drive himself into a frenzy. Suddenly he released her from the sexual embrace and dragged her by the hand towards her bed to push her none too gently down on to the mattress. He hauled her skirt up and spread her legs all in the same movement, his eyes glazing with lust when he discovered she was, as always, naked beneath her skirt.

The expression of near torment on his face as he clawed frantically at the fastening of his trousers caused such a thrill to tremble and prick inside Bridie that she discarded the idea she had of teaching Seamus some of the new ways of delight she had learnt. Instead she wanted Seamus to ravish her with his impatience and indeed, when he dropped his trousers, his organ did appear as a powerful weapon.

Within moments he was on top of her and there was no waiting, no preliminary fondling. He entered her swiftly and plunged deeply, his groan of satisfaction echoed by her cry of pleasure. His pounding was merciless, the force of each downward plunge jerking through Bridie's body and she relished every stroke. She knew he would reach his climax quickly and wanted to be there with him. The next time he reared back she slipped her hand between their bodies before he plunged downward again. Her finger quickly located the little peak of sensitivity about which she now knew so much. It was already engorged and sensitised, responding immediately to her touch.

Oh, yes. It was going to be soon. And for Seamus, too. Then she was suddenly no longer capable of coherent thought. There were only images and feelings and sweet burning delight throbbing to the rhythm of Seamus's pounding strokes.

When it was over he lay heavily on top of her, his breath a series of rasping gasps. Though the weight of his body crushed her, making her own breathing difficult, Bridie made no attempt to push him away. His manhood remained nestled in her sheath and she had no desire yet to deprive herself of its satisfying presence. With a secretive smile curving her lips she focused all her attention on their unity and began, slowly, consistently, to clench her internal muscles around the column of flesh they embraced. It was not going to be allowed to

53

relax out of her. Not yet. Bridie knew how to restore its strength.

A groan shuddered through Seamus's body and he pushed himself up on his hands to gaze down at her with an expression of agonised wonder. Giving him her impish smile, Bridie contracted her muscles again to hold him inside her as tightly as possible. She was rewarded with a second, louder groan and an almost despairing, 'By all the saints, Bridie,' before he was pounding her again. This time she slipped her hands beneath her buttocks to lift herself to meet every thrust.

Later she would be forced to deal with renewed pleas for them to marry but for now all she wanted was the intense physical activity to take her mind off Nat and his intended bride, because having sex with Seamus had only brought the other man more strongly to her thoughts. Just briefly, before she lost herself in another orgasm, Bridie wondered if the eminently suitable fiancée would have the ability to satisfy as sexual a man as Nat Durrant.

The horses picked their way slowly along the narrow path, lightly guided by their riders. They were docile animals who knew their way through the bush and were unlikely to be startled by lizards scuttling through the dry leaves or the sudden flight of a bird across their path. The young woman rode in front, as was her due. A mere painting master could not expect to ride ahead of or even abreast of his wealthy pupil no matter how intimate their relationship.

She had chosen their destination for she longed to capture on canvas the afternoon colours of the bay when the grey-blue water took on a molten sheen and the trees of the far side became capped with golden crowns. Lisette was passionate about her painting. Colours fascinated her and she gained immense satisfaction from reproducing on canvas the unique colours of the country-side. The praise of friends and family for her paintings meant little. What really mattered was that Mr Graham believed she possessed true artistic talent.

The painting master had come into her life six months previously after she convinced her parents that painting, to her, was not simply a genteel pastime in which she liked to dabble. Lisette had dreams of becoming a great artist. Mr Graham fostered those dreams and bemoaned with her that she must bow to the expectations of society and marry in accordance with her parents' wishes. His constant assertion that marriage would stifle her creativity had filled Lisette with doubts about her future life.

She glanced back over her shoulder to where he rode a few yards behind, leading a pack-horse which carried their painting equipment. Mr Graham would also be painting this afternoon. His forte was the human figure and Lisette was a willing model. Her talent for landscapes she considered poor compared with his for portraiture.

Mr Graham had painted an exquisite likeness of Lisette which had captured the unique greenish blue of her irises and the deceptive innocence of her wide-eyed gaze. In that portrait her golden hair was dressed artfully on top of her head to display the swan-like curve of her graceful neck. She had been painted in a gown of pomona silk which matched the colour of her eyes and revealed the creamy perfection of her shoulders and the dark mole which sat just above the neckline of her dress on the tantalising swell of her breast. All who had seen the portrait had exclaimed in wonder at the detail in the likeness and it had gained Mr Graham several lucrative commissions. That portrait now hung in temporary pride of place in the drawing room, to be given to her husband on their marriage.

There was another portrait that no one would ever see. The one in which her hair tumbled over her shoulders, her gaze was sultry and there was no garment to conceal the beauteous swell of her breasts. Lisette had not been allowed to see it until it was finished. She had been enthralled. To see herself portrayed so seductively had stirred such feelings of wantonness that she had claimed it for her own.

For as long as she could remember, Lisette had enjoyed looking at her nudity in the mirror. At a very early age she acknowledged nature had been generous in endowing her with physical beauty. The maturing of her body from its childish shape had kept her fascinated and she observed with wonder the gradual blossoming of her breasts and the appearance of golden down at the apex of her thighs. By the time she was sixteen Lisette had come to admire her body as much as she admired her face. Nor was it long before she discovered her narcissistic appreciation stirred exciting twinges deep inside her most intimate places.

Those thrills were as nothing to the ones she received on gazing at her nude portrait, at the rosy nipples, the lightly veined breasts and the dewy sheen of her pubic hair. There was the second mole, too, just above the golden curls. Lisette had despaired of those imperfections until Mr Graham had convinced her they enhanced both her beauty and her desirability. Mr Graham had declared his own desire and Lisette, aroused to an awareness of her sexuality, had succumbed. To a degree.

They came to the place Lisette had chosen on a sheltered rise overlooking the bay. They were still on her father's land yet far enough from the house to be undisturbed. While Mr Graham set up the easels Lisette tethered the horses, girths loosened, where they could graze. Her painting master was barely able to keep his seat on a horse. That the care of the horses must fall to her lessened him not in her eyes. She gazed at him now to wonder yet again at her fascination with him and compare him with the man she was to marry. There could be no two men less alike. Nat Durrant was all aggressive masculinity while Mr Graham was almost effeminate in appearance and manner. He adopted an artistic carelessness of dress and his light-brown hair was constantly disordered by his habit of running his fingers through it when concentrating. They were long, thin fingers. Everything about Mr Graham was long and thin. His face, his body and even his penis. Yet Lisette could not imagine him any other way.

'Where shall I pose?' she asked.

'I think on that rock with the trees behind you. If you were half seated, half reclining, I could portray you as a nymph in the woods.'

The idea of being portrayed as a nymph held appeal. The rough surface of the rock did not. That problem, Mr Graham declared, could be easily solved. He helped her remove the jacket of her nutmeg-brown riding habit then the skirt, which he draped over the rock. Lisette dealt with the remaining items of her clothing, folding each neatly before placing them in a pile beside the easel. Without self-consciousness she walked over to the rock and sat on her skirt. A sneaky cool breeze which sprang up from nowhere caressed her breasts as it shivered across the clearing. Lisette's nipples hardened in response.

'Nice,' approved Mr Graham when he saw them so rigid, 'but the areolae are a little puckered. They need to be plumped.'

He dipped his head to take one breast into his mouth, sucking gently and swilling the tip of his tongue around the nipple. To give himself support, he had placed his hands on the rock on either side of Lisette's body. She rested back on her own hands to thrust her breasts upward in welcome of the oral caress. With eyes closed she savoured the pleasure until she felt his mouth move away and heard him murmur, 'That's better.'

She looked down at herself then to see how rosy and plump the areola was and how her nipple had darkened and become even more erect. Mr Graham was giving his attention to her other breast and Lisette adjusted her position so that she could herself caress the breast which continued to tingle from his attention. She did so enjoy having her breasts caressed in any manner. To her they were the most erogenous part of her body. Even to stroke them herself aroused exquisite responses in the core of her femininity.

Having satisfied himself that her breasts had the blossoming look he wanted to capture on canvas, Mr Graham pulled the pins from her hair and used his long, sensitive fingers to fluff it around her face and swish it over one shoulder. His hands on her body, more arousing because they were impersonal, coaxed her into the required pose, half reclined, one knee crooked. He then returned to his canvas and began to paint.

The pose not being the easiest to hold, Lisette diverted her thoughts from the discomfort by thinking about the man to whom she had been promised in marriage. He would be returning to Melbourne on the morrow when their engagement would be made official. Her parents were giving a ball, to be attended by everybody who was anybody in the colony, at which the announcement would be made.

Lisette's feelings were in turmoil. In part she wanted to be married, quickly, so that she might experience that which she desired so intensely. No matter what else she did with Mr Graham she was determined to go to her husband a virgin. There was also the concern as to whether or not her husband would view her desire to paint with seriousness or dismiss it as a mere hobby. Either way Lisette doubted he would allow Mr Graham to remain with her as tutor. Though she had met Nat Durrant less than a half-dozen times Lisette was certain he was no fool.

An exasperated oath brought her sombre thoughts back to the present. Mr Graham was glaring at her, the hand which held the brush poised mid-air and the other raking through his hair. 'I am trying to paint a seductive nymph, not a scowling woman. What's the matter with you, Lisette? Where are your thoughts?'

The staccato words of censure, combined with the

increased ache in her muscles when she moved, exacerbated Lisette's mental turmoil to a degree which resulted in the formation of tears in her eyes. Being totally absorbed in the pursuance of his art, the sight of those tears exasperated Mr Graham even more. He flung down the brush in an overly dramatic gesture. 'I give up. You are being quite impossible. We might as well go back to the house.'

'No. I want you to paint my picture.'

'The light will not be right for an hour or more yet. What am I to do until then?'

'I will pose for you properly.' Lisette wiped her tears away with one hand and resumed her pose. 'It is just that I was thinking about tomorrow. And the future.'

Mr Graham's ire faded almost as dramatically as it had been aroused. He walked slowly over to Lisette. 'My poor Lisette. I understand. Shall I make you feel better?'

Without waiting for her to reply, he knelt, parted her thighs and plunged his tongue between her folds with an accuracy which swept all thoughts of her future husband from Lisette's mind. She very soon forgot about the aches in her muscles and the hardness of the rock on which she reclined. Mr Graham's talent with his tongue was excelled only by his talent with palette and brush. He stroked along her central crease and teased the folds with as many variations of touch as he would use to brush colour on a canvas. When he hardened his tongue to press it into her opening Lisette's body gave an uncontrolled twitch. His tongue became an erotic instrument which sensitised the soft inner flesh to send delicious darts of arousal stabbing through her groin.

Frustratingly, annoyingly, his tongue gave only a few brief flicks at the tiny peak which tingled more than any other part. Lisette's softly moaned, 'Oh, please,' was ignored. A few more deft, devastating strokes of his tongue and he rose to lean over her and press his lips against hers. He worked their mouths together so that she could taste herself and be doubly aroused by her own tangy flavour.

'Now you have the look I want,' he declared when he raised his head. He fluffed her hair, moved the placing of her right hand and walked back to resume his painting. 'Keep thinking about sex, darling, and don't move a muscle.'

Lisette was not able to think of anything but sex. She knew well how she must look for she had studied herself in the mirror when she had been sexually aroused, and had even watched while she pleasured herself. Her eyes would have darkened to the colour of a stormy sea, her lips would be full and ripely seductive, the expression on her face wholly sensuous. How could it be otherwise when her body was so inflamed with desire, so aroused, yet so unsatisfied?

Very carefully, so as not to break the line of her pose, Lisette shifted one hand between her thighs to continue what Mr Graham had started. Her fingers had barely made satisfying contact with her soft moist flesh before a sharp reprimand returned her to her pose. Lisette pouted but did not dare move again lest he leave her unsatisfied for the remainder of the afternoon. He had done that sometimes. Either made her wait an interminable time or left her aroused and unsatisfied simply to prove he was not a pawn to her pleasure.

While he might deny her what she wanted, he would never do what she forbade. To fall out of favour with Lisette, and therefore the elder Cunninghams, would be to see his career as a portrait artist falter. In the end Mr Graham would always bow to what Lisette wanted. Right at this moment she wanted sexual satisfaction. She simply could not wait. With a defiant pout she shifted her hand again and this time pushed two fingers into her warmth to give initial ease to the ache of need.

'I am not going to stop,' she declared when Mr Graham frowned.

'Then go ahead,' he said with infuriating indifference. 'I'll sketch some of the background while you're busy.'

And enjoy watching her masturbate. He did not need to say the words. She had touched herself for his pleasure before. The excitement of having him admire her in this manner manifested itself in a warm oozing which coated her embedded fingers. Lisette reclined fully in a more comfortable position with legs opened towards Mr Graham so that the petals of her feminine flower were fully revealed to his gaze.

The worst of her ache having been dulled, Lisette toyed with herself slowly, to prolong her own pleasure and to tantalise her painting master with what he could not have. All the time, while she toyed with her sex with one hand and caressed her breasts with the other, she kept her provocative gaze on his face. His gaze flicked back and forth from her to the canvas until she noted that it dwelt longer each time on her and only briefly on his work. Before long, he put his brush aside to come over to her, his expression one of tortured lust, his own arousal evident.

'Let me,' he begged, plunging a finger in with hers in an action so sexually shocking her body convulsed and she came near to losing control. She *was* losing control. She eased her own finger out so that she could rub her engorged nub. Mr Graham's finger remained motionless inside her. It did not matter. Within moments she was writhing with the delight of her orgasm. When it faded and he withdrew his finger she shuddered at the deprivation. Having closed her eyes at the onset of orgasm, she opened them to see him pulling open his trouser front. The determined expression on his face and the fire in his pale eyes sent a frisson along her spine. Lisette wondered if, this time, she had driven him too far. His cock was free and he was leaning towards her as if he would drive it into her in place of his finger.

'No!' Lisette cried. 'You cannot.' She turned swiftly on to her stomach, her feet reaching down to touch the ground, her buttocks lifted. There was a moment of real fear when she felt the velvety head of his penis rest against her crease. A sob caught in her throat and she cast a desperate glance over her shoulder. 'Oh, do not. Please. You know I cannot let you.'

He simply smiled and began to rub the tip against her softness and to flick it against her still highly sensitised nub until she was in a frenzy of desire and fear. Fear that she was no longer in control – of Mr Graham or her own body.

'You do want me right inside you, Lisette,' he cajoled. He pressed the very extremity of his shaft just between her sex-lips in a manner that induced an urge in her to embrace it farther. 'You can't deny what I can feel. How wet and warm and ready to be entered you are.'

Oh she was. Yes she was. But it could not be. 'Please, Mr Graham. You know – I told you – oh, please, please.' She was sobbing, the words disjointed, fighting herself more than she was pleading with Mr Graham.

'Please what, my dear? Please fuck you?'

'No!' she cried quickly lest she say 'yes'.

To her relief he pulled away and used his fingers to spread her sex-juice up between her buttocks. He smeared it around her anus before he worked his finger into that opening to stretch it and prepare her. As always, she cried out at his initial entry and the slightly painful stretching of the passage. By the time his long thin cock had penetrated her fully she was ready to give herself up to the delight of the only physical penetration she permitted.

His hands on her buttocks pulled them apart to open her and make easier his thrusts. Lisette's senses were swimming. When the rhythm of his thrusts changed to the slow withdrawal and forceful embedding which told her he was near his climax, Lisette pushed a hand between her abdomen and the rock so that she could plunge two fingers into herself. By pressing against the thin wall which separated the two passages she could doubly experience the piston action of his rod. Her thumb rubbed against her clit to intensify every sensation until she was quivering. Though in a near swoon with the ecstasy of her orgasm, she still registered Mr Graham's own climactic groans.

'One day,' he declared, 'you will drive me too far and I will take you in that virgin canal of yours no matter how much you plead.'

But Lisette, sexually sated, took no heed of his threat. They were simply words. Words she had heard before. Mr Graham knew that her maidenhead would only be breached by her husband on their wedding night. Nat Durrant would despise a bride who was not a virgin.

The O'Flynns' expressions of concern and disapproval were added to Seamus's pleas for Bridie to remain in Barkers Creek. All were to no avail. She packed her meagre possessions in a battered bag and hitched a ride with a waggoner to save herself the coach fare. There would, she reasoned, be better uses for her money when she finally reached Melbourne.

Being obliged to cook the man's meals and share his blanket at night in payment of her passage was no great hardship. Especially not the sharing of his bed. The waggoner was a giant of a man with a virility which matched his physique. While he lacked the finesse of Nat Durrant, he well knew the more a woman enjoyed herself, the greater was his own pleasure.

His company was to prove fortuitous in a far more practical way. Perched on the high seat of the waggon, gazing at the swaying rumps of the plodding horses, Bridie confided her dream of bettering herself in Melbourne, of rising above her poor origins to take her place in society. A grunt followed by silence had her wondering if he thought her foolish. Until he spoke.

'It's been done before, ordinary folks stepping up into society. Of course you need to have money –' he made a sideways glance at her profile '– though I might be able

63

to put you in the way of the right people. There's one or two that owe me a favour.'

'You would?' Immediately she was confident again, and cautious. 'Then you would consider I owed you a favour too.'

For answer he chuckled and drew back on the reins to bring the horses to a halt. There was an unmistakable gleam in his eyes. 'It could take us quite a few days to get to Melbourne, depending on how slow we go. Reckon that's plenty of time for you to show me just how appreciative you are.' He rubbed his hand suggestively over his crotch. 'Starting right now.'

Bridie's own eyes gleamed in response. She wasn't going to object. Not to anything.

Chapter Four

*F*ar more satisfying to Bridie than the admiring gazes of the men was the knowledge that not one of the illustrious company suspected her poor origins. Oh, they knew she was Irish. There was no disguising her generic features even if she had so wanted. Which she did not, for she had all the pride of her forebears. It was the lineage of those forebears about which Melbourne society was under a misapprehension, believing them to be a noble line which stretched back to the time of Brian Boru.

Bridie had come far in the world since months earlier, when she lived in poverty tending the land. Now, with the money from her sold homestead, and the pleasing find of the hoard under her bed, Bridie had changed – and become a much-lusted-after member of Melbourne society.

The people with whom she mingled believed her recently arrived in the colony, her presence explained as a mission to study potential investment opportunities for her wealthy father. This fabrication of her background, devised with the help of Mrs Winchester, had given her entry to a life she might otherwise have been denied. Mrs Winchester, that redoubtable dowager, had been a gem of a find. Under her careful tuition, Bridie had mastered all the social graces, learnt to dress with tasteful elegance and to soften her Irish brogue to a more cultured speech.

The good lady's own impeccable background and social standing had enabled her to introduce Bridie to the people by whom she had greatly desired to be accepted. The set of people with whom Nat Durrant would associate.

While the story of her interest in investments intrigued the men and caused the women to regard her with perplexity, they were by no means entirely false. One of the first things Bridie had done on arriving in Melbourne was to seek professional advice on how best to invest her money. The advice had been sound and with a number of her investments giving quick and profitable return she was now far wealthier than she had dreamt possible.

Not all her wealth, though, had been accumulated by wise investment. Bridie had discovered that she actually had the fabled 'luck of the Irish' when it came to cards. While gambling might not be considered to be quite proper for a young lady, Bridie pursued this pastime with profitable enjoyment. This despite the protests and dire predictions of Mrs Winchester. Her late husband's penchant for gambling had left her in the penurious state which had her grab at the opportunity to become the paid patroness and mentor of the rough-edged Irish lass. But this was one subject on which Bridie would not be guided.

On this night there would be gambling after dinner for those who wished to participate. Bridie already knew who would take seats at the tables and looked forward to what was undoubtedly going to be an exhilarating night. There were times when she considered the thrill of gambling to be almost as stimulating as sex.

At the moment she was enjoying the amorous attentions of several young men, responding flirtatiously to their flattery without giving any one cause to believe she might be persuaded to take a lover. One of the first things she had learnt was the importance of discretion.

Bridie did not take her lovers from her social set. There were other men she managed to meet who were only too happy to accommodate her sexual needs.

Unfortunately, accommodate her needs was all any of them had ever done. Not one had ever fired her body to passion. Not the way Nat Durrant had done. The suggestive flattery of one of her admirers recalled to her thoughts the night she had spent with Nat. She shifted uncomfortably, her body ever ready to respond to the memories.

To her relief, dinner was announced just then and the group made a move towards the dining room. It was then that Bridie saw him; the man she resented – and desired – above all others. He had obviously just arrived and was being greeted by their host. Bridie saw his gaze sweep the room as if in search of someone. It passed by the group she was with only to swing back quickly. His brows drew together slightly as if he was trying to place her face before his eyes widened in disbelieving recognition. At that moment his attention was claimed by the young woman who had hurried to his side. And that gave Bridie cause to draw her own brows together in a tiny frown.

There was no mistaking the intimacy of the girl's hand resting on his arm and the way she gazed up at him, nor the expression on his face when he gazed down at her with his hand moving to cover the tiny one which lay on his sleeve.

The immediate, uncontrollable, rush of desire Bridie had felt on seeing him drowned in a rising wave of resentment. So Lisette Cunningham was the suitable woman he had chosen to be his wife. Lisette had never told Bridie to whom she was affianced. Fast on the heels of Bridie's resentment came a surge of jealousy which caught her with such surprise that for a moment all coherent thought seemed to fly out of her head. Lisette was beautiful. A dainty, fragile creature of the type men longed to cherish and protect. Why would Nat desire her, a buxom Irish lass, when he had Lisette? And the worst of it all was that Bridie liked the other girl. Then another thought struck Bridie. Nat Durrant knew her true background.

Hardly able to concentrate on her dinner partner's chatter, Bridie allowed herself to be led to the dining room, relieved to discover she was seated too far away from Nat and Lisette for conversation to be possible. Yet she was as aware of him as if he was sitting next to her with his thigh brushing suggestively against hers as her partner's was now doing.

Although he could not hear her words, the lilt of her voice carried down the table to Nat. He realised her manner of speech had changed in accordance with her appearance even if her voice had lost none of its musical quality. He wished he was seated on the opposite side of the table so that he could feast his eyes on her. If he had thought he wanted her before, he wanted her tenfold now.

There were few times in the months since she had slapped his face and run out of the house that Bridie had ever been far from Nat's thoughts. He had not followed her because initially he had not really cared. Or so he told himself. Having spent a sexually magnificent night taking all her body could offer, he decided he had no need to complicate his life with a hot-tempered Irish wench.

Unfortunately, that very night, when he lay alone in his bed, his memories of her had been so vivid he had been brought to the humiliating state of having to manually render his own relief. Nor did things become any easier. Each time it became necessary to find a woman with whom to ease his sexual torment he regretted more and more that he had ever laughed at Bridie. If he had not offended her pride he would surely have been able to persuade her to be his mistress.

The shock of recognising her this night, in a place he

68

never expected her to be, had been so great it was with extreme difficulty he gave due attention to his fiancée and took intelligent part in the dinner conversation. Despite himself his gaze kept straying down the table to catch glimpses of her, apparently at ease and enjoying herself. He burnt with curiosity to know how she had raised herself to this status and where she had learnt to dress so elegantly as to be at ease in society. While his mind burnt with questions, his body burnt with desire. A desire so intense he realised he must exert considerable will power or he would be unable to rise from the table without causing himself considerable embarrassment.

Nat tried to put Bridie out of his mind. At least he tried to eschew images of her seductive body. Again and again he wondered about how she had wrought this change in her life. A rich husband perhaps? He decided to make a few discreet enquiries before he sought to resume a liaison.

Once or twice catching Nat's gaze turned in her direction, Bridie chose to pursue a policy of indifference. This was in part from fear of what disclosures he might make but mainly because this was what she had been planning from the moment she found the hidden money. Though she was less sanguine over the success of her plan now that she knew Lisette was his future wife, she still relished the notion of having him beg for her favours. On this resolution she adjourned speedily to the gaming room before Nat could speak with her.

Not that he had any intention of so doing. The knowledge of where she had gone gave him even more fuel for thought. Ladies did not usually gamble and he wondered, with an ache in his groin, if she had become some other man's mistress. Was she in the company of a husband or lover? If she was married, so be it. But he discovered he bitterly resented the thought of some other man having what he had turned aside. He knew he would have no peace of mind until he discovered the truth.

Lisette was the one who unwittingly provided him with all the information. 'Isn't that just like Bridie to rush away to cards before I had a chance to introduce you?'

The surprised, 'You know her?' that Nat almost uttered was hastily swallowed back. 'Who is Bridie?' he asked instead in a voice which strove for a tone of polite interest.

'A new friend. You must surely have noticed her when you arrived. She was the beauty in the blue velvet with the horde of admirers.'

'Ah. I think I know whom you mean. I was more concerned with looking for you.'

Lisette cast him a coquettish smile, not fully believing he had not noticed Bridie. Every man did. 'She is the most interesting person. Her father is of the Irish nobility and the family is quite wealthy. Bridie has come to Australia to investigate opportunities for investment. Quite unusual for a woman, don't you think? She is extremely clever.'

'You admire this woman?' This astonished Nat more than Bridie's fabricated background.

'Oh yes. I like her very much, too. In fact I am thinking of asking her to be one of my bridesmaids.'

Nat almost choked. What man's mistress had ever attended his bride? And Nat was more determined than ever to make Bridie his mistress. If Lisette possessed all the attributes to make him the perfect wife, there was no doubt Bridie was the perfect woman to take to his bed.

Bridie had not reappeared before the Cunninghams were ready to take their leave. Presuming the gamblers would be at their game until the small hours of the morning, Nat agreed to accompany the Cunninghams to their home. Once there, and after they had all enjoyed a nightcap, Lisette's parents retired to allow the betrothed couple a few minutes on their own.

Well aware that Mrs Cunningham would be back

70

downstairs if Nat had not departed within ten minutes, he was surprised when Lisette came to snuggle up against him in beguiling intimacy. When the customary chaste kiss deepened to something more sensual Nat hastily held her away. If he had not known Lisette better he would have thought she was attempting to seduce him. Then again, maybe she was. There was a sexual gleam in her eyes which had never been there before.

'I do wish we were already married.' Her body was pressing closer, her hand splaying across his shirt front in a totally unexpected gesture of intimacy. Every action was leaving him in no doubt as to why his betrothed wanted to be married. On that thought he realised he was fully prepared to wait for their wedding night.

'We will be in another two months, my dear. Are you becoming impatient?'

Her vehement and passionate, 'Yes,' both pleased and surprised him. He had not thought she would be such a passionate creature. In fact it would be the easiest thing in the world for him to take her, right at this moment, and he found himself wishing he felt at least a degree of desire. What better way to ease this ache that had been tormenting him all evening than with his future wife?

However, he was too aware of the relentless ticking of the clock. With Lisette's kisses becoming more urgent and his shaft reluctantly hardening, he held her firmly away and rose to his feet.

'It is late, my dear. Your mother will be down shortly if I do not leave. I will see you tomorrow.'

Nat's departure brought angry tears of frustration to Lisette's eyes. She had hoped so very much that he would respond in an ungentlemanly manner to her indication of her eagerness to be married. Lisette did not know how much longer she would be able to bear not having proper sex. Not only were her encounters with Mr Graham leaving her less satisfied each time, she was afraid she was now far less in control of herself. With Nat's return to town she had hoped to persuade him to pre-empt their marriage. Once he had taken her maidenhead and satis-fied himself she was a virgin, she would be free to do whatever she wished. And how she wished to have Mr Graham slide his steel-like rod into the opening between her thighs instead of the one between her buttocks.

In her bedroom Lisette allowed her maid to help her out of her elaborate evening gown and into her night-gown before she sent her away. When the girl had gone Lisette pulled her nightgown off again and stood in front of the mirror gazing at the reflection of her naked beauty. As they so frequently did, her hands caressed her body, stroking adoringly over the fullness of her breasts, and the tiny waist. They curved over her hips and toyed with the golden triangle of curls. Surely Nat would desire her when he saw her naked. Somehow she must make certain that he did. Then she would no longer have to suffer this torment of frustration.

Her gaze shifted to the painting which hung next to the mirror. It was her own landscape, of golden sunlight over the bay, and it was by far the best she had ever done. Hidden beneath it, in a clever frame that came apart, was the nude study Mr Graham had painted that same afternoon.

Lisette stepped closer to the wall and removed the clips that held the two paintings together. She lifted her own painting and set it aside so that she could admire her portrait. If her landscape was the best she had done then surely this study was the best Mr Graham had ever produced. Lisette considered it far superior to the one he had kept for himself. In that first nude study she was all seductive promise. In this one she had the sensual bloom of a woman who had been well and truly sexually satisfied.

Simply gazing at her portrait was sufficient to increase her desire and magnify that delicious moist tingling between her thighs. A shudder of intense longing was accompanied by a sigh of frustration. She could lie on the bed and pleasure herself while she gazed at her portrait

or she could – dare she? – creep up to Mr Graham's
room.

This was something Lisette had never before considered doing. Not only was there considerable risk of
discovery, but there was also her conviction that such a
course of action would weaken the control she held of
the painting master's desires. There had been times,
when her parents were out, when they had indulged in
sexual activity in the third-floor room which he had been
given for his studio. Most of the time their intimacies
occurred when they ventured out into the country so that
Lisette could practise her landscape painting.

The thought of going to his room, and the risk entailed,
gave such a delicious thrill of fearful anticipation it very
nearly created its own orgasmic reaction. Lisette pressed
her hand between her thighs, holding herself, and making up her mind. The latter was not so very difficult. In
the state she was in she would never be able to go to
sleep.

With only a light woollen robe to cover her nakedness
and with her feet bare to avoid making any noise, Lisette
crept cautiously out of her room, along the passage and
up the stairs to the third floor where Mr Graham occupied a bedroom next to his studio.

The danger inherent in what she was doing, and the
knowledge of the terrible consequences she would suffer
if discovered, enhanced her tingling anticipation of soon
being with her lover. Impatient though she was to surrender her virginity to her betrothed, Lisette's enjoyment of
the manner in which she was able to indulge in illicit sex
was close to becoming an addiction. She wondered, as
she crept silently up the stairs, whether Nat would be a
man to enjoy the same sexual pleasure. There was no
doubt in her mind that he was an extremely virile and
experienced man and she was looking forward to the
sexual delights to which he would undoubtedly introduce her after they were married. If not before.

What Lisette did not know when she softly pushed

open Mr Graham's door was that her beloved painting master was, that very night, going to introduce her to pleasures of which she had never dreamt.

The shock of seeing his pupil slip silently into his room jerked Mr Graham from his prone position on the bed. Sitting upright he stared without speaking, his mind working rapidly. There was no need to ask why she had come. He knew that well enough. Even if he had not, he would have realised what she sought when she slid off her gown to reveal her nakedness.

As always, the petite perfection of her pale-skinned body, the voluptuousness of her breasts, and sparse dusting of golden curls aroused him to desire. He wondered if he was at last to be allowed to have that which he had long ached for: the pleasure of encasing himself in the softness of her sex.

How many times he had been tempted to ignore her wishes and do just that – show her that she could not always have her own way even if her parents did indulge her every whim. Each time the memory of the ultimatum delivered the first time she had disrobed for him hardened his self-control. He believed her threat to cry rape if he ever did other than take her anally, and then he would be ruined, imprisoned. Possibly even hung.

So he had allowed this beautiful spoilt miss to torment him with her sex and amused himself between times with the scullery maid. That lusty wench was the reason he made no move towards Lisette. Any minute now Sally would also come sneaking through his door.

Mr Graham ran his hand distractedly through his hair, wondering how best to handle this situation. If he sent Lisette away she would consider herself spurned and who knew what she might do in a fit of pique. At the very least she would deny him totally and that would be more than his body would be able to bear. Despite the fact that she was spoilt, and was engaged to be married to a powerful and wealthy man, Mr Graham never wanted to be parted from his Lisette. On the other hand he trembled to think what she might say if Sally arrived.

Lisette had not seemed to be aware of his hesitation, of the tormented thoughts that had gone racing through his mind. She had stepped closer to the bed; so close he could smell the muskiness of her sexual arousal. Taking his hand she placed it between her thighs.

'Touch me,' she whispered. 'I need it so much tonight.' Her grip on his wrist urged him to probe her moist silkiness with his fingers. He felt her tremble and a spasm of raw animal lust, and something else, ran through his own body. Mr Graham, tormented too long, came to a decision.

'I want more than my fingers in there,' he declared, probing more deeply.

'No. No.' Yet her trembling increased and he knew her desire was too great for her to control.

'You are ready for it, Lisette.' His tone was seductive, persuasive. 'Your body needs to be properly fulfilled. It needs to be filled with my cock.' He took her hand and guided it to his rigid shaft. 'You have only to step across my lap, Lisette, and slide yourself down. Feel how upright it is. Ready for you. Reaching up to your loveliness. Come across me, Lisette. You need only lower yourself. Kiss me with your beautiful cunny then embrace me fully. You know it will feel good; that this is what you really want. Come, Lisette, come over me.'

He could tell his words were affecting her as deeply as his fingers were probing her. There were little moans issuing from her lips to accompany her trembling. With his fingers still within he drew her closer, his other hand on her hip ready to guide her on to his shaft. The sweet anticipation was heightened by his triumph.

'No!' Suddenly she broke out of her sexual trance to pull back away from temptation.

'Yes!' he declared, trying to urge her to him again. 'It is what we both want.'

Lisette shook her head. She continued to tremble and

75

he thought he saw the glitter of tears in her eyes. A little more persuasion and she would yet be his.

'I must go to my husband a virgin,' she pleaded. 'I will say you raped me. You know I will.'

The renewal of her threat brought him to unaccustomed anger. His deeper probing had shown him that the proof of her virginity was no longer intact. Considering the frequency of their sexual encounters, he was not surprised. Not that she would believe him if he told her that her caution had been for naught. And all these months when he had endured frustration for nothing. Miss Lisette was due for her come-uppance.

He withdrew his fingers to pinch her soft flesh hard enough to make her cry out in pain. His satisfaction turned to surprise when he felt the moist surge of her response to the pain. The knowledge brought a new excitement. It was past time he taught his spoilt young madam a lesson and Sally, when she arrived, would help.

'I won't do anything you don't want, Lisette. I promise. But there are ways of pleasure you have not yet tried. I believe you will enjoy a little pain.' He pinched her again, laughing softly when she gasped then moaned with desire. 'Yes, my dear, definitely a little pain.'

By alternately pinching and stroking the soft flesh of her sex he brought her almost to the point of climax, withdrawing the stimulation at the precise moment when to do so would cause her almost unbearable agony. At her distraught cry he gave a soft triumphant laugh.

'Pain, my dear, is the ultimate pleasure. But to enjoy it fully you must be in bondage.'

Only when she was indeed immobilised on the bed, her wrists bound together, tethered to some point behind her and her ankles secured with two of Mr Graham's silken cravats, did she begin to experience a slight degree of trepidation. With her thighs thus parted and her sex exposed she felt incredibly vulnerable. The curious thing

76

was how the combination of bondage, shivering nervousness and vulnerability created a keen pulsing response in all the parts of her that lay between her thighs.

The thought of what Mr Graham might do to her now that she was helpless had her turning a pleading gaze upward. He stood by the bed looking down at her, the almost feminine slenderness of his body dominated by his long rigid shaft. Since Lisette entered the room he had undergone some kind of metamorphosis, from the dilettante painting master she could order around to a man of sadistic power. She had seen his face express numerous emotions but never wear the strangely cruel expression it now held.

'I won't take your virginity, Lisette. Not unless you beg me to. Perhaps by the end of your lesson you will want it more than I have wanted it for many months. Are you ready for your lesson to begin?'

Lisette was incapable of answering. She was too confused, too aroused and – yes – too curious, in a fearful kind of way. She was so busy staring at Mr Graham's face and wondering at the change in him that she barely registered the sound at the door.

Mr Graham heard, and moved quickly across the room to open the door then step through into the passage. Lisette's rush of fearful anxiety over who might have come to the door was joined by bewilderment that Mr Graham had stepped out of the room naked.

In a few moments he was back with a woman following him through the door. Her presence gave Lisette so great a shock she was momentarily immobilised with disbelief. Then she shrieked, tossing and pulling against her bonds. How humiliating, that a maid should see her like this. If the girl talked! Lisette was near to sobbing. This could not be happening. It must be a nightmare, a bad dream brought on by unfulfilled desires. It must be that because, even while she struggled against her bonds, she could feel herself becoming so very wet between her thighs. A wetness Mr Graham also felt when he came back to the side of the bed to stroke her with the same kind of reassuring caress he might have used to brush her hair from her forehead.

'You have nothing to fear, Lisette. None but the three of us will ever know what goes on in this room tonight.'

Not knowing whether or not to believe him, Lisette gave up her futile struggles, her wide-eyed gaze going apprehensively from him to the maid. She expected the girl would be either embarrassed by or contemptuous of Lisette's situation. Instead her face was flushed with desire. She was now starting to remove her own garments.

'What is she doing here?' Lisette's voice was little more than a hoarse whisper.

'Well you see, my dear, I was waiting for Sally tonight. She gives me that which you withhold. Later you will witness what that is like and wonder at what you have missed.'

Lisette felt her eyes grow even wider. 'You are going to do it with her? In front of me? Is that why you brought her in?'

'Partly. Sally will help with your tuition.' He smiled, a thin sadistic curling of his lips. 'You came to me, Lisette, of your own free will. Now I will do what I will. But you will enjoy this night, my dear. I promise you that.'

Lisette swallowed hard, not game to ask for clarification of his intent. Sally, now undressed, stood beside him giving Lisette's body a lascivious appraisal which became more intent on her sex.

Never having seen another woman naked, Lisette, in turn, studied the maid's body. The girl was plump, her breasts sagging slightly, her abdomen well rounded. And where Lisette's mound was crowned with the finest dusting of golden curls, Sally's was a veritable jungle of black hair. While acknowledging the girl's body differed in its sensuality to her own physical loveliness, Lisette discovered she was as aroused by the other woman's nudity as she was by her own.

'Let us begin,' declared Mr Graham. 'My mouth has often pleasured you, Lisette; now your mouth must give me pleasure.'

'How do I –? What –?' Lisette's voice came out in a hoarse whisper. Her mind grappled with the knowledge of what Mr Graham meant. Only she had no idea of how she was to provide such pleasure.

'Show her, Sally.'

Sally cast a mocking glance at Lisette before seating herself on the edge of the bed and taking Mr Graham's shaft in her hands. She glanced up at him, gave him a slight smile, then bent her head forward to slide her lips over the end of his manhood.

Mr Graham's, 'Watch carefully, Lisette,' was entirely unnecessary. She could not tear her gaze away. The sight of his cock disappearing into Sally's mouth was almost unbearably arousing. The maid's mouth moved up and down the shaft, occasionally releasing him completely. At such times her tongue would flick at the tip and Mr Graham would emit a low groan, an expression of tortured delight contorting his thin aesthetic face.

'Enough,' he suddenly declared, pushing Sally's head away. 'I think Lisette must now know what to do.'

Lisette was neither certain that she did nor that she wanted to try. She thought she would much prefer simply to watch. However, she was to be given no choice. Mr Graham knelt on the bed astride her chest. His left hand lifted her head, his right guided his cock towards her mouth.

'Take me.'

'I –' Opening her mouth was a mistake. He plunged his rod into her cavity, causing her to gag when it reached the back of her throat.

'Relax. You're too tense.' He withdrew until there was only about an inch of him in her mouth. 'Come, Lisette. You watched Sally.' He placed his right hand behind her head also, guiding her to suck him in and out as the maid had done.

The sensation not being unpleasant, Lisette simply relaxed her mouth and allowed Mr Graham to manipulate the movement of her head. She thought she was doing quite well until a puzzled upward glance showed her that he did not appear to be as affected by the act as he had been with Sally. Was anything different?

'You're not doing anything, Lisette. That's the problem. Sally. Help Lisette.'

Lisette barely had time to wonder how Sally was going to help before her body was jolted by the shock of the girl's hand touching her sex. More astonishing was the way her flesh responded. Within moments she forgot that it was a woman's hand down there, stroking her, imparting pleasure, for it seemed that the greater the stimulation she received the more erotic became the action of Mr Graham's rod moving in her mouth.

Her passive acceptance became active participation. Feeling quite daring, she curled her tongue so that it brushed the underside of his shaft on each stroke.

'Better, my dear, much better. Now close your lips around me, suck me in and out. Yes. Aah. That's good.'

Yes, it was good. Lisette was loving the feel of his silky skin against her lips, of sucking him deeper and deeper, relaxing her throat now so that he could plunge into the cavern. And Sally's fingers were plunging into Lisette's canal, the action of one magnifying the pleasure of the other.

Then Sally was using both hands and Lisette's entire sex felt swollen. There was moisture everywhere – on the insides of her thighs and spreading back to her anus. A finger slid into that opening to magnify Lisette's sense of naughtiness even more. Her entire body was a mass of sexual sensation with every orifice the recipient of pleasure. Lisette felt as though she might drown in carnal delight.

Shockingly, suddenly, it was all gone. Both Mr Graham and Sally moved away. Lisette cried out in protest, and in agony, the pain of aborted fulfilment almost too terrible to bear.

The couple untied her ankles and helped her to a half-seated position before they rejoined her on the bed. Lisette was not long left in doubt as to what they intended. Sally lay on her back, head at the foot of the bed, with Mr Graham poised over her body. With her legs lifted, arms curled under her knees to hold them high and wide apart, every secret of her sex was exposed to Lisette's gaze until Mr Graham's downward plunge blocked her view of the bright pink opening.

She felt a vicarious shock, her body responding as if it was her canal into which Mr Graham pounded. Her breathing became as heavy as the maid's, her whimpers faint images of Sally's lusty cries of gratification. The girl was going into orgasm and so was Mr Graham, the pair of them bucking and jerking in a frenzy of coital movement. Lisette burnt and ached on the edge of an orgasm that would not come. Tears of frustration rolled down her cheeks.

'Poor Lisette, are you suffering?' Mr Graham asked when the couple parted.

'You know I am.' Lisette sniffed back her tears and opened her thighs. 'Please suck me,' she whispered.

'Sally will do that,' her tormentor declared and, before Lisette could protest, he had lifted her legs in the air and pulled them back behind her head. In an instant Sally's face was between them, her tongue hot and eager at the already too sensitised folds. It was too much. The second time Sally's tongue flicked against her clitoris, Lisette's frustrated desire exploded with an intensity that brought her near to swooning. Oh, bliss, bliss, to have those soft lips sucking out her juices, that clever tongue teasing to maintain the orgasm, then sucking harder until Lisette was limp and exhausted and could give no more.

She felt her legs being lowered and slowly opened her eyes. Mr Graham was gazing down at her, expression inscrutable. 'You have had your pleasure, Lisette, now it is time for pain. Go, Sally. I don't need you anymore tonight.'

Though patently not pleased by so abrupt a dismissal, the girl sullenly pulled on her garments. Mr Graham moved away from the bed, waiting until she left before he returned to Lisette. He was now holding a short birch rod in his hand. Taking hold of one of her ankles, he pulled her down until she was once again lying flat on the bed.

'For months you have tortured me, Lisette, by never giving me what I wanted. Even when you came here tonight you expected to be allowed to keep your virginity. Do you wish to keep it still?'

Lisette managed a hoarse, 'Yes,' her fearfully fascinated gaze on the birch.

'In that case I must be allowed to do whatever else I will.'

'Hurt me and I'll tell.' She knew that sounded childish but she was scared. The fear manifested itself in a renewed awareness in her sex. Even her breasts were tingling in apprehensive anticipation.

'You waste your breath, my dear. Even if you still want to carry out that threat when I have finished, there is Sally to consider. The word of two against one.'

He raised the birch as he spoke then brought it down to strike lightly across her nipples with a sting which caused her to inhale sharply. Twice more he delivered the stinging blows to her breasts and with each one her lower limbs twitched and she felt the sharp pain of each right down in her sex.

Her nipples were burning, sensitised to a degree they had never been before. So sensitised, so burning, that when he bent his head to suck lightly first on one then the other the pleasure was one of indescribable exquisiteness. That he should begin to stroke the birch along her crease while he suckled served to heighten the experience. Soon she was trembling, moaning with desire, thrusting her breasts upward to his mouth and working her sex against the thin rod of birch.

But she was not to be allowed pure pleasure for long. Instead of sucking her breasts, his teeth began to nip and the birch was flicked in stinging slaps against her sex. The combined pain brought tears to her eyes and agonised moans from her lips. She became incapable of focusing on either source of pain. There were too many other sensations which became mingled. Her body was again a shivering mass of sexual awareness, welcoming the sharp pressure of teeth on her breasts and the sting of birch against her. Each sharp contact inflamed nerve endings, sent darts of fire deep inside until her core began to melt and she was convulsing with an orgasm incredibly heightened by pain.

But he was not yet finished. Even while she was in the throes of her climax, he turned her over to position her on her knees with her buttocks raised to receive the sting of the birch. With her hands still secured and her face down on the pillow, her gasps and cries were muffled. After a few swats of the birch Mr Graham paused to push his fingers into her now throbbing canal and pinch her clitoris between thumb and forefinger before beating her again – pinching, then beating.

Lisette was no longer in control of her body or even her thoughts. All she wanted was for this mingling of pain and pleasure and sublime sexual sensation to go on for ever. Yet she did not think she could bear it if it did. Was that another orgasm or the same one? She could no longer tell. Fingers were pinching her clitoris, another penetrated her anus, working that opening in preparation for his entry. But the other opening was a burning aching void.

'Do it,' she cried. 'Do it properly.'

Then he was there, the head of his cock against her swollen sex, then within, sliding deep and true. He kept his thumb in her anus and continued to pinch her clitoris.

The feel of him filling her, thrusting in and out, his

strong muscle sliding smoothly against her own responsive flesh, sent her soaring to a pinnacle of sexual ecstasy so high she thought she might die if she fell back down.

Instead she lay in a half swoon hardly aware of her hands being untied. Mr Graham stretched out beside her to cradle her in his arms with her shivering body drawn against the comforting warmth of his.

'Dear Lisette,' he murmured, his voice incredibly tender, 'you were even more beautiful than I imagined. Now that you know your true self, we must do this again. Very soon.'

Chapter Five

*T*here was no reason for Nat not to assume his betrothed had retired to her bed for a chaste night's sleep. In fact she was gone from his mind by the time he had descended the steps of the Cunninghams' house and begun to walk along the deserted street. While the fair Lisette possessed all the attributes desirable in the wife of a man of his position, the woman who occupied his thoughts had dark hair, a fiery Irish temper and a sexual passion to match.

Nat had kept away from Bridie all evening for a number of reasons, not least of which was the need to control the surge of desire which threatened to cause him considerable embarrassment. By placing a few carefully innocuous questions to various people, he had expanded on the information Lisette had supplied to gain a clear picture of what Bridie had been doing since she disappeared from Barkers Ridge.

Thinking over all he had learnt, he found himself unsurprised by her success. He had always known she had spirit. That was what had attracted him from the start. It had been a desire to tame that spirit that impelled him to bend her over the table in the hut and take just retribution for Flannagan's larceny.

When he asked her to be his mistress he had it in mind to keep her, with her rough Irish ways, hidden away from the world and his peers, his alone to enjoy. Now she was a woman any man would be proud to call his mistress and he wondered with a surge of jealousy if any did. There had been no lack of admirers hovering around her all night, until she moved into the gambling room.

Beneath a street lamp he paused to check the time by his watch. It lacked but a few minutes to 2 a.m. He was only a hundred yards or so from the house where he had left her gambling. The lights shone brightly in the windows and he assumed the gamblers were still immersed in their cards. For how long would be anyone's guess. He considered going back into the house to watch and wait for her. Instead he hailed a passing cab and, on ascertaining the driver knew the whereabouts of the house named Rosalie, settled back against the seat to anticipate the pleasure of being reunited with Bridie, in every sense.

Only four players now sat at the table, the stakes having long since risen too high for the others. The atmosphere in the room was tense and the watchers marvelled at the calmness of the Irish heiress. Bridie had been winning consistently throughout the night, the few times she had lost having minimal effect on the end result.

Of the ones still in the game, one was a remittance man, his banishment from the family estates in England having done nothing to cure him of his propensity for frequently and carelessly gambling himself into horrific debt. He now laid down his cards announcing, with a shrug, that he was pulling out. The man opposite did the same.

'And you, Mr Jones?' Bridie asked. 'Do you withdraw, too?'

Every pair of eyes turned to the merchant. Sweat beaded his brow, his moon-shaped countenance even more florid in complexion than normal. The man had been losing as steadily as Bridie had been winning.

86

'Damn you, I will not,' he declared, discarding two cards and grabbing hastily at the replacements which were dealt. He relaxed visibly as he sifted them into his hand. Watching eyes turned back to Bridie, who maintained the same calm mien despite the fact that Jones might just as well have shouted out loud that he thought he now held a winning hand. He upped the stakes. Bridie met him and increased. Jones fidgeted. Every person in the room knew the man would have to put his warehouse at stake. If he withdrew he would lose anyway. He agreed to match Bridie.

The tension was now tangible. Breaths were held as Mr Jones fanned his cards out on the table, diamonds all of them, sequentially numbered. He smirked with triumph, 'Straight Flush.'

There was a hushed murmuring. Lady Luck had apparently decided to favour the old fool. Then all realised that Bridie had not so much as moved a facial muscle. They turned to stare at her, realising the immensity of the fortune she had lost.

'All mine, I believe,' Jones gloated, reaching across the table to draw the pile of cash and promissory notes towards him.

'I think not, Mr Jones.' The words were spoken with quiet calm. The man froze in action. Bridie casually fanned her cards across the table. 'A Royal Flush gives it all to me.'

For a long moment Jones, like everyone else, simply stared at the coloured cards before he collapsed back in his chair, his face as pale as it had previously been florid. He was gasping for breath, clawing to loosen his cravat. Someone hurriedly fetched a brandy, all fearing he was about to take a stroke. Only Bridie appeared unaffected by the man's distressed state. She gathered up her winnings, jammed them into her reticule and rose to leave.

'Wait! You can't do this to me,' bleated Mr Jones. 'Miss Flannagan, I'm a ruined man. You have ruined me.'

Bridie gazed down at him, her brows arched in disbelieving hauteur. 'I, Mr Jones? I did not ask you to gamble everything you own on the draw of a card.'

'You cheated.' The man was blustering now. 'You must have cheated. No one has your kind of luck.'

Spots of colour burnt in Bridie's cheeks, the glitter in her eyes betraying the degree to which she had been angered. The remittance man, who had been thinking salacious thoughts about Bridie all evening, stifled a groan. God, but she was magnificent when she was angry.

Her voice, however, retained the same cool disdain, her gaze sweeping the company. 'Does anyone else think I cheated?'

'No.'

'Of course not.'

'Perish the thought!'

There was a chorus of denials. Taking no heed of it, Jones struggled to his feet to shake his fist at Bridie. 'Well, I still say you did. You're nothing but a damned Irish trickster.'

There was a collective gasp of shock, everyone aware that if Bridie had been a man such an insult would mean pistols at dawn. A hardening glint in her eye suggested she would very much like to issue such a challenge. The remittance man was almost tempted to do so in her defence – until she spoke.

'I am sorry you think so, Mr Jones. You see I would have been quite happy for you to remain as manager of your warehouse for a generous salary. I see now that, feeling as you do, such an arrangement would not be feasible. My solicitor will contact you to arrange legal transfer to my name.' She glanced around the room. 'Good night, gentlemen.'

Bridie felt absolutely no compunction over the outcome of the evening's gambling. Jones was a fool, a contemptible toad of a man. She cared not one iota whether he had a family dependent upon him for their livelihood. From the day that she ran out of Nat Durrant's house she had vowed that no man was ever again going to use her. Bridie controlled her own life and the ease with which she manipulated men to gain what she wanted had bred within her considerable contempt for the opposite sex; even for Nat Durrant who had disguised his own base desires beneath the pretext of teaching her about her own sensuality.

While she waited for her carriage she thought about his appearance that evening at the dinner party. He had certainly been surprised to recognize her and while he had made no unpleasant disclosures of which she was aware she knew for certain he would seek her out. He was not a man to forgive a woman for slapping his face. Nat would want retribution for that if nothing else and Bridie knew exactly how Nat would demand she make amends. Well, Bridie had long craved retribution herself and she would have Nat Durrant begging on his knees before she allowed him to have sex with her again.

Her carriage was rolling to a halt when the remittance man came hurrying to her side. 'Miss Flannagan, may I have the pleasure of escorting you home?'

Bridie gave the man a cool appraisal. Her opinion of the Honourable Harold Beechmont was about on a par with that of Mr Jones. However, the Honourable Harry possessed a certain dissolute charm which held a degree of appeal. In her own carriage Bridie had no need of an escort, yet she well knew why the man had made the offer. On deciding she was not averse to the notion of taking him as a lover, she allowed him to accompany her into her carriage.

The Honourable Harry wasted no time, kissing her forcefully the moment the carriage started to roll down the street. His lips quickly parted hers, his tongue thrusting into her mouth eagerly. To her own astonishment Bridie's arousal was rapid, her responses heightened from the intense hours of gambling. Add to that images of her night with Nat and she was more than ready for sex.

She was also in a reckless mood and a half mile from her house she moved out of her would-be lover's embrace to order the carriage to stop. The Honourable Harry was suitably puzzled.

'It is a beautiful night,' declared Bridie. 'I would like to walk the rest of the way. With you to escort me I know I will be safe.'

A flash of white teeth acknowledged her intent. They both dismounted to watch the carriage depart before they started to walk slowly in its wake.

'Do you often do this?' Harry asked.

'Only on the rare occasions when I have an escort. Usually I wait until I am home and walk in the grounds of my estate.' She sensed his puzzlement and smiled up at him. 'The night air clears my head, helps me to sleep better.'

'There are other things beside the night air that will help you sleep.'

'I abhor alcohol and other soporifics.'

'I was thinking of sex.' He stopped walking and turned to pull her hard against him so that she could be in no doubt as to how ready he was to provide her with that commodity.

Bridie was more than ready herself. Taking his hand, she led him off the road and down an overgrown path. They passed a mansion that was in darkness, continuing on until they reached a small open-sided pavilion. There was an air of neglect about everything.

'Whose place is this?' Harry asked, gazing around with considerable curiosity.

'The owner died and left it to his family in England. No one has ever come to live here.'

'How come you know about it? Have you been exploring?'

'A friend told me about it. She gave me a painting she had done which featured this pavilion.'

'I see.' He gave the leaf-strewn floor a ruminative study. 'Wouldn't your bed be more comfortable?'

'Without doubt, except that I rarely take my lovers to my house. Besides which I have a desire tonight to be wicked.'

'Wicked enough to lie on this dirty floor while I pound into you?'

'Ah, but it is not necessary for me to lie on my back. You must use your imagination, sir.'

'My imagination has been seeing you naked all night. Will you deny me that pleasure?'

'Not at all, but you must help me with my gown.'

The expertise with which Harry performed that chore proved him to be a master in the art of undressing a woman. When bodice, skirts and petticoats were thrust aside he bared her breasts to his lascivious gaze and lecherous mouth. While he suckled and tongued her nipples, his hand found the way inside her drawers to stroke her moist folds.

Bridie shivered. She wanted sex so much that just the touch of his hand was sufficient to precipitate an even greater moistness. On feeling it, Harry raised his head with a groan.

'I want to taste you. Take these garments off and give your sex to me so that I can.'

Wanting his mouth on her, sucking out her juices, Bridie turned and bent forward from her thighs. She supported herself by resting her hands on the back of a dusty broken bench and bracing her feet apart.

Looking back over her shoulder, she gave Harry a provocatively inviting smile. With a half rueful one of his own he knelt on the floor and quickly parted her drawers, his thumbs twin instruments of pleasure that parted her folds. His tongue jabbed and licked then feathered up and down from side to side until she was gasping from the effect it was having on her external flesh and the more dramatic one it was creating internally. She came almost too quickly and, before her orgasm was over, he had risen to drive his freed rod into her pulsing core. He pumped quickly and powerfully and Bridie,

91

who had intended simply to enjoy the physical act, found herself thinking of Nat. When she orgasmed again it was the image of his face that whirled with all the other fractured images through her mind.

The Honourable Harry wanted more. The first urgent need having been satisfied, he attempted to persuade Bridie to finish disrobing and allow him to enjoy every inch of her body. Bridie declined, knowing full well that to deny him would make him even more eager. It amused her to tease her lovers to keep them ardent. Harry must wait before she gave him rein to do with her what he willed.

'It's late,' she said now. 'If I do not reach home soon my servants will become concerned.'

'Let me come with you. There must be some way I can slip discreetly up to your bedroom.'

'You can help me dress, sir, then escort me to my door. The carriage will be waiting to take you back to town.'

Despite his chagrin he was too much of a gentleman to force himself on her against her wishes. He bade her a formal goodnight at her door and spent the journey back to his lodgings with his thoughts switching between pleasantly erotic images of Bridie and ways of recouping the money he had lost that night. If he didn't have a winning streak soon he would be in serious trouble.

The last thing Bridie expected to be told on her return was that Nat Durrant was waiting for her in the library.

'I am sorry, ma'am,' her butler apologised. 'The gentleman insisted it was of the utmost importance he speak with you tonight.'

'That's quite all right, Rogers. I will see Mr Durrant immediately.'

He was standing gazing at her portrait, when she entered the room. There was such unguarded desire in his eyes Bridie experienced a surge of raw sexual hunger, a hunger which almost made her forget her resolution and send her running across the room into his arms. If she had not so recently been well shafted by the Honourable Harry she might indeed have done so. As it was, she was able to assume a mask of courteousness.

'You wished to see me, Mr Durrant?'

He turned slowly, his gaze admiring. 'How beautiful you are. I always knew you would look well in finery.'

'Indeed?' Bridie was stripping off her gloves to lay them on the desk with her bag. 'Surely you have not come here at this hour to pay me compliments.'

'Who painted your portrait?' he asked, his gaze flicking back to where it hung. 'It is an excellent likeness. It almost does your beauty justice.'

Bridie wondered what Nat would say if he knew the artist had begged to be allowed to capture a great deal more of her beauty on canvas.

'Mr Graham,' she replied. 'You know him, surely.'

'No. Should I?'

'He is Lisette's art teacher. He lives with the Cunninghams who have provided him with a fine studio. In addition to tutoring Lisette, he does very well from portraiture. He is much in demand.'

'I can see why,' murmured Nat in a tone which told Bridie he plainly knew little or nothing of Mr Graham's existence. There was something else of which Bridie was certain Nat knew nothing. Lisette had not been shy of posing naked for her tutor. Mr Graham had shown Bridie that portrait when he had been attempting to persuade her to remove her own clothes. While she had continued to decline, she had often wondered if the relationship between artist and pupil had been responsible for the sensuality of Lisette's expression.

That was one of the reasons it had given her such a shock tonight to realise Lisette was Nat's betrothed. If only he knew the true nature of the girl. Well, he would no doubt find out in due course and the knowledge of how he would feel gave Bridie a great deal of satisfaction. A glance at the clock showed her it was nearing 4 a.m.

'It is late, Mr Durrant. Please say what you have come to say. I would like to go to bed.'

'I would like to come with you.' His words were quiet, his expression hot with desire. 'I don't think I have ever wanted any woman as much as I want you.'

The way he was gazing at her, the suggestive sibilance of his words, were melting Bridie's insides. Her heart was beating faster and for long, silent moments she fought the urge to give in to her own escalating desire. But the moment she was undressed he would know she had already been with a man that night and that was not the way she wanted it to be.

In those moments of silence he had stepped closer and now his knuckles stroked lightly across her breasts. Bridie trembled at the touch, remembering all the other ways he had touched, all the places his hands had caressed her body. Every one of those places was aching now with the memory.

Nat's head was bending closer, then his mouth was passionate upon hers, his arms going around her to mould her body against the length of his so that she could be in no doubt as to the strength of his desire. It required every ounce of Bridie's will power to keep her response minimal, to hide the fact she wanted nothing more than to be closer to him with no layers of material between; flesh against flesh; flesh inside flesh.

When Nat raised his head the self-control which had stood her in good stead at the gaming table came to her rescue. Bridie stepped out of his embrace and pulled the bell cord. Her butler came so promptly she suspected he had been hovering outside the door.

'Rogers, show Mr Durrant out, will you?' She then turned back to Nat. 'Thank you for calling.'

He was standing rigid, his face suffusing with angry colour. There was not a damned thing he could do and he knew it. With a curt 'Goodnight' he stalked out of the room.

Bridie waited until she heard the front door close then

with a sigh she gathered up her gloves and reticule and went slowly up to her room. The first flush of triumph had soon turned hollow. The ache in her womb told her it was going to be a long, restless night. She almost wished she had not sent the Honourable Harry away.

The ache in Nat's groin was vicious. As vicious as his temper. He had been close to telling the butler to get lost and taking Bridie there and then on the library floor, thus putting an end to her little game. And there was no doubt in his mind she was playing games.

Well, she had won tonight but he would make damned certain she did not do so again. No trumped-up wench was going to get the better of Nat Durrant. He wanted her and he would have her, again and again, until he had got her out of his system. There was plenty of time on the long walk back to town to think on all the ways in which this could be achieved. Unfortunately such lurid imaginings exacerbated the ache in his groin.

He was still some distance from his lodgings when a slight form stepped out of a shadowed doorway.

'Would you care to step inside, sir? 'Tis a nice clean establishment we have.'

Though he had given no thought to alleviating his need with such a person, the opportunity having presented itself, he followed the woman into the building and up a narrow flight of stairs. A discerning survey of the room showed it to be as clean as her person.

Nat gave a curt nod. 'Get undressed,' he said and walked over to extinguish the lamp. The woman was not in the least attractive and, she being merely the means by which he would achieve sexual release, he had no desire to gaze upon her face. He stripped off his own garments, ignoring the woman's gasp of appreciation when his aching cock sprang free of the restraint of his trousers.

'Oh lordy, sir, that do look big. I'm getting all wet and excited looking at it. I'll do anything you want.'

'Shut up and bend over the bed.' Nat snapped the

commands. He didn't want to listen to the woman any more than he wanted to look at her. A nice wet receptacle for his throbbing cock was all he wanted and she certainly provided that. His entry was swift, the smooth feel of her enclosing his shaft extremely satisfying. When he began to pump he was further pleased by the way she thrust back against him, rotating her pelvis at the same time to maximise the pleasure to them both.

Bridie had done that. Bridie! Nat groaned. This should be Bridie's delicious canal into which he pounded. Closing his eyes, he imagined that it was and his anger and frustrated desire had him pounding savagely into his partner. He barely registered her climax, and was not aware that each deep thrust which gave him his own was accompanied by the cry, 'Bridie – Bridie – Bridie.'

The woman whose body he pounded, who was experiencing the greatest orgasm she had had in many a night, was not the least upset by the cry of another woman's name. A man who possessed such a wonderfully hard organ of pleasure could call her any name he liked.

The hours after Bridie went to bed were every bit as restless as she had anticipated. When she did finally go to sleep, sometime after dawn, it was to toss and turn with erotic dreams of being with Nat. By the time she awoke, close on midday, she was in a torment of sexual need.

She wondered if she would have the will power to continue to deny Nat until he was driven to beg. Probably not if she did not find someone with whom she could enjoy a satisfying union. With a sigh, she wished she knew where the Honourable Harry lodged. He would be more than willing to oblige.

The sudden realisation that what would work for her might also work for Nat gave her a moment's pause. It was only for a moment. Nat might find someone else with whom to assuage his physical arousal but Bridie knew him well enough to know that he would return. His pride would dictate he prove himself her master.

When, mid-afternoon, Rogers knocked on the door of her private sitting room to announce she had a gentleman caller, she did not even ask his name. Telling the butler to show her visitor up, she put aside the letter she was writing, closed her escritoire and steeled herself for her next encounter with Nat.

But the man who entered the room was not tall, dark and sardonic. He was stocky, red-haired and achingly familiar.

'Seamus!'

'Bridie.'

They both moved, meeting with a clasp of hands, pleasure beaming in the faces of both. A discreet cough made Bridie aware of Rogers hovering in the doorway.

'Will madam require refreshments?'

'Yes. Yes, of course, Rogers.' She hardly took any notice of the man's departure, all her attention on Seamus as she led him to the sofa. 'I can't really believe it is you. When did you come to Melbourne? Why didn't you let me know?'

'I wanted to surprise you. Now I'm thinking more that you have surprised me. Bridie, this house, all this.' He lifted a hand to indicate the elegant furnishings of the room. 'Does it all belong to you?'

'Indeed it does. I have done well, Seamus. I have discovered I have a good head for business and know how best to invest for quick profit.'

'You cannot have made so much out of what you were paid for the farm.' There was an unspoken question behind the words. Seamus's blue eyes held a sullen jealousy.

'I am not a kept woman, if that's what you are thinking. Everything I have has been gained by honest means. But tell me about yourself. Why did you leave Barkers Ridge? No, wait,' she added when there was a knock at the door. A maid entered with a tray set with tea things and plates of delicate sandwiches and cakes.

'Thank you, Mary. You may leave it there and tell Rogers I am not to be disturbed for the rest of the afternoon.'

'Yes, ma'am.'

The maid having departed, Bridie poured the tea, carefully adding the milk first then passing the cup to Seamus. His somewhat bemused expression brought a teasing smile to play around her mouth. 'You never expected me to become a lady, did you?' and without waiting for him to answer, demanded again that he tell her about himself.

'There's little enough to tell. I kept thinking about you saying you wanted a better life for yourself. I thought that if I left Barkers Ridge and made something of myself I might persuade you to marry me. But now –'

'Now, what?'

'I'm thinking I'll never have the money to match this and you –. You're not the same, Bridie. You'd not want me now.'

'Wouldn't I now?' Bridie rose, walked over to lock her door then turned to face him, her smile more provocative than teasing. 'Shall I show you, Seamus O'Flynn, how wrong you are? I am still the same Bridie.'

The rush of colour to Seamus's face betrayed his eagerness as did the irrefutable evidence of his arousal. The knowledge of how eager he was to have sex with her not only pleased Bridie, it renewed the sense of power over him she had first experienced in the hut at Barkers Ridge. While she had less intention now than ever of marrying Seamus, her pleasure at his eagerness was genuine. As a lover Seamus had satisfied her well enough and there was already a plan forming in her mind by which she could keep Seamus by her side and in her bed. But there was the matter of his arousal and her own tingling urgency to be dealt with first.

Bridie walked slowly back to where Seamus had risen

98

to his feet. She touched one hand to his face and the other to the bulge of his trousers. 'How eager you are, dear Seamus, and how I long to have the pleasure of you inside me. But we have all afternoon.'

Seamus groaned. 'You have changed. You are more of a seductress. Have you had tutors, Bridie?'

A light, secretive laugh answered his jealous query. 'I have had tutors in many things.' Her fingers moved to the buttons of his coat. 'We will undress each other slowly, to draw out the anticipation of the final pleasure.'

'I don't want anticipation. I want you. Right now.' He caught her close, grinding their abdomens together to demonstrate just how quickly he wanted to satisfy his urge.

With her hands trapped against his chest and the pressure of his hard column against her abdomen creating a throb of eagerness between her thighs Bridie tilted her head back to return his hot gaze with a taunting one. 'Then you had better start undressing me.'

Because she had risen late and had no intention of leaving the house, Bridie was dressed simply, though the flounced silk skirt and the embroidered muslin caraco bodice she wore were grand indeed when compared with garments she had been wearing the last time she saw Seamus.

The bodice and the chemisette she wore beneath were quickly removed and tossed carelessly aside before Bridie removed Seamus's coat. Her chemise barely covered the swell of her bosom and, when Seamus's coat was discarded, Bridie caught at his hand and brought it up to press against her right breast. His other hand quickly followed so that both her breasts were cupped, his thumbs rubbing her nipples through the fabric.

They hardened immediately into tight peaks of wantonness and Seamus's sharp intake of breath matched her own. He dipped his head to take one breast into his mouth, sucking on the nipple through the material. Bridie's surprise that he was capable of such an erotic action equalled her pleasure. To have him sucking her through the material and to feel it wet against her breast when he moved to her other nipple was more arousing than if his mouth had been on her bare flesh. Only when she began to shiver with the intensity of her delight did he cease.

'Your skirt now, I think.'

Garment by garment they removed each other's clothes with Seamus's mouth returning constantly to Bridie's breasts to ensure the muslin covering stayed wet and her nipples hard. Bridie having more layers of clothing to be removed, they reached a stage where Seamus was naked and she was still clad in drawers, chemise and lightly boned stays.

By then Bridie's sexual awareness had been heightened to an almost unbearable degree and Seamus, she knew, was experiencing the greatest difficulty in refraining from falling upon her to unite their bodies in urgency. When he would have unlaced her stays she demanded he remove her drawers instead. To have her upper torso encased in chemise and stays while her hips and lower limbs were naked was a state of undress which never failed to raise her sexual awareness by several degrees. It also had the added benefit of doing the same for her partner. The expression on Seamus's face was as heady as any aphrodisiac. She was so moist, so pulsing, she knew she was going to enjoy sex with Seamus more than with any of her other lovers. And she was going to give Seamus as much pleasure as she expected to be given.

Bridie reached for Seamus's penis, curling her fingers around the eager column. He followed suit by sliding a finger between her thighs to lie along the silken dampness of her crease. For a moment it rested tantalisingly where it was before pressing between the folds to probe upward to her warmth. Bridie sucked in her breath in approval, adjusted her stance slightly wider, and tilted her hips forward to give that erotic digit more room for movement. Two fingers pushing inside her were more exciting than one. She moved erotically over Seamus's probing fingers and lightly circled the pad of her thumb over the tiny eye of his cock.

He pressed his other hand against the back of her head to draw her nearer for a kiss in which his tongue probed in coital action inside her mouth. At the same time he began to plunder her rapidly with his fingers, the combination of thrusting tongue and fingers bringing her to a trembling state of expectancy. It was Bridie who pulled away. She did not want to climax, not yet, not like that.

'Kiss me again,' she demanded. 'On my sex. Probe your tongue into me the way it probed my mouth.'

'Would you take me into your mouth?'

'Of course.' In an instant she was on her knees, his cock steadied in one hand, her lips closing over the glans in little sucking actions that had Seamus gasping in astonished delight.

'By all the saints, Bridie. I didn't think you would. Aah! You are magnificent. Aah! Cease, woman, cease!'

Strong fingers in her hair pulled her head away. On lifting her face, she saw from his tortured expression he had been close to his climax. With a smile of satisfaction she sank back on her heels then swung her legs around so that she could lie back on the rug. Knees flexed, opened wide, she gazed up at Seamus who needed no verbal invitation to give her the intimate kiss she desired.

Kneeling between her thighs, he grasped her legs to drag her towards him, lifting her knees over his shoulders so that she was semi-inverted with only her shoulders on the rug and her sex open and deliciously vulnerable to his mouth.

Bridie was now the one to be astonished, a fleeting curiosity as to where Seamus had learnt such a thing swamped by an incredible onrush of sensation when his mouth lowered to suckle her sex. The pleasure Nat had been the first to teach her to enjoy was magnified tenfold by the eroticism of her inverted position. This lifting and opening made her nerve endings more responsive to the soft movement of his lips, the harder teasing of his tongue and the gentle nibbling of his teeth. Such was his expertise, she was soon trembling uncontrollably from the build-up of her climax then shuddering with its release. Lost in the kaleidoscope of colour and symphony of sound which always accompanied such intense orgasm, Bride seemed this time to also hear the chiming of a bell.

Seamus's mouth was fastened hard on her, drawing out her orgasm. The moment it began to ease he moved to take his body over hers, his shoulders pushing her legs back against her own torso to tip her pelvis even higher before he plunged his shaft into her. The entry started her orgasm all over again, the angle of penetration stimulating places within her that were not normally sensitised by the piston action of a male organ. Nerves jumped to life and Bridie thought she might swoon from the sheer magnitude of her delight.

Nat rang the doorbell for the second time with an impatience that sent the chime reverberating throughout the house. When the butler finally opened the door Nat's impatience gave his words an edge of abruptness.

'Inform Miss Flannagan I am here to see her.'

Rogers was unperturbed by the testy command. 'I am sorry, sir, Miss Flannagan is not at home.'

Uttering an exclamation of exasperation, Nat was about to ask when she might return when his attention was caught by an unguarded expression in the butler's eyes. While not able to define exactly what it was Nat was suddenly convinced the man was lying on his mistress's orders. Bridie had asked Rogers to show him out a mere eight or so hours earlier. Had she given instructions he was not to be allowed in the house again? Nat's lips compressed.

'I commend your loyalty, man, but I am not convinced your mistress is out. I need to see her about a matter of some urgency.' That was no lie. His latent desire had been rekindled so strongly the previous night that he thought he might go mad if he had to spend another one without losing his flesh in the remembered sweetness of Bridie's. Though she had often been in his thoughts he had not imagined that on seeing her again his need for her would be so all consuming.

'I am sorry, sir,' Rogers said again. 'I have my orders.'

Nat pulled his notebook out of his pocket and withdrew a few banknotes. 'I will make it worth your while.'

Rogers grew tall with indignation. 'I do not take bribes, sir. Even if I could be tempted it would avail you nothing.'

'Why is that?'

'It is not my place to say, sir.'

The expletive Nat uttered caused the butler's features to assume an even more haughty arrangement. Of which Nat took no notice. Anger and frustration had him just about ready to push the butler aside and storm into the house in search of Bridie. Only one consideration gave him pause.

'Is she with someone?' he asked, then, no answer being forthcoming, came close to losing his temper. 'For Heaven's sakes, man, I am only asking a simple question.'

Rogers almost took a step backward. 'The gentleman is an old friend, I believe.'

It was the one word, gentleman, which stopped Nat because he formed an unpleasant suspicion as to exactly how Bridie might be entertaining her visitor. Nat discovered he had no desire to see her in intimacy with another man. Just to think of her in such a situation stirred emotions with which he had never been familiar.

He turned abruptly and strode down the steps, not looking back when he heard the door shut.

Four hours after Nat – unbeknown to Bridie – had rung her doorbell, she was leading Seamus across the park-like grounds of her estate to a small cottage.

103

'What do you think?' she asked after they had both stepped inside. 'It is only small but as you can see it is quite comfortably fitted out. You can have this for your own if you will stay and manage the warehouses for me.'

Seamus looked around the cottage, which was small only in comparison with the main house. The large front room in which they stood was the full width of the cottage. One door led into a good-sized bedroom, another led into a kitchen, while a central passage between those rooms led to the rear door.

He knew he would be a fool not to accept both the cottage and the offer of employment. Yet Bridie's generous offer bruised his pride. Despite her frequent declarations that her feelings towards him had not changed, the libidinous woman with whom he had just spent a carnally satisfying afternoon was not his Bridie. Seamus was well aware that she was, in a way, buying him – offering him employment and a house so that he would be there for her when she wanted sex.

For that reason he felt humiliated, but if the afternoon had shown him nothing else it had emphasised Bridie's addiction to sensual pleasure. He also knew he could not easily walk away from this woman who fascinated him with her ability to revel in sex. He wanted to enjoy a lot more of her and maybe, just maybe, he might persuade her to change her mind about marriage.

Chapter Six

*B*eing obliged to dine with the Cunninghams again that evening did not suit Nat, who would far rather have been spending his time in pursuit of Bridie. For the past twenty-four hours she had been like a canker in his system, something which had always been there but which had now grown to uncontrollable proportions. How different his feisty Irish lass was from Lisette; dark haired and passionate to his fiancée's fairness and gentle nature.

Caught up on his possessive claim to each, he admitted to himself that he really did not know either woman very well. True, he knew every delicious inch of Bridie's body but he knew nothing of the way she thought, of the real person beneath the sensual exterior. Lisette he knew no better, never having bothered to learn any more about her other than that she possessed all the attributes he deemed necessary in a wife. Whether or not she would enjoy the physical side of marriage had never been a consideration. Not when he could avail himself of the delights of a mistress of Bridie Flannagan's calibre.

For the life of him Nat was unable to form any mental image of Lisette's naked body. He would learn the reality soon enough, sooner than their marriage perhaps. If

Lisette showed herself still to be willing to pre-empt their marriage vows perhaps he would endeavour to find a way for them to be alone together.

But when he arrived at the Cunninghams', it was to be greeted by a reserved and pale-faced Lisette who appeared to shrink even from the touch of his hand. Nat was compelled to wonder, firstly, if he had imagined her ardency the previous night and, secondly, if he would be able to enjoy sex with his wife at all or if he would constantly lust for the woman he was determined to make his mistress.

Far from being eager to coerce her future husband into intimacy, Lisette had spent the day in trepidation of meeting him again. She felt certain he would take one look at her and know her for what she was. Yet exactly what she was she had no idea. Lisette did not even know if there was a name for a woman who enjoyed sex with both a man and a woman.

Those early morning hours in Mr Graham's room had been a beginning, an awakening. How she had enjoyed the careful way he inflicted pain to drive her into a sexual dementia which demanded the satisfaction of having him drive himself into her. Then later, after he had held her quivering body in his arms he had aroused her again. Gentle and tender this time, entering her, pleasuring her, as if she was the most precious creature on earth. He told her that he loved her and would only ever do things to her, or demand acts of her, which would give her the greatest sexual joy. He promised her many.

That very afternoon she had discovered another. On going to Mr Graham's studio she had been both surprised and peeved to discover Sally posing naked as she herself had done. Her perplexity as to how the girl even came to be there at that hour of the day was clarified by the explanation that it was the maid's fortnightly half day off.

Mr Graham had put aside his palette and brush to kiss

the sulky pout from Lisette's lips. 'Do not be put out, my sweet. I have something in mind to please you. You enjoyed Sally's touch last night. Undress and let her fondle you again. You do not have to return her caresses, simply lie back and enjoy.' He smiled gently at the wide-eyed gaze she turned upon him, reading in her eyes the excitement she was unable to deny. 'I am going to watch. And sketch.'

Lisette's narcissistic sensuality had been drawn to the notion like a moth to a flame. With Sally caressing her body with an erotic expertise and Mr Graham watching, Lisette had felt herself at the apex of her sexuality, incredibly seductive, beautiful, sensual. Following Mr Graham's advice she lay back and enjoyed.

'Suck her, Sally,' the artist ordered. 'Lisette loves me to bring her orally to her climax but when I am occupied with tasting her I cannot see the expression on her face. Give her an orgasm, Sally, so that I can watch her features contort with the ecstasy.'

The sensually evocative words had almost been sufficient to bring Lisette to her climax, a state Sally's clever tongue quickly invoked. Lisette found herself moistening her lips with her tongue while wondering what Sally would taste like if she was to do the same to her. Her curiosity, however, was not sufficient to coax her to experiment. Lisette thought she would prefer to remain the passive recipient of pleasure rather than an active instigator.

Having set aside his pad and charcoal, Mr Graham undressed and came to join the two women. The sight of his erection had Lisette moistening her lips again. She remembered the erotic experience of taking him in her mouth, the even more wonderful sensation of his hard shaft penetrating her. She wondered which he would want now.

He wanted neither. Ignoring Lisette, he pushed Sally on to her back on the floor and raised her sex to his mouth to give her the pleasure she had just given Lisette.

Fascinated, longing, Lisette watched the spasms of orgasmic rapture pass across the maid's face. Her own sex had throbbed with a vicarious thrill so intense she had begun to whimper with her own unbearable need.

Only when Sally was spent had Mr Graham turned his attention to Lisette. He made her kneel on all fours. Positioned behind her, he had spread her own sexual juices around her anus. When his thumb was deliciously embedded in that orifice his cock thrust in the other. Lisette had near swooned in delight. Always before it had been his cock in her anus and his finger in her hole. This way thrilled her more and her thrill soon became even greater.

Absorbed in the sensations within her own body, Lisette had taken no notice of Sally wriggling around until she felt the maid's tongue flick against her sensitive nub. Shock, amazed delicious shock, arched her body. She dipped her head to look between her swaying breasts to discover Sally was simultaneously teasing Lisette's nub and licking Mr Graham's shaft as it slipped in and out. The unbelievable carnality was far too heady a stimulant. Lisette, senses swamped by the increased pounding of Mr Graham's shaft and the cleverness of Sally's tongue, soared on the heights of a magnificent climax.

All the sexual images of the past hours remained vivid in Lisette's mind and kept her body in an unabated state of arousal which she felt certain Nat must detect. In all, she was in a terrible quandary, not for a moment regretting the things which had happened yet terrified of what Nat would say when he learnt his bride was not a virgin. Heaven forbid that he discover anything else about her sexual activities.

Lisette was no longer even certain she wanted to be married. A wife's duty to her husband, even one as virile as Nat Durrant, must surely be boring when compared with the licentious pleasures to which she had been introduced by Mr Graham. She could find no solution to her dilemma. Her fear of Nat's certain anger, her confusion over her experiences with both Mr Graham *and* Sally, her great need to continue to enjoy forbidden pleasures and explore others about which she fantasised, kept her quiet and withdrawn throughout the evening.

In fact, by the time Lisette pleaded a headache and asked to be excused, Nat was only too pleased to take his own leave of his future in-laws. He walked back to his lodgings toying with the idea of going to Bridie's house and forcing his attentions upon her if necessary. He was certain any resistance would be merely token.

Tempting though the idea was, it was discarded within moments of entering his lodgings and receiving the message which had been delivered earlier. Muttering several imprecations, he crushed the sheet of paper in his hand. The last thing he wanted to do right now was return to Barkers Ridge. Neither could he remain in Melbourne while his cattle were being shot. Especially when he was almost certain of the identity of the culprit. He'd wager his desire for Bridie it was Lucas Martin.

In spite of all Mrs Winchester's careful tutoring, Bridie was very much on the verge of reverting to her origins and giving her tongue free rein with her anger. And wouldn't this pompous little barrel of a man be shocked out of his polished boots then. Using contempt to control her anger, Bridie ran her gaze dismissively up and down his corpulent person in a manner which would have made a less self-opinionated person shrivel to silence.

Not so Jonah Jones, junior. He stood his ground, the lecherous expression on his moon face having no effect on Bridie other than to further lower her estimation of both father and son. Bridie was a shrewd judge of people, an asset which contributed greatly to her success as a gambler. Mr Jones, senior, was an addicted gambler and his son imagined himself the answer to every woman's dream. Even dear ordinary Seamus was a Prince Charming compared with Jones, and Nat Durrant's physical attributes far excelled both.

However, it was obvious Jonah Jones was not in the habit of comparing himself unfavourably with other men. Bridie wondered how many women, if any, succumbed to his sleazy advances or if his sexual encounters were only ever conducted for an exchange of money.

'You are not thinking clearly, Miss Flannagan,' the man explained in a tone more suited to addressing a none too bright child. 'But then I must forgive you, you being only a woman. A very beautiful woman, of course. You would decorate any man's home and I am quite willing to overlook your little misdemeanours when you are my wife.'

While understanding perfectly well he was referring to the way in which she had gained ownership of the warehouses, Bridie gave him a challenging stare, her dulcet tone dripping with false sweetness. 'What misdemeanours are those, Mr Jones? Are you saying that if I became your wife I would be at liberty to take lovers more physically appealing than yourself?'

The insult struck home, the floridness of the man's complexion deepening and travelling upward to colour the scalp beneath the thinning hair. The lechery of his gaze changed to something closer to hatred. 'A lady would not speak in such a loose manner, but then we both know you are not a lady. No lady sits at a card table with men.'

'What would you have done if it had been a man to whom your father had lost everything?' Bridie continued as if he had not spoken. 'You would not then have been able to attempt to coerce marriage to regain possession.'

'I would have dealt with a man differently.'

'Really?' Bridie raised haughty brows, almost laughing at how readily he had laid himself open to the next insult. 'I cannot imagine any man quailing under any threat you might make. Or would you use sexual coercion with a man, as well?'

110

Jones appeared about to take a fit. He advanced, spluttering with rage, to within a pace of Bridie who gazed unflinching at his contorted face.

'You affirm your true nature, Miss Flannagan, with your talk of lovers and sex. You taunt me so that I will forget I am a gentleman and take you now. You're hot for it and I'm happy to oblige. I'll show you how long and fat my cock is and what it can do for a woman. You will like it so much you will gladly marry me for more.'

Oblivious to the increased contempt in Bridie's expression, he began fidgeting with his trouser fastenings while he spoke. Bridie lifted both hands to shove against his chest using a force which sent him staggering back to lose his balance and land unceremoniously on his backside on the floor. The genuine surprise on his face did make Bridie laugh though there was little of amusement in her mirth.

'Your attentions, Mr Jones, are even more unwelcome than your visit. I have only the utmost contempt for both you and your fool of a father. Did he tell you I would have kept him as manager if he had not accused me of cheating?'

'And rightly so. There is no other way you could have won,' declared Jonah Jones, scrambling to his feet and attempting to recover his dignity. 'There is only your word that you didn't cheat.' He was advancing towards her again, malice overlying the lechery. 'Be nice to me or I will set the police on you.'

Bridie turned away and took the few paces to the bell cord. 'I do not take kindly to being threatened, Mr Jones, and I advise you to take care what you say. Rogers will show you out.'

The butler appeared on her words, Seamus following in his wake. Bridie gave Seamus a quick smile before addressing Rogers. 'Mr Jones is ready to leave.'

A venomous glare acknowledged defeat. 'I'll be back,' spluttered Jones. 'I will expose you for the cheating whore you are.'

Seamus came to the defence of Bridie's honour by using his right fist to put Mr Jones back on his rear on the floor. He then hauled him roughly to his feet. 'You'll be apologising for those words.'

'I will not,' shouted the man. 'I bet you're in cahoots with her, and in her bed too, no doubt. I saw the way she looked at you.'

Seamus raised his fist again. Bridie intervened.

'No, Seamus. Just escort the creature to the front door.'

'With pleasure,' declared Seamus and frogmarched a spluttering, cursing Jonah Jones from the room.

Bridie gave the astonished Rogers, who had remained standing just inside the door, a rueful half smile. 'Mr O'Flynn is very protective of me. I am certain he did not mean to usurp your duty. If that odious man ever comes here again he is not to be allowed to do so much as put a toe inside the door.'

'I understand, madam.' Rogers departed a moment before Seamus returned, still exhibiting a good degree of anger.

'I was of a mind to help him down the stairs with my boot to his rear. Instead I gave him a good shove. Will you be telling me what it was about, Bridie?'

'He is the son of the man whose warehouses I now own and which you are going to manage. You are, aren't you?'

'Of course I am. I want to be with you, Bridie, and if that's the way it's to be I'll not say no.'

'You are a good man, Seamus O'Flynn. I count myself fortunate to have you for my friend.'

'I'm thinking it pleases you to have me for your lover, too.' While the statement was positive, his tone held a query.

'Very much,' Bridie assured him. 'Surely you have no doubts about how much I enjoy being with you.'

'Perhaps I need you to show me again, Bridie. I missed not being able to be with you last evening.'

'I have many social engagements, Seamus.'

'Today then? Now? Look at me, Bridie, and you will see how much I want you.'

'So you do, dear Seamus, and I would not be unwilling if I did not need to consult urgently with my solicitor. I must ensure my ownership of the warehouses is made legal. Mr Jones was kind enough to bring me the deeds even if he did not expect to leave them in my hands.'

'Will you be gone for long?'

'For some hours, I imagine. Do not fret, Seamus,' she added on observing his disappointment. 'I will put aside time for you later today. I give you my promise.'

She wound her arms around his neck and pressed her mouth on his, her tongue playing seductively over his lips then pressing between in tiny thrusts. Seamus responded by grabbing her buttocks to grind their pelvises together. Moisture tingled between her thighs and she wondered what Seamus would say if he knew her own desires would first be satisfied by another.

After Bridie had departed in her carriage Seamus strolled back to his cottage. He continued to have difficulty in accepting both the change in Bridie's fortunes and in her person. He was annoyed with her for kissing him in a manner she knew would arouse, then walking away from him apparently unaffected. Chafing at the notion he was being used by this woman who was so familiar yet now so much a stranger, he vowed to control the sex the next time they were together. He forgot that Bridie had always been the stronger of the two of them both in spirit and determination.

Such were his thoughts when he entered his cottage to find a maid in the act of making up his bed. She gave him a smiling greeting.

'My name's Meg. I was given orders that I was to do for you, sir.'

'And what would you be doing for me, Meg?' asked Seamus, giving the maid's plump figure a suggestive appraisal.

The girl dimpled knowingly. 'Anything you want, sir. I've not finished the bed yet.'

'How long can you stay?'

'Long enough, sir.'

'Good. But I'll not be having you call me sir. Seamus is my name.'

He was removing his coat and pulling off his shirt as he spoke, the maid's eagerness in discarding her garb showing him she would be more than able to relieve the ache that made his organ project so stiff and hard from his body.

'How do you want it?' Meg asked. 'I am very good at pleasing a man with my mouth.'

While he had no doubt that she was, Seamus found himself more fascinated by a pair of breasts so plump there was scarcely a hair's-breadth of space between.

'Would you like to fuck me between my breasts, sir – Seamus?' Her hands cupped and lifted her heavy breasts. 'I'd like to surround your cock with these.' She heaved her breasts even higher, her tongue snaking out to flick first at one nipple then the other.

The effect on Seamus's aching member was dramatic. He bore Meg backward on to the bed and scrambled across her torso to press his cock against her breastbone. She immediately pressed the fleshy mounds together to encompass him fully.

Closely encased, aroused by the erotic novelty of something he had done so few times, Seamus began to pump vigorously. He watched the head of his shaft thrust to view above those plump breasts then disappear again. Meg also raised her head to watch, her incredibly agile tongue waiting to flick at his glans each time his shaft was pushed close. A bare half-dozen times of the erotic tease was sufficient to make Seamus lose control. His semen sprayed over her throat and on her face and Meg's delight became more obvious with each creamy spurt that landed against her skin.

The sight of his seed sprayed all over Meg's face kept

Seamus aroused when normally his shaft would have begun to relax. This time he wanted to fuck her properly and the discovery of how wet and ready she was when he reached a hand behind his body to feel would have had him moving to enter her if she had not begun to massage his shaft with her hands.

Her cleverness at that task was making it ache all over again and swell to such a degree he wondered if it was possible for the skin to split. Still astride her chest, he half turned his upper body so that the hand he had reached back was able to feel her. Pushing three of his fingers inside, he frigged her so rapidly she was soon uttering gasping cries of pleasure.

Knowing she was more than ready, Seamus moved back and pulled her over to be on top. Meg rapidly positioned herself to slide over his rod then bounce up and down with a gusto that had the bed creaking in rhythm and their climaxes quickly achieved. Seamus was very well satisfied. Meg would more than compensate for the times when Bridie was not available. The added knowledge that with Meg he would be in command did much to compensate for the uncomfortable image he was developing of himself as Bridie's kept man.

As always William Rosen greeted Bridie courteously and prepared to attend to the business purpose of her visit. He always put business before pleasure. Bridie understood that, therefore he was surprised when she declined to disclose the reason she was in his office and began instead to unpin her bonnet.

'I have a feeling you might not be pleased with what I have done, William, therefore I want to make certain you are in an agreeable frame of mind. Besides which I am impatient for you today.'

The lawyer's brown eyes gleamed. 'What have I done to be honoured with your eagerness?'

'Nothing, other than to be a man. And I do need one, so very badly.'

Straight, firm lips quirked. 'That is hardly flattering, Bridie. You might just as well have told me any man would do.'

Bridie flashed a provocative smile at the fair and handsome solicitor. 'I am not totally wicked, William. Only a man as presentable as yourself will find favour with me.'

'Good looks and a good cock, Bridie? Is that what you are saying?'

'Perhaps.'

'How many lovers do you have?'

For answer she gave him another smile and discarded her bodice. Her skirt was coming off before she spoke. 'Why do you just stand there, William?'

'I am trying to figure you out. Besides, I am enjoying watching you undress.'

Her petticoats were going the same way as her skirt and he saw she wore only a hip-length chemise under her stays. The dark hair on her pubis and the fair skin of her thighs were revealed to his ardent gaze. The gleam of desire in his eyes gave Bridie the same delicious thrill of power she experienced whenever she was the object of a man's sexual ardour.

She knew well how much William liked to have her like this, feet encased in boots, body constricted by stays, a covering of fine cambric over her breasts and her sex in full view. It was a degree of undress she found highly stimulating herself and the fact that William remained fully clothed rendered it even more erotic.

Feeling unusually wanton she ignored the sofa which normally couched their sexual ardour to perch on the edge of his desk. She rested back on her arms and lifted her feet to the edge of the desk in a silent invitation for him to explore the petalled folds opened to his view. Those folds were now tingling so much and William delayed so long she was on the verge of begging him to touch her before he moved.

When he did it was to kneel in front of her to part the

soft flesh with his fingers. Almost as if he was exploring visually and by touch secrets with which he was unfamiliar. This clever toying with her sex imparted just the right degree of delight to arouse and pleasure without tumbling her over the edge.

Bridie sighed with satisfaction. 'How clever your fingers are, William. True instruments of pleasure.'

'Would you rate my tongue as highly?'

'Mmm. Perhaps you should remind me.'

'What would you do if I was to decline?'

'I would be angry with you.'

William chuckled. 'That I cannot have.'

The deft touch of his tongue against her central crease evoked another sigh of delight. Bridie gave herself up to the delight, closing her eyes to concentrate on that very special pleasure. How she loved having a man's mouth on her sex, her flesh far more responsive to the caress of a clever tongue than a finger. The orgasms thus achieved were always highly satisfying and – dear Lord! – if William kept on plying his tongue so expertly she would orgasm very soon.

Bridie opened her eyes and lifted her head to gaze at the fair one between her thighs. She stemmed the onrush of arousal precipitated by the sight with a damning statement. 'I was gambling the other night.'

William raised his eyes though his tongue continued to tease her before he replied. 'Did you lose?' His tongue flicked little darts of delight again. 'Is that what this is all about?'

Since he hardly paused in his lingual teasing of her most sensitive nub, his eyes holding hers, Bridie barely managed to say 'I won,' before gasping from the pleasure. Because his eyes remained fixed on her face she propped herself higher on her hands to be aroused even more by watching the action of his tongue.

Dear Lord, she was so close; she could feel all the delicious little fires within coming together ready to explode in the conflagration of orgasm.

'Are you ready to come?' asked William, smiling when she cried out in protest at removal of the stimulation. 'Why has winning created a problem?'

Bridie knew she would receive no further satisfaction until she told him. 'I won a shipping warehouse.'

'Whose?'

'Jonah Jones.'

'Ah,' said William, in a tone which indicated everything was now clear.

'Please,' Bridie begged, far more concerned with what was happening – or rather, not happening – between her thighs.

'You plead so delightfully, my dear, and taste so delicious, too.'

And he tasted her again, inserting his tongue into her opening then flicking it against her nub. The cry sprang from Bridie's throat, her body arching with the initial pseudo painful onset of her orgasm. William's mouth sucked harder. Bridie sank farther and farther back on her hands until she was lying flat on the desk, aware only of William expertly prolonging her orgasm to give her the greatest possible delight.

Her eyes were still closed, her internal pulsing not yet faded when he moved and she felt his glans press against her. On opening her eyes she saw that his clothing had been disarranged only sufficiently for him to free his shaft. His lips glistened with her juices and Bridie's own pouted in sensual response. She allowed him to spread her legs high and wide and sucked in her breath in satisfaction when his shaft slid into her.

'I gather Mr Jones was unhappy over the outcome of your card game.' William made the assumption while beginning a rhythmic stroking that was so extremely pleasurable as to make Bridie want to forget all about poker games and warehouses. 'Is he ruined?'

Bridie managed to convey an affirmative reply.

'Ah,' said William once again, except this time the exclamation was not occasioned solely by mental enlightenment. The sound indicated a degree of physical satisfaction as well.

To Bridie's relief he dropped the subject of Mr Jones to concentrate on increasing the ardency of his thrusts. Bridie banished Mr Jones from conscious thought, too. Of far more importance were the wonderful sensations being imparted by William's shaft, the friction that was reigniting her internal fires. She surrendered herself to a second, less intense but equally satisfying, orgasm.

'I should be angry with you,' William declared some time later. 'What if Jones had held the winning hand? You would have lost everything.'

'Not everything. I am not so foolish as to put all I own at stake. Besides which, such a thing is never likely to happen. I gamble with my head, William, not my heart.'

'I sometimes wonder if you even have a heart. We have been lovers almost since we met yet I have the feeling that to you all I provide is sex, no feelings involved.'

'I am very fond of you, William.'

'Only fond,' he scoffed. 'A sentiment dictated by your head, not your heart.'

'Which is how I gamble.'

'With people's lives as well as the cards. Be careful, Bridie, of what you do. I know your past. What matters little to me will provide great fuel for gossip with others and the means for some to bring you down. Jonah Jones and his son could prove to be vicious enemies.'

Bridie gave a dismissive shrug. 'I am not worried by their threats. The pair are contemptible fools.'

'Even so, I am worried by this business.'

'You worry too much.'

'Isn't that what you pay me to do?'

'Perhaps.' Bridie patted her hat into position and placed a lush kiss on William's mouth. 'Thank you for everything. Give my regards to Mrs Rosen.'

'Witch,' he declared, grinning when she cast him a saucy look before gliding gracefully past the door he held open. Closing it behind her, he gave a chuckle. Bridie knew perfectly well that his wife also took lovers. What he had never disclosed was their pact to relate to each other every detail of their sexual encounters and how such tales heightened the thrills of their own lovemaking.

Chapter Seven

*T*he Settlers Inn, located in one of the less salubrious back streets of the town, was not the type of establishment Jonah Jones, junior, would normally frequent. He sidled through the door having the greatest difficulty in refraining from wrinkling his nose in distaste. Everything around him, the odour of unwashed bodies, the smell of stale ale and the general seediness of the place, was an offence to his fastidious sensibilities. However, he had entered the inn of his own free will.

Though immediately aware of the curious and overtly antagonistic gazes directed at the expensive coat which had been tailored to fit perfectly around his rotund belly, he took several more hesitant paces into the bar. He had been told he would find here a man prepared to carry out certain tasks, no questions asked, for the right amount of money. While he did not doubt several of the inn's customers would be prepared to rough up the Flannagan woman for a monetary gain, Jonah Jones found their collective appearance somewhat intimidating.

He was still trying to gather the courage to approach someone – anyone – when a deep, surprisingly well-educated, voice spoke from somewhere to his right. Initially it was the unexpected, cultured cadence which caught his attention. Jones was turning to identify the owner of the voice when the actual words the man had spoken registered in his brain. A flush of nervous excitement emboldened him to push roughly past a group of three uncouth types to confront the speaker.

'Excuse me, sir.' Jonah Jones fawned before the man whose height, breadth of shoulder and swarthy, scowling face were sufficient to intimidate a braver man than the merchant. 'Did I hear you asking after an Irish woman?'

The man turned incredibly pale, almost colourless eyes towards Jones. 'You know this woman?'

'I know a woman who might be the one you seek. She calls herself Bridie Flannagan.'

'That is her true name.' The pale eyes began to gleam with an expression that had the merchant swallow nervously then take a fumbling step of retreat when their gaze hardened to a stare directed at him. 'How well do you know her?'

Jonah Jones swallowed nervously again. 'I – er – We've met.'

'You are not a friend of hers, are you?'

Indignation and seething resentment swept away most of Jonah Jones' nervousness. 'Most certainly not.'

The stranger seemed pleased, nodding his head thoughtfully. 'Can you tell me where I will find this woman?'

'I'd first like to know your business with her.' By now Jones was certain the stranger was no friend of the Flannagan woman's, either. This was confirmed when the man, after several moments ponderous silence, answered the question.

'She stole something of mine. I want to get it back.'

This time it was Jonah Jones who pondered. 'Why haven't you gone to the police?'

A half-humorous sneer twisted the man's mouth. 'The police are bumbling fools. I prefer to deal with this myself.'

The unspoken intimation that Bridie Flannagan would

come off second best in any dealing decided Jonah Jones. He gave the stranger detailed directions to the house called Rosalie and, when asked, provided an equally explicit and lewdly graphic description of the woman who had humiliated him in the worst possible way. There was only the slightest change in the man's expression but it was sufficient to give Jonah Jones a great deal of satisfaction. The Flannagan woman would not be pushing this man away or having her Irish rough-neck march him out the house.

Inhaling a deep breath of the considerably fresher air in the street, Jones watched the pale-eyed stranger stride purposefully ahead. There was something about the man's face which tugged at a chord of memory but for the life of him Jonah Jones could not figure out why he should seem familiar. Not that it mattered. The only thing of importance was the man's determination to settle a score with Bridie Flannagan and, in sending him straight to her, Jones felt he had done a great deal towards settling his own score. While he had been denied the vengeful pleasure of getting on top of her – and in her – he now gained considerable vicarious glee from imagining her lying helpless beneath that pale-eyed stranger.

There was such a pleasant breeze, the afternoon air so clear and balmy, that Bridie decided to walk beyond her own grounds to take the path through the bush, past the empty house, and on to the neglected pavilion. The sight of it evoked pleasantly erotic memories of the Honour-able Harry and she wondered what he had been doing since that night. She had fully expected to meet him at the card table the previous evening and had been mildly disappointed when she did not.

Daily, since the night she won Jones's warehouse then celebrated the event with Harry in this pavilion, she had expected him to call. When he took his reluctant leave of her at her door he had made it very plain how much he

123

wanted to see her again, in a situation where their mutual physical pleasuring could be conducted far more comfortably. Even though she now had Seamus, Bridie would have liked to get to know the Honourable Harry a little better.

Harry, Seamus, William. All of them expert lovers, each with his own special way of giving her pleasure. Yet none of them knew as many ways as Nat Durrant of arousing her sensual awareness. A queer sensation quivered in Bridie's stomach when she thought of Nat. While she had expected Harry to call, she had been absolutely certain Nat would return. At every ring of the doorbell she waited to be told Nat was seeking her. Each time she assured herself it was not disappointment which left her unsettled.

The temptation to question Lisette had been set aside for fear of appearing too interested in her friend's fiancé. Bridie would like to know how often Lisette had seen Nat in the week since Bridie sent him from her house. A week in which so many unexpected things had happened. Meeting Nat again, the arrival of Seamus, the acquisition of Jones's warehouse, Harry, William and Seamus again. Bridie's thoughts became centred on her lover-friend. She brushed the leaves off a seat and, resting back, thought over the happenings of the previous night.

As always after an evening of highly successful gambling, she had arrived home too exhilarated to be able to sleep. Though it was already in the early hours of the new day and Seamus would be rising with the sun to go to the warehouses, Bridie needed more than a walk in the cool air to clear her head and calm her for sleep.

She dismissed her maid the moment she had no more need of her, completing the task of undressing by herself. Her hands lingered on her body as she did, cupping her breasts in her chemise and sliding down to press the material of her drawers against the moistness which was already pooling between her thighs. When her garments were removed and she stood entirely naked, her hands repeated the caress. Turning her head sideways to the mirror she saw how strongly her nipples stood out – hard little peaks darkly shadowed against the creamy white cones of her breasts.

The act of rubbing her fingertips lightly over those rigid points sent delicious shivers of desire quivering through her body. Her hands slid down to press again between her thighs, this time to explore the intimate folds and not just feel their dampness. One finger found the nub of her pleasure, the lightest touch evincing a moan of need. How desperate that need, how great her desire for fulfilment, for the orgasmic rapture which would calm her restless body.

For such a need her own hands could not give satisfaction enough. A man's hard muscle, filling her, stretching, stroking and banging into her until she was in a state of mindless ecstasy, was what Bridie craved. And she knew exactly where that manly muscle was to be found. Seamus would not deny her.

Tying a robe over her nakedness, her hair hanging loose to her waist, Bridie slipped quietly out of her room and just as quietly out of the house and across the grounds to Seamus's cottage. She was about to enter when she was halted by a low moan followed immediately by a louder one. They came from Seamus – unmistakable sounds of sexual gratification. A flare of anger surged through her, to be quickly quelled. Did it matter if Seamus took other lovers? All she could demand was that he was available to satisfy Bridie's needs first. And she wanted them satisfied now.

Silently pushing open the door, she stepped inside the cottage and moved softly to the bedroom. Seamus lay on his back on the bed, hands pillowed behind his head, eyes closed, with an expression of extreme sexual euphoria on his face – proof of the expert manner in which he was being fellated.

Bridie did not at first recognise the girl; after all, she

only ever saw her servants in uniform. Then she realised it was the maid Meg who had been told to look after Seamus's needs. She was doing that with undoubted expertise.

Absorbed as they were – Seamus in his pleasure and Meg in maintaining and heightening that pleasure – neither was aware of Bridie's presence. Nor had she immediately made it known. Observing the couple gave her a vicarious thrill which set her sex pulsing in anticipation. She had not known that watching others perform a sexual act could be so arousing. Too arousing. She wanted her lips over Seamus's organ instead of the maid's.

'That's enough,' she declared, the unexpectedness of the exclamation bringing the maid to her feet in shock and Seamus to open his eyes, the initial surprise in them replaced by an expression Bridie could not quite define. Instead of trying she turned her attention to the girl. 'You can go now.'

The girl opened her mouth to protest against the command, something Bridie knew she would not have done if her own salaciousness had not been fully aroused. Bridie was unmoved by her plight. Meg must satisfy herself whatever way she could. At that moment Bridie's only concern was her own throbbing need. 'Leave this cottage now or leave my employment.' The maid went.

Seamus resumed his pose with his hands pillowed behind his head. The interruption having in no way diminished the tumescence of his manhood, he gave Bridie a mocking look. 'Do you aim to finish what Meg started?'

He was totally unabashed, taunting her with the fact he was intimate with the maid. 'Come now, Bridie, you know how much I enjoy seeing my cock in your mouth. What else did you come here for?'

Bridie did not answer immediately. Her gaze was on his upright organ, on the glans still moist from Meg's mouth and the pearlescent drop which seeped from the eye. The moisture which had been steadily increasing between her own thighs surged forth in a rush of desire. Returning his taunting gaze with one of her own, Bridie discarded her robe and stepped the few paces to the bed.

'You know me well enough, Seamus, to know I prefer a man to pleasure me. If he has pleasure in the process that is good but my own pleasure is paramount.' So saying, she knelt across his pelvis, lowering herself until his glans was held lightly at the entrance of her sex.

The sigh which escaped her could not be withheld. How delicious it felt to have him just there, the contact all the more erotic for being so light. Bridie allowed her body to sink slowly lower and relished the feel of him sliding into her. Not fully. Only an inch or so to take the urgent edge of her desire for sex.

For a half dozen times she moved up and down on the top of his cock before she leant forward to take her weight on her hands. Her hips were raised so that once again the glans was all that remained enclosed. Very slowly she began to rotate her hips, teasing Seamus, exciting herself, sensitive tissue flaring with erotic delight.

She saw Seamus close his eyes and watched his features contort with the near agony of her tormenting. Suddenly his pelvis surged upward to drive his shaft fully into Bridie's canal, the hard, hot strength of him showing how well Meg had done her work. Seamus was on the brink of his climax.

But Bridie wanted her pleasure. He was not to be allowed to spoil it for her. Though she had been enjoying herself immensely, and relished the force with which he had plunged home, she quickly lifted free. Strong hands reached for her in an attempt to make her encompass him again but she was too quick. On her feet she looked down at him. Her hands caressed her breasts in provocative invitation, her pelvis thrust slightly forward to bring his gaze to the damply glistening curls of her mound.

127

'I came here for my satisfaction, Seamus. You will not spoil it for me by coming too soon. I'm hungry for sex tonight. I want it to last. I want you hard and strong to take me again and again.'

Seamus studied her for a moment, the expression in his eyes once more that strange one which disturbed her slightly. 'I believe I mean no more to you now than an instrument of sex. Well, you'll have your pleasure again tonight, Bridie. One day though, I'll show you I'm not a man to be used.'

He sat up, his hands measuring her waist to draw her closer to the bed. They curved over her hips and around her buttocks, his fingers parting the cheeks to rub the valley between and to tease lightly across her anus. For a moment she tensed lest he force the intimacy she always refused.

His fingers passed over that opening to press between her thighs from behind. They toyed with the moist folds, yet never reached quite far enough to touch her sensitive nub. Bridie could feel it swelling, tingling with anticipation. Seamus gave a soft chuckle and bent his head forward. His tongue darted out to flick at her navel and feather into the indentation. All the while, his fingers parted and stroked her pulsing flesh. All the while, Bridie ached for him to caress her clitoris. Winding her fingers in his hair, she pressed her pelvis forward and attempted to force his head lower.

'Please, Seamus. Do not tease.'

Seamus looked up at her, a mocking question in his eyes. 'Tease, Bridie? Surely I'm giving you what you want.'

'You know you are not.'

'Then what is it you're wanting? Tell me, Bridie.'

'Pleasure me with your mouth.'

'Will you pleasure me with yours?'

Bridie shook her head, aching for Seamus to do as she asked.

'That is not being fair now.' He had shifted his hands

so that one was now in front of her and both played with her sex. They teased and tweaked, occasionally rubbing lightly against her nub until she was trembling from head to toe, her entire body a mass of awakened nerve endings. She thought he was going to tease for ever unless he could extract her promise to take him in her mouth, for his gaze continued to challenge.

Suddenly he seemed to change his mind. He pulled her on to the bed and tipped her on her back with her legs dangling over the side. Simultaneously he moved to kneel on the floor between her thighs. Fingers pushed into her opening; fingers that were not gentle, but which twisted and probed with a ruthlessness which left her gasping – and stirred her already awakened nerves with a brutal excitement which evoked the familiar tight sensation deep within.

'Oh, no,' she cried, 'not like that.' She did not want his fingers to be the instrument of her climax.

'How then?'

'Your mouth. Oh please, with your mouth.'

'Beg me.'

'I beg you. Please, please, Seamus, stop teasing. Oh!' The last exclamation was jerked from her when Seamus suddenly lifted her legs over his shoulders to bring her sex within an inch of his mouth. Although there was no actual contact between them, there was an almost tangible sensation of touch, like the lightest, most elusive brush of his lips against her flesh.

For how long he held her like that she did not know. Perhaps it was only seconds. For Bridie it seemed like long minutes of the most exquisite tortuous frustration, her nerve endings reacting more strongly to the erotic suggestion than they would have to direct touch.

When it came it was a feather-light touch, his tongue sweeping along her crease from bottom to top, passing so quickly over her clitoris she was barely given the chance to savour the delight. He teased her mercilessly, the touch of his tongue calculated to the right degree to

129

send her into a frenzy until she was writhing half on, half off, the bed, her legs over his shoulders and his hands clasped firmly around her thighs.

Her little cries and sighs soon became despairing moans, disjointed pleas for him to give her release. Only when she was near demented with frustrated desire did he give his full attention to her tingling bud. The peak of his tongue teased rapidly until all the tiny fires which already burnt magnified and melded into a flaming mass of exquisite sensation. Bridie cried out and Seamus's mouth closed over her pulsing quim to suck hard while his tongue delved deep in her crease to draw out all the nectar of her ecstasy.

When her convulsive movements eased he gave her only a few moments respite before he started again. This time Bridie's cry was one of protest. Her orgasm had been too intense for her to bear having another so soon. In vain she tried to push Seamus's head away. He would not be budged. Then it was too late. The heat within was welling and flaring afresh with almost painful intensity. Bridie was too drained to move her hips or writhe and buck as she had done during her first orgasm. Was this torture or ecstasy with her body feeling like it was breaking apart?

She could only whimper while Seamus drew orgasm after orgasm out of her. Then, when she thought she could bear no more, he turned her over, face down on the bed. Limp and exhausted she had not the strength to move of her own will. She allowed him to lift her legs so that she was kneeling on the bed, face against the mattress, buttocks raised.

Seamus stood up and she felt him guide the head of his cock between the swollen lips of her sex. Firm hands grasped her hips and she was pulled back at the same time he thrust forward. His rock-hard shaft drove strong and certain to her innermost depths. Over and over he thrust, working her hips back and forth to maximise each penetration. Powerless to do anything, Bridie could feel his balls slapping against her. Somehow that aroused her afresh and she closed her eyes to surrender all thought to the magnificence of sex.

She had craved strong sex and Seamus was giving her everything she had craved plus more. Though she had had several orgasms, albeit some were only tiny, he appeared nowhere near his climax. Bridie had wanted him hard and enduring and that was how she was getting him. He was indefatigable, ceasing his pumping to stand motionless and rotate her around his stationary shaft, then to pull free to tease his glans against her clit until her flesh was screaming and another orgasm seemed imminent.

Sensing when she reached that point, he eased the stimulus until her raging body quieted. He then pushed back into her, thrusting hard then suddenly stopping, pushing deep, holding himself embedded while he curved a hand under her abdomen to pinch her burning nub lightly between thumb and forefinger.

Bridie's gasp was closer to a scream. Hot searing pleasure-pain shot through her body, flooded her, burnt her, and she wondered if she had ever really had an orgasm before. Within a heartbeat she was incapable of thinking anything. All was sensation, physical euphoria, magnificent orgasm, perpetuated by the strong rhythmic action of Seamus's cock pumping in and out. Faster, harder, until one great thrust welded them together and they were both crying out loud, giving voice to the mindless delight which encompassed them both.

That sexual encounter had brought a shift in their relationship with Seamus the one in control. Sitting in the pavilion, Bridie wondered if she was losing her hold over him before quickly telling herself control was not what she wanted. All she asked of Seamus was undivided loyalty. The presence of Meg in his cottage and the way he had refused to submit to her will gave Bridie cause to suspect Seamus was no longer entirely her loyal

131

friend. If she had changed since coming to Melbourne, then so too had her childhood companion.

Bridie was still pondering the possible future of their relationship while she strolled back to her house, so absorbed in her thoughts she emitted an instinctive gasp of fright when her way was blocked by a man. Within the deep shadow of the trees her initial surprise gave way to a rush of joy that Nat had returned, to be as quickly followed by wariness when she realised the man – though of a similar build to Nat – was a stranger.

The eyes which gazed so intently at her were not a warm dark brown. They were like chips of ice, their paleness against so dark a skin and beneath heavy black brows slightly sinister.

'You are Bridie Flannagan,' he stated, his pale gaze giving careful scrutiny to her face and the feminine curves of her body. 'The description did not do you justice.'

'What description? Who are you?' Then belatedly, because his appraisal was too intimate and her body too responsive from her reminiscing, 'What do you want?'

'I want what is mine.'

'Yours?' Not only was Bridie puzzled, she was beginning to think she must sound quite witless. 'I do not understand. Do you think I have something that belongs to you?' Her mind was working rapidly, reviewing all her gambling bounty. This man fitted nowhere. 'You are surely mistaken.'

'I am not mistaken, Bridie.' The familiar use of her name earnt him a repressive glare to which he responded with an amused smile. 'Even though we meet for the first time I feel I know you well. Flannagan spoke a great deal about his daughter.'

'You knew my father?' Bridie's interest was intrigued.

'We did some work together.' The satirical emphasis on the word 'work' confirmed Bridie's growing suspicion. Her face again betrayed her, the man's amusement turning to a hard grimace which fluttered fear in

132

her stomach. 'I see you understand. Flannagan was minding some money for me. When I went to collect it I discovered he was dead and both daughter and money had disappeared.'

'I didn't know. I thought it all belonged to Pa.'

'That man didn't have the brains to plan a robbery but he had his uses.'

'I will give you back the equivalent of what was there,' Bridie said quietly. 'Tell me where you can be contacted and I will have the money sent to you.'

He laughed. A short hard laugh. 'You are not going to be rid of me so easily. You will just as likely set the police on to me.'

'I won't.'

'You won't be given the chance. I have seen the outside of your house and imagine the inside is equally as grand. It will be pleasant after some of the places I have been forced to live in over recent years.'

Bridie's mouth drooped in shock. 'You cannot live with me.'

'I both can and fully intend to. You will be wise to play the perfect hostess and give me everything I want.'

'What if I refuse?'

He reached out to rub his knuckles across her breasts, smiling again at the shiver she could not control. 'You won't refuse, nor will you want to after the first time I take you.'

His arrogance should have made Bridie angry. Instead she acknowledged his claim by asking his name. Even though he frightened her a little, he excited her sexually and it was not simply because she had been reliving that scene with Seamus. After the dark stranger had taken his pleasure – and she had taken hers – she would offer him enough money to persuade him to leave.

The cool disclosure of his name was sufficient to tell her she would not be able to manipulate this man. Lucas Martin! Of course, Bridie had heard of the notorious bushranger. She was surprised he had ever trusted the

133

likes of her father. Lucas Martin was reputed to be a hard and dangerous man and one for whom every red-blooded woman was willing to part her legs.

Lucas Martin wasted no time in proving the stories of his sexual prowess were not exaggerated. By the time he had been in her house a day and a half even thoughts of Nat slipped to the deeper recesses of Bridie's mind and the Honourable Harry was forgotten altogether.

Seamus posed a problem which she solved by sending him far out into the country to negotiate the purchase of more wool for export. By the time he returned, Lucas would surely have left Rosalie. Despite her enjoyment of the sex he provided, Bridie knew she was his pawn. While she did not believe he would ever cause her harm, she realised he was a man who would be even more ruthless than Nat in obtaining his own way.

Lucas had given Bridie instructions on what to say and how to behave. He never revealed himself to any visitors to Rosalie, his face being on too many wanted posters. The few servants who saw him believed him to be Bridie's reclusive brother. And he was still in her house when Seamus returned from the country.

Bridie sent the young Irishman away with the excuse it was her time of month. He would have to be satisfied with Meg for as long as Lucas remained.

Neither Bridie nor Lucas knew that Jonah Jones was at that very moment gazing at one of the wanted posters, wondering how best to use his knowledge of the bush-ranger's whereabouts to engineer the Flannagan woman's downfall.

Chapter Eight

*T*he soft moans issuing from Bridie's lips were of mingled pleasure and frustration. Lucas was in the mood to torment, to continually arouse her to an unendurable need only to leave her unsatisfied and her quivering flesh untouched until the sharp edge of desire had blurred. His powerful, clever fingers would then begin their devastating teasing again. And he knew she was helpless to do other than surrender to whatever he willed in the way of sex. The complete control he had so quickly gained over her body was why Bridie had not entirely lost her fear of him. Whatever Lucas demanded she gave, whether he wanted to take her quickly, brutally, or subject her to this sadistic sexual manipulation. Sex with Lucas was intense, carnal and magnificent, but never tender or loving. He commanded her body and her body controlled her mind.

He was sitting on the edge of the bed now, watching her, strong fingers rolling the folds of her sex together, his forefinger curving upward to stroke against her engorged clit, maintaining a degree of arousal just insufficient to bring her to a climax. Her body writhed on the bed, desperate for the release he maliciously withheld. Soon she would begin to beg – again! Every time he reduced her to the tormented state of pleading for release she vowed to herself she would break free of his sexual dominance. Yet over and over she succumbed to his will. Bridie was Lucas Martin's sexual pawn.

With a mass of aching nerves tingling in her core, Bridie raised her eyes to plead silently with the ice-like ones which observed her torment. A faintly cruel smile twisted his mouth to send a shiver along her spine. Not for the first time she wondered why she had allowed herself to become involved with this man. 'You're a bastard,' she whispered.

'And you enjoy it,' he countered. 'Admit that you like what I am doing to you.'

He flicked his finger rapidly over her wet clit once more. Bridie moaned, hoping he would take her all the way this time. It seemed he would. She gasped when his finger touched sensitive internal places then cried out with shock when the door of her room banged open.

Seamus stood in the doorway, glowering.

Lucas moved quickly to spring to his feet and face the intruder, his magnificent naked body tensed for self-defence. A shudder of absolute longing went through Bridie. He was so primitively virile, unconcerned by his rampant nakedness.

The high colour in Seamus's face might have been embarrassment or anger. Bridie knew which when he spoke.

'So it's true what Meg said. Am I no longer good enough for you, then?' He glowered at her with such resentment she wished there was something she could grab to draw over her nakedness, stupid though it was to feel self-conscious in front of Seamus.

'Who is this man?' Lucas asked, his glance sliding slightly towards her while never leaving Seamus. He was not embarrassed by his nakedness and Bridie noted the interruption had done nothing to lessen his arousal. To look upon that magnificent column was to incite her

136

inner flesh to lascivious anticipation. She became angry with Seamus.

'Go away, Seamus. You've no right to come to my room without being asked.'

'There's a lot I'll be asking you, Bridie Flannagan, of that you can be certain. But I'll go now I know why you've not wanted me this past week.'

'No.' The hard-bitten denial came from Lucas. The two men eyed each other warily and Bridie looked from one to the other then back again. Lucas spoke carefully. 'No one but the servants was supposed to know I was here. How do I know this man is to be trusted, Bridie? Especially if he is a jealous lover.'

'He's a friend. He won't say anything. Will you, Seamus?' Her eyes pleaded for understanding. 'I'll make it up to you. I promise, she said.'

'He stays.'

'Why, Lucas?'

'Of course!' Seamus's enlightened exclamation startled Bridie and made Lucas go very still. 'I was thinking I knew the face. Now what would you be doing with a wanted man in your bed, Bridie?'

Even while Bridie mentally struggled with how to explain, she noted that Seamus exhibited no fear of the other man. In fact he appeared very much to be silently taking his measure as indeed Lucas had been assessing him.

'Now that you have recognised me,' Lucas said, 'I definitely cannot allow you to leave unless you can prove without doubt you are to be trusted.'

'He can be,' declared Bridie, gaze darting from one to the other again. There was an undercurrent of something which disturbed her, a silent communication between the men.

'I cannot take your word, Bridie. Seamus – that was the name? – will need to prove it himself.'

'What proof are you asking of me?' Seamus's voice was quiet, his steady gaze holding the other man's.

Lucas gave a slow, deviant smile. 'I think you know.'

Seamus shut the door and began to take off his shirt.

For agonisingly long moments Bridie found herself speechless before she could shakily demand to know what was going on, even though her mind had already reached an accurate conclusion. A conclusion so carnally shocking her titillated body had almost gone into immediate orgasm.

Surely she could not want this – both Seamus and Lucas to have sex with her at the same time? But while her mind told her one thing, her body decreed another. She was becoming strangely excited and when Lucas leant over to stare into her eyes she could only gaze helplessly back.

'Can you satisfy us both, Bridie?'

Bridie managed a brief nod. She had sometimes fantasised about having two lovers together but had never expected such a situation to ever arise, or to feel such excitement now that it had.

'If that is a promise, Bridie, you shall have your pleasure first. I have tormented you long enough this evening.'

Seamus, naked, had come to stand at the other side of the bed and Bridie saw that he was as ready as Lucas to deliver pleasure. The difference in their nakedness was in itself arousing: Lucas was swarthy all over, his organ darkly rampant, the tip reaching to his navel; Seamus, meanwhile, was fair-skinned, his shorter, thicker shaft hotly aroused.

There was only one question to trouble Bridie. 'Why are you doing this, Seamus?'

'Remember the last time, Bridie? I told you then I would show you one day I'm not a man to be used.'

In silent agreement they half sat, one each side of the bed. Lucas took her hands to position them on the pillow behind her head, giving Bridie the understanding she was not to participate but to simply lie still and enjoy.

Both men caressed her body, one hand of each mould-

138

ing and kneading a breast, the other sliding up the inside of a thigh. Bridie, her hands where Lucas had placed them, closed her eyes to better savour the unfamiliar, totally wonderful experience of having four male hands on her body. They made her feel so deliciously wanton.

When the hands on her inner thighs moved higher to touch the outer folds of her sex she allowed her legs to fall wider apart and tilted her pelvis upward. Fingers stroking jointly along her moistened crease imparted pulses of magnified pleasure. Still she did not open her eyes, wanting nothing to distract her from her total absorption in this unique eroticism.

She knew whose fingers probed, her flesh receptive to the individual style each man used to arouse the sensitivity in her inner flesh. Those fingers probed and teased and all the time the massage of her breasts continued. Her nipples were so hard they were aching, her entire sex pulsing and tingling. Being stirred ever closer to a climax she moaned a little and thrust her pelvis towards those wonderful fingers. Yet, at the same time, she tried to hold herself back, not wanting the pleasure of the dual caress to end too soon.

When both men pushed fingers inside, together, she knew she could not deny herself much longer. Her entire body began to quiver. Then there was only Lucas's finger thrusting rapidly in and out while Seamus rubbed her swollen clit to take her to the point of no return. Bridie's hands clenched into fists. She cried out. Her body strained upward, and held tensely while the two men took her through an orgasm that left her limp, burning and wanting more. Definitely wanting more.

They tossed a coin while she recovered and it was Lucas who claimed the right to be pleasured first. While she had thoroughly enjoyed having both men do things to her, Bridie was not so certain about fellating either man while the other watched.

Having won the toss, Lucas quickly stretched out on the bed, hands beneath his head, his masculine projection a glorious temptation. Bridie was very tempted, the uncertain glance she cast at Seamus greeted with a twisted, hard smile that did not belong on the face of her Seamus.

'You'll do what you're told, Bridie. I've watched you take my cock in your mouth many times and I know how much you enjoy it.'

Bridie knelt and leant over Lucas, her face turned away from Seamus to pretend he was not there. Though Lucas's shaft was of a rigidity that needed no support, she curled both hands loosely around the base while she ran her tongue lightly over the smooth skin of the head. Her mouth never moved any lower, her lips sucking on the glans or her tongue licking and teasing the tiny eye.

This was Lucas's pleasure. Seamus preferred to be taken deep and when his turn came he stood beside the bed so that he could thrust into her mouth. All the time, while she pleasured first Lucas, then Seamus, neither man touched her body. She was beginning to feel so deprived she tensed in anticipation when Lucas moved behind her.

Bridie was lying on her side, propped on one elbow to raise her head to the level of Seamus's groin. Lucas pushed a leg beneath her lower one and lifted the other over his hip. He rubbed the head of his cock along her crease several times before he pushed slowly to his depth. At that point Seamus pulled away to become the watcher once more.

There was nothing then to distract Bridie from the pounding muscle between her thighs. It was pulled back with taunting slowness then rammed with force as deep as it would go. Over and over with the same deliberate action. Each time her body was jerked along the bed, and she did not even know when Lucas climaxed – whether it was before or after her own.

When Lucas rolled away, Seamus grabbed her thighs to slew her around, across the bed. Her legs were pulled around his hips, her pelvis lifted from the bed, her still-throbbing sex brought into contact with his. There was no slow deliberation with Seamus. His thrusting was fast and furious.

Again Bridie closed her eyes, this time against the onset of another imminent orgasm. She did not know how much more her body could bear until Lucas rubbed his finger across her nub. The world fragmented around her with the epicentre of the eruption deep within her core.

With her return to reality she thought the men would then be satisfied. They were not. Their libidos seemed so untiring Bridie was soon wondering if she would ever again, after this night, have the energy for sex.

It was the sensation of something heavy pinning down her leg which brought Bridie slowly out of a deep slumber. She opened her eyes to discover Seamus asleep beside her, his hand resting on her crooked knee. With the realisation it was not Seamus's leg which pinned her other to the mattress there came full remembrance of the night's carnality.

Swamped by erotic images and the awe of her own licentious behaviour, she twisted her head around to find Lucas watching her from half-closed eyes.

'Lie still,' he commanded softly, an arm reaching over her hip to hold her on her side. Lazy fingers played with her pubic curls to heat her internally. The full length of Lucas's body was pressed against hers to enable her to feel the ready hardness of him move against her buttocks.

With a soft moan of desire Bridie rolled fully on to her front, her hips pressing back in silent invitation. His fingers touched her briefly before he adjusted his own position to drive his cock into her eager moistness. He felt so very good as he slid deep, flesh so recently rendered highly sensitive responding in burning delight.

Bridie's sighs of approval woke Seamus. For several moments he lay looking at her face before he rolled on his side to face her fully. He took her crooked leg and lifted it to enable him to move closer. Behind her, Lucas, the rhythm of his thrusts barely altered, settled full length again.

The head of Seamus's rod rubbed on Bridie's most sensitive peak. She felt it press against her opening and she cried out in disbelief at what he was trying to do. Lucas had withdrawn and she found herself trembling from the totally unexpected, carnally intoxicating, sensation of two hard organs seeking her sex. They had not done this to her before, satisfied throughout the night to take her one at a time.

Shocked, trembling, excited, she clasped her crooked and raised leg to pull it back and open herself even wider. In unison, moving as if they were one gargantuan phallus, the two cocks pressed steadily. By slow degrees they penetrated her canal, stretching her so fully that tears swam in her eyes and her gasps were almost sobs.

Her senses were swimming; all her being concentrated in the reaction of her sex. Then she was no longer even able to think. She was all carnality; all sex; soft, burning flesh pulsing against two throbbing shafts; turning to liquid fire – a fire which melted thought, swamped every sense with sexuality.

Those sex-sated senses were only just returning to reality when there was a loud knock on her bedroom door. The realisation of what she had done, the horror of being discovered by her maid with not one but two men in her bed, caused so great a concern she was incapable of answering and could only gaze helplessly at Seamus then twist to look at Lucas.

While Seamus appeared to be equally as horrified by the risk, Lucas's face had become a still mask, his eyes narrowed, suspicious, cautious. He gave a low-voiced command. 'Tell your maid you do not want to be disturbed.'

Before she could, the knock was repeated more loudly and it was Rogers' voice which called, 'Miss Flannagan.'

To have her butler wake her was unprecedented. Bridie

shot a startled glance at Lucas, who had become even more still. She found it necessary to moisten her lips and swallow to bring saliva to her mouth before she could answer. 'What is it, Rogers?'

'The police are downstairs, ma'am. They are demanding to see you.'

Bridie's heart pounded. Again her gaze sought Lucas. Whatever his crimes, despite the fear she had never quite lost, she did not want to see him taken by the law. Both knew it was Lucas for whom they had come.

'You will have to go down, Bridie. Delay them for as long as you can.'

In a voice that was less than steady Bridie told Rogers to inform the police she would be down shortly. They heard his footsteps move away. Lucas moved too to pull his robe over his nakedness. He must first return to his room to dress before he could make his escape. Could she delay the police long enough?

'Take care,' she whispered, surprised when he caught her to him to kiss her hard and briefly.

'I'll use the side entrance but I'll be back, Bridie. You've not yet paid me in full.'

Then he was gone, slipping cautiously out of her room to make his stealthy way along the passage. Seamus, now dressed, followed in his wake. All the time he had not spoken but at the door he paused to gaze back at her with a troubled expression. Bridie sensed his puzzled regret for sharing her with another man and knew their relationship would never again be the same. However, what was done could not be undone and, if not for the certain ruin of their friendship, she had no regrets. All she could say was to softly ask him to also use the side entrance.

Bridie waited only a few more moments before she rose and rang for her maid. A half hour later she descended the main staircase. The two policemen awaited her in the library, one pacing in obvious impatience while the other, older officer, appeared to have spent the waiting time in an appreciative study of the room's valuable contents. Rogers stood on duty near the door, giving Bridie the whimsical notion he was on guard over the law enforcers.

With a brief nod of dismissal for her butler, Bridie swept into the room with a falsely welcoming smile. 'I do apologise for keeping you waiting, gentlemen.'

'We must apologise for disturbing you so early, Miss Flannagan. Us working folk tend to forget the hours privileged people like yourself are accustomed to keep.'

Bridie was not about to tell him she knew all about the hours the poorer working classes kept. 'I am not always so late in rising, sergeant. I had a very tiring night,' she added with a provocative flutter of her eyelids.

While the roving gaze of the younger man over the curves of her body showed he was indeed wondering about her nocturnal activities, the older man was not to be deflected from the purpose of their visit. He pulled a sheet of paper from an inner pocket of his jacket and unfolded it for Bridie to view. At that moment she came close to losing her poise. It proclaimed a two-hundred pound reward for the man whose dark, compelling face stared from the wanted poster.

'I see I do not need to ask if you know this man, Miss Flannagan. Your face gives you away. We have been informed that you are harbouring this criminal. We want to search your house.'

'Most certainly not. I have nothing to hide. This man is not here and I will not have you traipsing through my house for no reason.'

'We have a warrant for your arrest, Miss Flannagan, as well as for the arrest of Lucas Martin. It will do you no good to try to obstruct the execution of our duty.'

'You would be wasting your time.'

'Really?' The sergeant pursed his lips. 'If Lucas Martin has tried to leave the house he will not have got far. I have men posted outside. We will wait here until he is brought back in, then I will arrest you for aiding and abetting a criminal.'

Fear churned in Bridie's gut as she visualised herself imprisoned. This was not an eventuality she had considered when Lucas came into her life, her home and her bed. Too late, she cursed herself for the loss of cool reason; for allowing her flesh to rule her mind. But then Lucas was far too forceful a man to ever be denied. She needed someone equally as forceful to help her now. There was only one who could.

Even as Nat's image pushed the unpleasant ones from her mind, the door was flung open and he came striding into the room, his expression arrogant and grim. 'What the devil is going on?'

Bridie's reaction was purely instinctive. Relief precipitated her across the room, his arms enclosing her in their sanctuary though his eyes flickered in surprise. He redirected his hard stare at the police sergeant.

'I asked, what is going on?'

'May I know of what interest it is to you, sir? And your name.'

'Nat Durrant. Miss Flannagan is a particular friend of mine.'

Nat's identity evidently came as a surprise to the sergeant. A widening of his eyes before a mask of polite efficiency was assumed indicated his awareness of the influence Nat held in high quarters. 'No offence, Mr Durrant, but we believe Miss Flannagan guilty of harbouring a wanted man.' He passed over the wanted poster. 'We have been informed he has been living in this house for the past week.'

When Nat looked at the poster his arm tightened around Bridie's shoulder. She felt the tension in him, the curbed anger. 'That is impossible. I returned last night from Barkers Ridge where he has been causing problems for the settlers. And shooting my cattle.'

'Did you see him at Barkers Ridge?'

'No,' Nat admitted. 'I did not see him myself. But there

145

are so many people in the district who swear they did there is no doubt in my mind. This man cannot have been in Melbourne.'

'Who told you he was at Rosalie?' Bridie asked the sergeant, her confidence restored now that Nat was by her side.

'I am not able to tell you his name.'

Nat bit out an expletive. 'You cannot accuse Miss Flannagan without doing her the courtesy of knowing the identity of this informant.'

The sergeant stared at Nat, taking the other man's measure, acquiescing to what he saw. 'Mr Jonah Jones.'

Bridie's gasp of outrage brought her the questioning attention of both Nat and the sergeant. 'Why, there you have your answer,' she declared, at the same time stepping out of the security of Nat's embrace. 'I recently had business dealings with Mr Jones who was far from happy with the outcome. In what I thought was merely pique he voiced certain threats.'

'Were they threats of violence, ma'am?'

'Not at all. I did not take his rantings about getting even and making me pay as more than an extension of his disgruntlement over our deal. I understand now that he meant every word.'

'I see. Under the circumstances we should perhaps have another word with Mr Jones.' The sergeant glanced at Nat then back to Bridie. 'You are fortunate you have someone of Mr Durrant's standing in the community to vouch for you, Miss Flannagan,' but there was a speculation in his eyes which renewed her unease.

'Do you realise just how fortunate?' Nat asked in brittle tones the moment they stood alone in the library. 'I saved your lovely neck for you, my dear. Just how long has Lucas Martin been in your house?'

Bridie jerked back at the harsh question. With an implacable set to his features, eyes stony hard, he awaited her reply. She prevaricated while her mind raced through

146

a multitude of questions to which it sought the correct answers. 'You said he was at Barkers Ridge.'

'He had been at Barkers Ridge. He was asking a lot of questions about Flannagan – and his daughter. That is one of the reasons I hurried back here.'

'Was the other to see Lisette?'

His eyes narrowed at the mention of Lisette's name. 'At the moment she is the least of my concerns. Do you realise I was actually afraid that Martin might hurt you?'

'He would never do that.'

'Aah! So he has been here. Where is he now?'

'Gone. He has escaped the police again.' Bridie knew that to be true. If he had been captured he would have been brought back to the house then nothing Nat said would be able to save her from arrest. She shuddered anew at the imagined horrors of prison. 'I am very grateful to you, Nat.'

'Is that the reason you rushed into my arms? For a moment I thought you were pleased to see me. Or was it simply for the benefit of the police?'

What could she say? Bridie's shoulders lifted in an uncertain shrug. Having vowed so vehemently to bring Nat Durrant to his knees she had ruined all by rushing into his arms out of fear and relief. Yet held so tightly those first brief moments then protected within the circle of his arm, she had re-experienced the rightness she had felt the first time she lay in his embrace.

'You have not answered me, Bridie. Do you still want to send me away? Do you plan to continue to punish me?' He gave a soft laugh at the startled widening of her eyes. 'I know you too well, Bridie. You wanted to make me suffer for the insult I gave your pride by laughing at you.' A subdued groan followed the words and he caught her to him in a fierce embrace. 'I will never laugh at you again, Bridie. I want you too much. Admit that you want me, that it hurt you, too, to send me away that night.'

He began to kiss her, giving her no chance of reply.

Firm lips parted hers, bruising their softness, compelling her to open her mouth for the erotic thrust of his tongue. It plunged in and out to leave her in no doubt how desperately he wanted it to be his cock plunging into her other sweetness. That part of her was quick to respond, causing her to wonder briefly how her body could flame with such desire when she had so recently been with two other men. Together.

Firm hands gripped her buttocks to mould her lower body against his and send liquid fire racing through her veins. Nat's tongue ceased its plundering of her mouth.

'Don't send me away,' he pleaded. 'I can wait no longer to have you naked in my arms.'

His hot carnal mouth trailed kisses down the column of her neck, the only flesh visible above her high-necked gown. Suddenly she wanted his lips on all of her flesh, wanted them trailing over her skin to delight every vulnerable nerve-end. If Nat had not exactly gone down on his knees to beg, the desperation of his desire was slave enough to her pride.

'Bridie,' Nat groaned again, 'I don't think I can wait.'

Nor did he, sinking down on the nearest chair with her lifted across his lap, clothing disarranged only sufficiently to enable him to slide her over his shaft. With her hands gripping the top of the high-backed chair, Bridie rested her head on his shoulder and savoured the feel of him within. Why did Nat feel so different, so perfect? What was it about the shape of him that made it seem as if his cock had been moulded specially to fit within her?

Just to have him there, encased in her flesh, was giving her the greatest joy. She clenched her internal muscles around him to embrace him more tightly and was rewarded by his groan of pleasure. Her own pleasure was insurmountable and, with Nat doing little more than flexing his buttocks to push his organ deeper within, Bridie quickly brought them both to climax.

'You are the most wonderful woman in the world,

Bridie Flannagan,' Nat declared, taking her face between both hands and holding her so he could look into her eyes. 'Let us spend today together. And tonight. Then all the other days and nights.'

'Today and perhaps tonight,' said Bridie. Even though her heart soared with joy she would promise him nothing until she was certain his feelings had turned from ones of lust to love. 'We won't stay here,' she hastened to add. She wanted so much to renew the special joy of being with Nat and was reluctant to do so in the bed so recently shared with Lucas and Seamus. 'I will order my carriage to take us somewhere in the country.'

'I know of a pleasant inn at Geelong.'

Thus it was arranged, with only one request for Bridie to make before she left Nat to make herself ready. 'I want your promise that you will do nothing which will lead to Lucas's capture.'

She saw his face harden, and knew he was jealous even while understanding it was something he would never admit to. 'Why do you want him to remain free?'

'Partly because, in an indirect way, he gave me the means to become the woman I am. To me he was not an outlaw, he was –'

'What?' barked Nat.

'My lover.' Revenge was sweet. Nat's expression was thunderous.

'For that alone I would see him behind bars. Or any other man who touches you. You belong to me, Bridie.'

His arrogance stirred Bridie's quick temper. She was not yet ready to forgive him completely. 'I belong to no one but myself. Make no mistake about that, Nat Durrant. You might have been the first to teach me about sensual pleasure but do not think that everything I know was learnt in your bed.'

With every word she watched his expression grow harder and harder and triumphed at her ability to inflict hurt. She would yet bring this man, who had taken her heart and thrown it away, to his knees. 'I have had

149

several lovers. Some have merely satisfied a need. Others have led me along exciting paths of sexuality. I have been loyal to none. Neither have I restricted myself to enjoying individually all they had to offer.'

Nat's face paled then darkened to an almost purplish hue. There was such pain in his eyes Bridie almost relented. Was she going too far in her desire to pay him back for her own hurt and humiliation, for the fact that despite everything he could still claim her heart if he chose? 'That's right, Nat, I have had sex with two men at once and one of them was Lucas Martin. Would you still now call me yours?'

'I could kill you for that,' he declared with suppressed passion.

'But you won't.'

'No. I will fuck you to death instead. Just wait until we are at the Settlers Inn, Bridie Flannagan. I will show you that you will have no need for two men to satisfy your lust for sex when I am your lover.'

Chapter Nine

*I*n a way Seamus was relieved it was a Sunday and he had no need to go to the warehouse, for he was certain he would not be able to keep his mind on his work. All he had been able to think about since he left Bridie's room in the wake of Lucas Martin was of sharing her with the other man and of her being eager to be pleasured by both and give pleasure in return.

This morning, when he had woken to find Lucas already inside her, he had acted instinctively, not giving any thought to what he was doing until his cock had been pressed hard against Lucas's and they had pushed in unison to enter Bridie's sexual warmth. There had been a brief rational moment of shock that he could do such a thing before sensation took over. Never for as long as he lived would he forget that experience. He doubted if Bridie would, either.

The perturbing question was whether either of them would want to do it again. He did not think he would. Of Bridie he was uncertain. Seamus was beginning to realise exactly how much she had changed, and how little he really knew her. But perhaps he had never really known her and this licentious wanton was the real Bridie.

He found it hard to believe how short a time it was

since he had been planning to marry his childhood friend, envisaging them as a loving couple in a neat cottage raising their children. That would never be. Not now. The new Bridie would neither want to live in a cottage nor share her life with only one man. On the other hand, Seamus admitted he was not averse to sharing either her body or her wealth. He too had changed. The new Bridie inspired his lust, not his love.

These thoughts, and the many questions which occupied his mind, were what set him walking away from Rosalie along the path leading to the deserted house. He intended to bypass it and continue down through the bush, convinced he would think more clearly far away from Bridie. At the sound of a girlish giggle he halted, puzzled, then moved forward cautiously. His first thought was that the house must be occupied and whoever dwelt there might object to trespassers. He quickly saw that neither the woman who giggled nor her companion expected anyone to come by.

They stood on the unkempt lawn facing the house. The woman was painting, her brush moving with deft strokes over her canvas. That in itself would not have been surprising except the woman was near to naked, clad only in her undergarments, her breasts bared to the hands of the man who stood behind. His trousers hung around his ankles, his buttocks and legs bare, his cock hard with arousal. Seamus's own organ stirred in quick response to what he was witnessing.

The man bent his knees to thrust his rod upward through the opening of the young woman's drawers. Seamus knew it had found its mark when the girl gave a gasp. Apart from her initial cry of pleasure she took no further heed of being shafted, continuing to dab colour on her painting of the house. The man was not pumping her, nor doing anything to disturb the steadiness of her hand. While he continued to fondle her breasts, he ground his pelvis against her buttocks in a way that would have his shaft working inside her.

Eventually he took the palette from her left hand, the brush from her right, and dropped them gently on the ground. By a gentle push to her shoulders, he coaxed her to lean forward and rest her hands on the top of the easel. His hands sought the opening in her garments that had given his penis access. They pulled it wide to bare the pale swell of her buttocks. He began to thrust slowly, his fingers digging into her fleshy globes.

Seamus heard the girl's whimpers and realised the man's long fingers were deliberately inflicting pain – a pain she obviously welcomed. The hands disappeared inside her drawers somewhere beneath her body. A sharp cry told Seamus her nub was being pinched, the continuation of her cries indicating she was close to her climax. Still the man continued with slow steady thrusts until the time he pushed extra hard and held himself embedded. The girl straightened with him still encased and half turned her face as she reached up a hand to touch his cheek.

That was when Seamus recognised her. He knew her name; knew she was Nat Durrant's fiancée. And he had never forgiven Nat Durrant for being the first with Bridie. He walked out of the concealing bush into full view.

Lisette's shriek was one of pure horror. When the red-haired man greeted her with a challenging, 'Good morning, Miss Cunningham,' she near fainted with shock. She had pulled the cambric back over her breasts and noted from the corner of her eye that Mr Graham had pulled up his trousers. He also appeared far less concerned than she at having been discovered actually having sex. In fact, he appeared to be waiting for her to handle the situation. She moistened very dry lips and made two attempts to speak. The way the man was looking at her was having a most disturbing effect.

'How do you know my name?'

'Bridie told me. I have seen you at Rosalie.'

'Oh.' Lisette realised the man must be Bridie's new

employee though she thought him over familiar. 'You won't tell anyone you saw – saw me here, will you? Please.'

'That depends,' replied Seamus.

'I will pay you anything you want.'

'Will you give me anything I ask?'

In startled comprehension Lisette's gaze flew to the bulging front of the Irishman's trousers and unbidden came the thought that there was a great deal more bulk than Mr Graham's stretching the material. She moistened her lips again.

Mr Graham placed an arm around her shoulder. 'Take his promise of silence, my dear, then give him what he wants.'

Lisette dragged her bemused gaze from Seamus's trousers to her beloved painting master's face. 'He wants to have sex with me.'

'I know, and I will sketch you together.' He smiled softly, tenderly, and slid a sly glance towards Seamus to gauge his response. 'You enjoyed being with Sally for my benefit and you will enjoy being with this man. Won't you, my dear?'

'Yes,' breathed Lisette almost on a sigh. 'But can we go inside in case anybody else comes along?'

Since the day Mr Graham found the key to a side door hidden behind a loose stone, they had made this place their own. All the rooms remained fully furnished, the furnishings protected by sheets, though all was covered in a thick layer of dust. Mr Graham led the way upstairs and along a passage. A sound, not unlike the closing of a door, startled them all to stillness. Mr Graham relaxed first giving a dismissive shrug. 'A loose window banging somewhere. No one else is in the house.'

In that assumption he was wrong. Lucas moved away from the door he had just closed to stare out of the window and scan the bush between this house and Bridie's. Lack of any sign of the police did not necessarily mean they had gone away. If they thought he was close they would be watching her house.

Though it had happened sooner than he planned, he would have to leave Melbourne. Leave Bridie. A rueful smile touched his mouth. He had enjoyed the taste of luxury, and he had enjoyed Bridie's sensuality. She was not only beautiful, she was wholly sexual. The only other woman he had known who could take two men at once and enjoy the experience had been a rough-spoken tavern slut.

Despite her upbringing, Bridie Flannagan was now a true lady – cultured, clever, commanding respect. It was the contrast between lady and wanton that made her so sexually exciting. Lucas was sorry it had to end so soon. He would have liked to stretch Bridie to the limits of her sexuality. The eagerness with which she had accepted both him and Seamus convinced him she would be a willing participant in anything he suggested. One day perhaps he would come back for her.

In the meantime he needed both food and money and Bridie was his only source. When Seamus had finished with the blonde nymphet he would ask him to take a message to Bridie. On that thought Lucas stretched out on the bed, hands behind his head, and entertained himself imagining what was going on in some other room in this house. She was certainly a hot little piece. He would like a go at her himself but he valued his life too much to risk betraying his presence to strangers.

In the other bedroom Mr Graham took control. Any notion Seamus had of having Lisette panting beneath his thrust was soon set aside. The painting master was serious about his art.

'I want you to take a position then hold it until I have finished the outline sketch. There will be no fucking, no orgasms, until I permit. First, Seamus, you will sit in that chair with your leg lifted over the arm. Yes, that's right. Your cock and balls are fully visible. You will kneel in front of him, Lisette, but not to block his cock from my view. Hold it with your left hand and run your tongue up the stem. You may do that more than once. Raise your eyes and look up at him. Seamus – ah yes, that's what I want: your head thrown back with that expression of sexual gratification on your face.'

His charcoal flew rapidly across his sketch pad, the faint sound it made magnifying Lisette's desire. She was thrilled to be posing in sexual positions, and she tingled with the anticipation of Mr Graham watching when Seamus was finally allowed to thrust his rod repeatedly into her until she orgasmed.

The next position Mr Graham requested was for Lisette to seat herself on Seamus, back to his chest, her left leg lifted over his to open herself enough to slide over his shaft. She discovered his cock fitted more tightly than Mr Graham's, even if it did not spear so deeply. At Mr Graham's command, work-roughened hands cupped her breasts and Seamus began to lick the side of her neck.

Only he did not simply lick her neck. The tip of his tongue feathered against her skin with a suggestiveness which made her wish it was on her sex and teasing her clit. Though neither of them moved she could feel his penis pulsing within her. To be like this, joined, unmoving, was so highly erotic she began to clench herself around Seamus's shaft until Mr Graham realised what she was doing and ordered her to stop. He reminded them that they were not to orgasm.

They changed to another position, then another. Again and again they moved apart, only to rejoin again some other way. They sat, stood, knelt and lay on the bed with Seamus entering her from every possible angle. Though she again took him in her mouth, never once did his tongue tease her sex. His shaft would fill her and remain static while Mr Graham sketched and her aching need for action became almost unbearable.

She knew Seamus was also finding it increasingly difficult to hold the static poses Mr Graham demanded.

They were lying on their sides on the bed, Seamus behind Lisette, when Mr Graham said, 'Lisette likes it in her rear passage. Take her that way.'

When Seamus rolled her face down she drew her knees under her body to raise her buttocks. His hands parted the mounds and she felt his cock press against her bottom-hole. It had already been probed several times by his fingers so it was stretched and lubricated. Even so, his entry was difficult, making her eyes smart with tears as he stretched her to her limit.

'By all the saints,' he cried, 'I've not done this before. It's so tight. Aah!'

Then he lost control, pumping in her with wild cries that stirred Lisette to her own frenzy. Her shoulders were on the bed, her head turned sideways looking at Mr Graham, whose charcoal continued to fly across his sketch book. She slid both hands beneath her pelvis and pressed a finger in her sex to feel the movement of Seamus's cock in the adjacent passage.

His cries became louder when he felt her finger, his thrusts more urgent. Lisette was gasping also, using her other hand to rub her swollen nub, her wild cries joining Seamus's as she tipped herself over the edge of ecstasy.

'Meet me here tomorrow,' Seamus begged later. 'I want to see you again.' He glanced towards Mr Graham, who was strapping the easel on to the saddle of his horse. 'Without him.'

'Why must I be on my own?'

'There are things I want to talk about.'

'Only talk?' she asked with a pout.

'We'll do more than talk.'

Anticipation trembled through Lisette and she wondered briefly why she should feel no shame at her behaviour. Since the day Mr Graham had first persuaded her to pose naked she had become more and more enthralled by her sexuality. She loved to have her beautiful body admired, to have her flawless skin caressed and her lustful flesh aroused to wanton exultation of her desirability. Lisette preferred to have things done to her – to be the recipient of sexual attention rather than the giver. Even when she was in bondage and Mr Graham was skilfully inflicting pain, her enjoyment was boundless. She wondered if Seamus would be willing to do that to her; tie her to the bed, and drive her mindless by doing wicked things to her body. 'Tomorrow is Monday. Surely you will be working?'

'Bridie is the only one I have to answer to. I'll be here. Will you?'

'I don't know if I can. I am not allowed to leave the house alone.'

'You'll find a way, I think. Like me, you're wanting more.'

'You are very quiet,' Mr Graham said. They were almost back at the Cunninghams' and Lisette had not spoken since they left the deserted house. 'I do not think you have even seen where you were going. Your face is closed, your thoughts turned inward. What troubles you, Lisette?'

She gave a slight, helpless shake of her head. 'I have a lot to think about.'

'Including your forthcoming marriage.'

His perception did not surprise her. Many times she had thought Mr Graham knew her better than she knew herself. 'Nat will expect me to be a virgin.'

'Are you sorry you are not?'

'No – yes – I don't know.'

'I do. You should not marry him, Lisette. You are not meant to be a wife and mother. You should let your spirit be free. Embrace a lifestyle that will allow you to be your true hedonistic self, that will enable you to realise your full artistic potential. You could be a great artist with the right tuition, and the best teachers are in Paris.'

Startled, she gazed at him, moved by his vehemence. His next words gave her a shock.

'I was planning to go to Paris immediately you were married. Cancel the wedding, Lisette. Come with me.'

Tears trembled on her lashes at the thought of a life without him. She had believed they would find a way to remain together or at least see each other. 'You never told me you were going away.'

'Nor did I intend to. If you married I was simply going to go. A farewell would be too painful.'

'You said "if". There has never been any doubt I will marry.'

'Ah, but there has, my dear. On that night you came to my room I became certain you should not marry and you began to have serious doubts yourself.' He pulled his horse to a halt and reached for the bridle of her mare to bring it to a standstill. His long aesthetic face held earnest appeal. 'Come to Paris with me, Lisette. Not only for the sake of your art. I adore you. I want to spend my life helping you to fulfil every one of your desires. With me you can be your true self. With Nat Durrant you will have to be the woman he imagines you to be.'

'I know,' she admitted quietly.

'So?' His eyes challenged her to make the decision. Again she gave that helpless shake of her head. To break off her engagement and run away to Paris was not as simple as her beloved Mr Graham made it sound.

For the first time since becoming mistress of Rosalie, Bridie felt disinclined to trust her servants. She knew the police had questioned them and was almost certain at least one had admitted that the wanted man had been staying in the house. There was also the strong probability the police knew how intimate her relationship was with Lucas Martin. One could never keep secrets from servants and, over the past few weeks, she seemed to have cast her normal discretion aside.

The message Seamus had brought caused both surprise and concern, the one because Lucas was so near and the other because to remain had put him at greater risk of being captured. There was also another, personal concern.

She had spent more than a day and a night with Nat, the thirty or so hours they were together even more wonderful than the night she had spent at his homestead when she was an innocent discovering her sensuality. Her greater experience had enabled her to perform the erotic acts which pleased and aroused without need of Nat's instruction.

When they parted a few hours earlier he had not, as before, asked her to become his mistress. He had begged instead to be allowed to return to Rosalie as soon as he was able. Bridie wryly acknowledged she would never bring Nat to his knees. An arrogant declaration he must be allowed to make up for the months they were apart could hardly be considered to be begging for her favours. But why should he when she had given so readily, her own need of his body too great for her to pretend otherwise?

She had known many lovers: Lucas, Seamus, William, the Honourable Harold Beechmont; all highly sexed men who knew how to make a woman's flesh tremble with delight. When Nat made her flesh tremble it was more than sex, it was special. It was so very special Bridie knew she wanted no other lover than Nat. The Honourable Harry had disappeared, William did not matter, Seamus she could handle and Lucas, whose sexual dominance she could not withstand, was far away from Melbourne. Or so she had thought.

Now she was like a thief in her own kitchen, gathering up a parcel of food, taking from here and there in the hope none would be missed. Already she had put together in a pouch all the money she had in the house. Because it was not a large sum, William having advised her of the wisdom of keeping most of it in the bank, she had added a few jewels.

With her bounty in a flour sack she started across her estate to the bush track. Though it was only early afternoon she did not want to delay longer. Lucas had given his message to Seamus the previous morning and declared his intention of remaining in the vacant house until Bridie came with the money. He must by now be wondering if she ever would. Even though Seamus had taken him food there was always the risk Lucas might decide to return to Rosalie. The sooner he was gone the better it would be for his safety, and her peace of mind.

The moment she was hidden by the trees from any watcher, Bridie began to hurry, anxious to deliver her parcel and send Lucas on his way. With any luck he would be well away from Rosalie before nightfall, before Nat returned.

On rounding a bend in the path she was startled to see a woman moving with furtive haste ahead of her and astonished when she realised the woman was Lisette. There was no sign of Mr Graham. Nor was Lisette likely to be painting in so fashionable an afternoon dress. Bridie's curiosity was aroused for there was no doubt Lisette had also come from the direction of Rosalie. Slowing her own pace to a more cautious one, Bridie followed the other girl.

True to Seamus's prediction, Lisette had found a way to keep their assignation. By an incredible stroke of luck her personal maid was called away to visit her ailing mother. Lisette expressed her need to go shopping and asked for the maid, Sally, to be allowed to accompany her. While the request surprised Mrs Cunningham and caused raised eyebrows and mutterings in the servants' quarters, Lisette, as always, was given her way.

Sally was an eager conspirator who accompanied Lisette in a cab to Rosalie and promised to return with the cab in two hours' time. No one would think it strange that Lisette had gone to visit her friend alone. She might even call on Bridie later to give truth to her deception. Before that she would revel in Seamus's sexual adoration of her body.

* * *

The way Lisette hurried to the side door of the house and went inside without even glancing over her shoulder told Bridie her friend was very certain of where she was going and what she was doing. Curiosity and a niggling disquiet made Bridie follow quietly. She, too, stepped through the door into a small entrance hall – in time to see Seamus haul Lisette against his body, hands gripping her buttocks to hold her against the suggestive thrust of his pelvis.

Lisette responded with a girlish giggle. 'You are impatient.'

'So will you be when you see the surprise I have for you.'

'I like surprises.' She wriggled against Seamus, acting the brazen nymphet. 'Is it this nice hard column in your trousers?'

'It's two of them. I've got one and he's got the other.'

'Who? Oh.'

Lucas had come into the hall apparently unconcerned by anything other than his lecherous anticipation of an afternoon of sexual games with Seamus and Lisette. 'At your service, miss, in whatever way you want to be serviced.'

Bridie gasped. Three heads swivelled to where she stood just inside the door. Three faces registered three totally different reactions. There was fright on Lisette's, defiance on Seamus's and cool amusement on Lucas's. He was the one who spoke.

'So, you have managed to tear yourself away from your new lover long enough to come to me. I planned to enjoy you again before I left. Now –' he paused, his pale eyes gleaming. 'Will you join us to even the numbers?'

Both women gasped though it was difficult to tell which of the two was the more shocked by the suggestion. Whatever else Lisette might do, Bridie could not imagine she would want to indulge in that kind of intimacy with her friend any more than Bridie wanted to share a sexual romp with Lisette. Her voice was tight with distaste.

'You are sexually depraved, Lucas. And you are no better, Seamus. Here,' she thrust the bag at Lucas. 'There is food and money. If you have any sense you will leave straight away. I think the police are still snooping around.'

Lucas, taking the money pouch out of the bag to stuff it in a pocket, gave her a malicious smile. 'Are you really concerned about me, or yourself? I know who you've been with, Bridie, and you wouldn't want him to know about me, would you? After all, I have been shooting his cattle.' He laughed in cynical amusement. 'Who would have thought it, eh? You and me, then you and Nat Durrant.'

'Nat?' squeaked Lisette who had listened in amazement to the interchange. 'You and Nat are lovers?'

'Why so surprised,' Bridie snapped, turning on the other girl. 'At least with me he knows what he's getting but he's going to be damned surprised when he finds out about you. Oh, no. I'll not be telling him. If he goes through with your marriage I shall take great delight in imagining his humiliation and anger on your wedding night.'

She had worked herself into a right temper, not even reasoning it was brought on by the certainty of her love for Nat and her continuing uncertainty of his feelings for her. Long having suspected Lisette was no innocent, this proof of her licentiousness rekindled the hurt Nat inflicted when he laughed. His eminently suitable fiancée was living a lie. Except in her parentage, she was evidently no more worthy than he considered Bridie to be his bride.

'My, my,' declared Lucas, now highly amused. 'What a wonderful turnaround. You did not tell me this enchanting nymphet was Durrant's fiancée, Seamus.'

Seamus, who had been all but struck dumb by Lucas's

revelation and Bridie's outburst, managed to mutter, 'Didn't know you knew him.'

'We know each other very well. I have a score or two to settle with Nat Durrant. Which makes the prospect of savouring the delights of this lush miss all the more enticing. I will derive considerable satisfaction from knowing I was one of the men to have had Nat Durrant's bride.' He turned a cool gaze back to Bridie. 'But I do not think I can let you go if he is waiting for you. Somehow I am no longer certain you can be trusted.'

'He isn't and I can be. After what we have shared you must believe me.'

'Why should I? Your professed loyalties are apparently no more genuine than this delectable nymphet's.'

'I'm not like her.' Bridie's eyes flashed blue sparks.

Lucas chuckled. 'I would like the chance to make the comparison. I –' He ceased speaking, body suddenly tense, expression alert. 'What was that?'

Swiftly, silently, he moved to peer over Bridie's shoulder before quickly shutting the door behind her. His hand on her shoulder propelled her forward. 'The police must have been watching you. Unless you brought them?'

'Of course not!'

'I'd like to believe you but either way you are going to be my ticket out of here.' Not loosening his grip on Bridie's shoulder, he gave Lisette a rueful half smile. 'I regret I can't stay to enjoy your charms, sweetheart, but the police will come barging in here any moment. Keep her happy, Seamus, and the police occupied if you can. You –' he tightened his grip on Bridie's shoulder '– are coming with me.'

'We'll have to go, too,' Lisette urged when Lucas had bundled Bridie through another door and out of their sight.

'There's nowhere we can go. We'll have to stay here.

164

I've no mind to go anywhere until I've had what I've been thinking about all day.'

'But the police?'

'You heard Lucas. You like an audience well enough, Lisette, and you'll no doubt soon have one.'

He grabbed her hand as he spoke to pull her after him to the nearby dining room. There he dragged the dust cover off the huge table while urging her to undress.

Half fearful, excited, aroused, yet not knowing what to expect, Lisette fumbled with nervous fingers at the buttons of her blouse.

'Hurry up,' Seamus snapped.

'I'm trying to.'

Seamus made an exasperated sound. With the strength of his blacksmith hardened hands he literally tore the skirt from her hips and wrenched her bodice open. He silenced her cry of protest with the promise to fetch her a cloak of Bridie's when they were finished.

Her drawers were rent in two before she was lifted on to the table, her legs parted for Seamus to bury his face between her thighs. His tongue struck her tiny sensitive peak with uncanny accuracy, convulsing her body with delight. It continued to flick and probe so expertly she was soon heedless of anything except the pleasure for which she had come to this house.

Even when the three policemen barged through the open door her main interest was in the erotic image she presented, a minor flutter of uncertainty banished by the rapid change to their expressions.

'Well, well,' declared one. 'This is certainly not what we expected. We were looking for an outlaw.'

Seamus briefly lifted his head. 'There is no one else here.' He returned to Lisette's tingling quim with an ardour that had her gasping again and the police exclaiming in lewd approval.

The three came closer to the table and Lisette's pleasure increased tenfold. To have three pairs of hot male eyes avidly watching the action of Seamus's tongue darting at her folds rendered her flesh highly responsive. Knowing she must soon orgasm, she writhed against his mouth, her gaze first seeking that of the policeman who had spoken, then each of the others. She moistened her lips with her tongue, taunting them, increasing her own arousal.

The first policeman gave a lecherous chuckle. 'The lady likes an audience. Christ, you're hot,' he exclaimed.

But Lisette barely registered his words because the heat was inside her body, consuming her, melting her sex against Seamus's mouth. Her eyes were closed, her body arched. She felt his mouth leave her sex, then cried out in protest. Then the nuzzling began again to carry her farther through her orgasm.

The second time there was a brief cessation of the oral pleasuring she realised it was when one man left and another took his place. The knowledge they were taking turns with tasting her sent her spinning into an even wilder orgasm, one so totally consuming she was barely aware of the remaining garments being pulled from her body and her boots and stockings taken from her feet.

Hands raised her legs and held them high. Lips no longer nuzzled her sex. The hot head of a male organ pressed there instead. Lisette opened her eyes to see it was Seamus between her legs and two of the policemen who pulled them wide to open her. The third was discarding his jacket and Lisette understood that they all intended to take their pleasure with her; that this was what the man Lucas had hoped would happen.

The warm juices of anticipation seeped from her. Once again she moistened dry lips with her tongue, her gaze going from Seamus's face to each of the officers then back to Seamus again. 'Yes,' she whispered. 'Oh, yes.'

Seamus thrust into her and she cried out her delight at having his thick shaft banging hard inside her. And thoughts of how the others would also bang into her had her panting quickly and thrusting up to meet Seamus each time. She wasn't aware how her eyes sparkled with sexual excitement.

Chapter Ten

*T*he fear which held Bridie in a heart-racing grip was on behalf of Lucas. For all he had done, for all his crimes, she did not want to see him behind bars. He was the most sexual man she knew; far more sexual than Nat, who would never countenance another man joining him in his pleasure, even if it added a unique dimension to Bridie's own. True, she had wished to be rid of Lucas, to free herself from his sexual dominance but not at the price of his freedom.

Therefore she went willingly with him, through the shrouded rooms of the house and the cold cheerless kitchen. At the kitchen door he tightened his grip on her upper arm to hold her slightly in front of him when they stepped cautiously into the overgrown kitchen garden. Beyond it lay an equally overgrown orchard into which the native bush encroached. There was only a short distance of open space to traverse.

They had almost reached the concealing overgrowth in the orchard when the shout they feared told them they had been seen. Lucas whirled around. Bridie was hauled back against his chest and the revolver he carried in his hand pressed to her temple. The policeman who had shouted stood near the southern corner of the house, rifle raised, ready to fire.

'Drop it or the woman dies,' snarled Lucas, pressing the cold end of the revolver even harder against her temple. In that moment Bridie had no need to act the part of hostage. She was terrified; that the policeman might attempt to shoot and that Lucas would carry out his threat. He sounded so very serious.

When the policeman carefully set down his rifle, Bridie's racing pulse slowed only slightly. Lucas began backing away, drawing Bridie with him, issuing cold instructions to the policeman warning him not to follow or she would still be shot. Bridie knew then why she had never quite lost her fear of Lucas. He would use anyone to gain his own ends.

Then they were running, Lucas almost dragging Bridie behind him as he threaded his way through the trees. Skirts and petticoats were not designed for such reckless flight. There was nothing she could do about the twigs that caught and tore her clothes. Only when one ripped a stinging scratch on her cheek did she cry out.

Lucas glanced back and noted the thin line of dripping blood with little sympathy. 'Watch where you're going.'

'Me watch?' cried Bridie, almost stumbling when he jerked her after him again. 'How can I watch anything with you dragging me along?'

'I'm not letting you go.'

'Why? The police aren't following. You're safe now.'

'Only for as long as they think I still have you.'

'I'll hide and delay going back to Rosalie until they've gone. Oh!' An exposed tree root tripped her. She stumbled badly, saved from pitching forward by Lucas's painful yank on her arm. Tears smarted her eyes.

Lucas swore with impatience. 'For Chrissake be careful. I don't need you with a twisted ankle.'

'You don't need me at all,' Bridie raged back.

His lips curled slightly, his eyes holding a mocking promise. 'Oh, yes I do.'

168

She was crushed against the hard length of his body, one of his hands on her buttocks pressing her pelvis intimately to his. The other hand gripped her hair. His mouth came over hers, his tongue thrusting immediately inside. The erotic embrace lasted just long enough to leave Bridie trembling. Lucas's eyes continued to mock. 'I've not tired of you yet. You're coming with me.'

He started off again, still dragging her in his wake until they reached the edge of a steep gully down which they slipped and slithered. A small creek trickled through the bottom, its water clear and sweet to drink. There, in the cool green of mosses and ferns, they paused to catch their breath. The only sounds were those of nature; the rustle of a lizard through the undergrowth; the songs of birds; the sighing of the breeze in the trees.

'I think we are safe now,' said Lucas.

'But you are not going to let me go,' Bridie stated wearily, the silent look he flashed at her all the answer she needed. 'Where are we going?'

'To find somewhere to stay for the night. Shelter should not be a problem, only you might have to manage without food. You should have brought the bag.'

'You should have,' Bridie retorted. 'And you forget that I have not always supped at a sumptuous table. I know what it is like to live from hand to mouth.'

His firm mouth pursed in agreement. 'We should do well together, then. You won't quail at the hardness of the life I normally lead. Lisette, now, would be a different matter. That was a spoilt and pampered miss if I ever saw one. She takes what she wants without thought to the consequences.' He gave a harsh laugh. 'You were quite right, Bridie. Nat Durrant is going to be extremely disillusioned on his wedding night.'

The mention of Nat brought an ache to Bridie's heart. He would learn what had happened to her and might even believe she had gone willingly to Lucas. After all, she had taunted him with her admission of enjoying the kind of sex Lucas devised. Perhaps he would care no more than for the loss of a compatible bed partner. He had never said he was not going to marry Lisette.

'What was Lisette doing at the house?'

'Do you really need to be told? She had been there yesterday with a man I believe was her painting master. Seamus arrived and demanded her favours for his silence.'

'Did Seamus tell you that?'

The crooked smile touched his mouth again. 'I was an interested observer. I did not speak with Seamus until after the couple left and then it was only to give him the message for you. He told me then that he had arranged for the girl to return alone. Since we did not know when you would be back and he assured me Lisette would agree to anything –'

He allowed the unspoken words to hang in the air and Bridie again knew anger that Nat should be so deceived. Not that she was condemning Lisette for her libidinous ways. If the girl had been betrothed to any other man Bridie would not care in what sexual activities she indulged.

There was something else which she now recalled – something which put a different perspective on Nat's fury over her defiant boast of enjoying sex with Lucas. 'You said you had a score to settle with Nat. What did you mean? Somehow I have gained the feeling you two know each other very well.'

She saw the cold, hard mask settle over Lucas's face and her stomach curled again with the knowledge he would be a vicious enemy. Whatever lay between the two men, the hatred, on Lucas's part at least, went deep.

'We grew up together, the best of friends. Our fathers were close friends, too. Or so I thought.'

'What happened?'

'Nathan Durrant, senior, ruined my father. He quite callously took him for every penny he owned, drove him bankrupt then bought his land for a song.' He paused, the bitterness of years etched in his face. 'My father could not face himself as a failure. He took his own life. The shock gave my mother a stroke. For two years she lay without moving or speaking before she joined him in the grave. I vowed then that Nathan Durrant was not going to enjoy a long life.'

Bridie's mouth was dry. 'Did you kill him?' she whispered.

'Not directly. I hit him in his shoulder and his horse bolted. He was thrown and badly crippled. I had my revenge. Both Nathan Durrant and his son knew I had fired that shot.'

Bridie was silent. Now she understood the callousness in Lucas and the hardness in Nat. Without being told she knew the vendetta had not stopped there. Boys who were once friends were now men who hated.

The recounting was apparently too disturbing for Lucas. He made a dismissive sound and changed the subject. 'Since we weren't followed, I presume Seamus managed to distract the police.' He smiled at her questioning look. 'Use your imagination, Bridie. When the police searched the house they would have found Seamus and Lisette in the throes of sex. Seamus would have invited them to join in and I've no doubt the nymphet would have been very willing.'

Shock showed on Bridie's face. 'Seamus would not do that. Why, it's –'

'What, Bridie? Something you would like to try yourself, to provide the pleasure for several men?'

'I most certainly would not!'

Lucas chuckled. 'Want to make a bet?'

'The situation is never going to arise.'

'I know what has arisen.' His hand curved over his groin. 'I was stuck in that house for two days without a woman.'

The look Bridie slanted at him was meant to show how little she cared. 'Was that so hard to bear?'

'For me, yes. Especially when we had been interrupted

at a most enjoyable time. I'm going to do that again, Bridie, have you with another man, before I let you go.'

'Then you will never let me go because I will never agree to it again.'

'We'll see.' He had opened his trousers, his cock springing hard and free. 'Right now I need to bury this in your lushness.'

Bridie found herself tipped on her back, her skirts hauled up and her undergarments ripped from her body. 'You won't be needing these while you are with me. When I want you I don't want the bother of fumbling with layers of clothing.'

He was poised over her, his downward swoop straight and true. He had not tested her readiness. Perhaps he knew there was no need, for his talk of sex had already aroused some deep inner part of her, wondering what it would be like with several men, before such images were firmly rejected.

Lucas appeared interested only in releasing the built-up tension of his two-day abstinence. Supporting himself on his hands, his body not touching hers, he pounded with gasping urgency to attain his release when Bridie was only halfway to the peak of hers. He withdrew to leave her unsatisfied and aching for more. Her expression said it all.

His lips curled in mockery, Lucas hauled her to her feet. 'We've been here too long already. You will just have to wait.'

Lisette was in a sexual euphoria. Male organs had pounded, thrusted and twisted in her for what seemed like hours and she was not yet ready for them to stop. The bawdy encouragement the men gave to each other, and to her, kept her libido at peak. Responding to their lechery, revelling in her own salaciousness, she arched her body, caressed her breasts and slid her tongue provocatively around pouting lips in uninhibited enjoyment of being the recipient of so much sexual attention.

Only the precipitate arrival of a fourth policeman interrupted her absorption in herself but, as Seamus had begun to thrust into her again in such a wonderful manner, she barely registered the angry words about Lucas Martin escaping while the three officers amused themselves with a whore. The use of that word did not shame Lisette. If possessing a beautiful body, being sexually desirable to men and relishing the joys of the flesh was being a whore then she was worthy of the name.

'Well, he's far away by now,' declared the newcomer, 'so I might just as well discover for myself what has kept you all from your duty.'

He approached the table, fumbled his penis from his trousers and thrust it towards Lisette's face. His own leered down at her. 'A lush like you must know how to suck cock, too. Come on, my beauty, take me deep.'

For several moments Lisette simply gazed up at him, her eyes wide with the falsely innocent gaze she employed so well. She circled fingers over her nipples and ran her tongue over her lips, satisfied when she saw the tightening of lust in the man's face. She provoked him further. 'I cannot reach it, officer.'

Seamus made certain she could, pulling one of her legs down and tipping her on her side. Without withdrawing completely, he straddled her lower leg, pushed the other vertical with both hands and resumed pumping with greater vigour.

Propping herself on her elbow, Lisette clasped the waiting shaft with her free hand to steady it for her eager mouth. She would show this man and the three who watched just how well she could suck cock – as he had so crudely phrased a woman's pleasuring of a man.

Mr Graham had taught her well. Before long the recipient of her expertise was panting and Seamus was thrusting harder and harder to the rhythmic clapping of the three who watched. Steadily, inexorably, they increased the tempo of their clapping, adding a repetitive chant, the same word over and over. Lisette could feel it beating through her blood. It stirred the two who were doing what the others chanted and they jerked in unison, Seamus in her canal, the policeman in her mouth. Harder, louder, faster, pounding, climaxing in her mouth – and her own orgasm racing out of time to the steady clapping.

The police left, their low conversation no doubt contriving excuses for having allowed Lucas Martin to escape. Seamus assisted Lisette in the restoration of her appearance to that of a young lady who had been visiting her friend rather than experiencing her wildest sexual fantasy.

'I used to dream about that,' she confessed to Seamus. 'I often tried to imagine what it would be like.'

'Was it as you imagined?'

Lisette's eyes shone. 'Far, far better.'

'Then tell me why you are planning to marry Nat Durrant. You'll not be doing anything like that as his wife.'

His words brought back that amazing confrontation with Bridie. A tiny frown puckered her brow. 'Bridie never told me she knew Nat. Was that because she has always been his mistress?'

'That I cannot tell you, though I doubt it. She always declared she hated him.'

'But she can't have known him long having so recently come from Ireland.'

Seamus belatedly remembered Bridie's fabricated background. 'There's things about Bridie you don't know but I'll not be the one to tell you those, either.'

With her head tilted to one side, Lisette regarded him speculatively. There was a hunch forming in her mind that the information he would not disclose might help her resolve her own dilemma. 'She did not sound as if she hated Nat this afternoon.'

Seamus shrugged. 'Bridie likes sex as much as you do. She doesn't refuse any able-bodied man.'

'You sound bitter.'

'Why not? Bridie would have married me if Nat Durrant had not got to her first.'

'And now?' asked Lisette after she had absorbed the import of Seamus's statement. A woman could care deeply for her first lover, as she well knew.

'I'm not wanting to marry her now. Bridie uses me for sex and from now on I'll be doing the same with her. But you've not answered my question.'

Lisette's expression became troubled. 'The marriage was arranged. Nat decided I had the upbringing, background and social position to make him a suitable wife and my parents agreed.'

'Did you have no say in the matter?'

'Oh yes. I was happy to agree. After all, Nat is everything a woman could desire in a husband. He is wealthy, virile. I intended to go to him a virgin.'

This time Seamus was surprised. 'From virgin to wanton. When did you change?'

'When I discovered my true self.'

'Then why marry Nat Durrant?'

Lisette hesitated. 'I can think of no reason to call the marriage off.'

When Seamus gave her a searching stare she flushed and turned her face away to fiddle with her dress. The tears in the skirt were not as bad as she had expected and could be hidden by careful folding and the rearrangement of her fichu concealed those in her bodice. In truth she could think of several good reasons for calling off her marriage but, whether she married Nat or not, she would inevitably have to face his anger.

She certainly never expected to come face to face with the man himself when Seamus and she returned to Rosalie. He was standing on the driveway in discussion with the four policemen and the blood that was already draining from her face rushed completely away with the lewd smirk one sent in her direction.

Beside her Seamus spoke quietly. 'I'll do the talking.

175

You just agree. That lot will not be saying anything to get themselves in trouble.'

By then Nat had become aware of their approach. His brows drew together in a frown. 'I didn't know you were here, Lisette.' His questioning gaze went from her to Seamus, who stood protectively close.

Lisette tried to stammer a reply, relieved when Seamus took up the explanation. 'Miss Cunningham was visiting Bridie. They were walking near the old house when they were accosted by that man, Martin. I found Miss Cunningham in a distressed state and Bridie apparently taken hostage.'

'Are you all right?' Nat gave Lisette a searching look.

'I am now. I was so scared before.' From beneath trembling lashes she stole a furtive glance at the police who stood gaping at her act of timid maiden. They would not, she saw with relief, say anything to contradict Seamus's story.

'How did you come to Rosalie?' Nat asked. 'I have not seen any conveyance.'

'I came by cab. My maid will be returning with it shortly.'

'Good. I am glad you are not going home alone after such a terrible experience.'

Lisette's glance slid to the police again, who stood with bland expressions on their faces, and she almost giggled. They all knew her experience had been anything but terrible. 'Will you be visiting us tonight, Nat?'

'That all depends.'

'On Bridie?'

He gave her a sharp look, reading some surprising things in the simply query. 'Yes.'

Much later that night, while Lisette confessed to Mr Graham what she had done and willingly accepted the punishment he deemed applicable for acting without his consent, Seamus slept soundly in his cottage and Nat rode north, certain Lucas Martin would return to the region of Barkers Ridge.

At the same time, Bridie and Lucas were sheltering in an abandoned settler's shack, the slab walls and bark roof intact enough to keep the damp night air at bay. They had no blankets and their clothing made their bed. Lucas had wanted her naked, had insisted he feel her skin against his. They were as close now as they could be, with Bridie sprawled on Lucas's chest, able only to moan at the pain of his fingers digging into her buttocks and the powerful upward thrust of his hips as he brought her to yet another climax.

Chapter Eleven

*B*ridie woke in the grey hours of early morning to find herself alone. Dressed in her torn and tattered dress, she looked outside to discover there was no sign of Lucas. Rather than being relieved she became apprehensive. She had no idea where they were nor, if Lucas had left her, how to find her way back to civilisation. There were far too many stories of people disappearing in the bush never to be seen again for her not to feel some fear.

While her mind attempted to make a rational assessment of her situation, she attended to her most basic needs, washed her face in the nearby stream and drank by cupping her hands to scoop the water. She was wondering if she would be able to retrace their route when Lucas came riding from the bush behind the hut, leading a second horse with a bloody piece of meat hanging from the saddle.

'Transport and breakfast,' he declared. 'Courtesy of a nearby farmer.'

'You mean he gave them to you?'

Lucas chuckled. 'I didn't ask. Hopefully he won't miss his horses or his beast before we have eaten and are on our way.'

A fire was quickly lit with the slice of beef rump

threaded on to a green stick to be turned and roasted over the flames. With Lucas deeming it safer not to wait until the fire had died to perfect roasting coals, the outside became blackened. And if the centre was a little too rare, Bridie was not complaining. She ate ravenously, tearing at the meat with her teeth and not caring that blood and grease dripped on to her skirt.

For four days they rode steadily north towards Barkers Ridge before turning east towards high country. By the second night Lucas had obtained food and clothing. Men's clothing. Strange though they seemed at first, Bridie soon discovered the practicality of wearing trousers when riding astride. Without any undergarments she had needed to pull her skirt between her legs to prevent her thighs and more tender flesh from being abraded by the saddle leather.

Lucas also made her hide her hair under a hat and turn up the collar of her coat to shield her face from the too curious who might realise she was a woman. They stayed in inns after the first night and went openly into the little towns to buy food. While most seemed to accept them simply as travellers, Bridie was amazed by Lucas's arrogant unconcern. Once when she saw a wanted poster she was certain he must be recognised. He laughed when she voiced her concern, his mouth twisted in cynicism, his cold hard eyes giving her the thrill of fear that so excited her sexually.

'In ten years the police have not caught me and they aren't smart enough to do it now. It will take a good man to track us where we are going, Bridie.'

What neither Lucas nor Bridie knew was that such a man was at that moment less than a day's ride behind.

Around midday on the fifth day their journey ended. With the horses carefully picking their way they had ascended to where huge boulders shrugged aside the trees. A damp shrouding mist reduced visibility and made the rocky terrain treacherously slippery beneath the horses' hooves. Skilled rider though she was, Bridie was in trepidation of her mount stumbling. If she was pitched from the saddle she would either strike her head on one of the rocks or go tumbling down the mountain edge to certain death.

At last they passed between two steep-sided rocks to begin a more gradual descent into a small, high-walled valley. There was a cluster of crudely built huts away to their right, built back against the almost sheer rock, out of the main force of the strong wind which whistled through the gap.

Bridie gazed about in awe. 'What is this place?'

'Belongs to the Dunn brothers. Jack and Mick. We'll be safe here.'

'Are they outlaws, too?'

'That depends on your definition of outlaw. They have no liking for the police.'

Within a few yards they were challenged. The very appearance of the man who sat on his horse blocking the path sent a shiver of fear down Bridie's spine. His face was marked by scars, mean black eyes pierced from beneath equally black brows and a drooping moustache framed a mouth of yellowed teeth. The bandolier of ammunition slung across his shoulder, the guns on his hips and the rifle he carried in his hand completed the lawless image. Bridie considered her recent question well and truly answered.

'You get uglier every time I see you, Jack Dunn,' Lucas declared while pushing back his dripping hat to reveal his own face.

The man grunted in recognition and Bridie had the distinct impression no one but Lucas could have made such a comment and gotten away with it. 'Ain't seen you in a while. Who's the lad? You usually work alone.'

Lucas had started to reply when a sudden stronger gust of wind whipped Bridie's hat from her head. Her long hair tumbled free, to be tousled by the same wind. Unable to do anything about it, Bridie noted with a tightening of her gut how Jack Dunn's eyes had narrowed to threatening slits and his expression had become even more aggressive.

'A woman,' he growled. 'You know the rules about bringing a woman here.'

'I know,' said Lucas quietly.

'Does she?'

'She'll do what I tell her.' Lucas had turned his horse to retrieve Bridie's hat from where it hung on a tree branch. He handed it to her, the eyes he kept on her face carefully void of any expression.

'She'd better. I don't want no trouble. You can go on down to the hut. I've got things to do.'

He set his horse forward, his cruel little eyes searching her face when he drew level. Everything about the man made Bridie wish Lucas had taken her anywhere else but here. However, there was little she could do except set her horse to walk behind Lucas's mount. When the path became wide enough she moved up beside him. She had had time enough to reflect on Jack Dunn's words.

'Would you mind explaining that conversation? Am I expected to become a drudge?'

Lucas glanced at her, eyes cold, lips drawn together. 'You will be expected to cook, and do other things.'

'Such as?'

'Women rarely come here. The ones who do are usually of a certain type.'

'I see.' Bridie spoke quietly and Lucas, whose knowledge of her was restricted to the carnal side of her nature, did not realise that such quietness of tone was a sure sign her temper was beginning to boil. 'These women have been happy to accommodate both of the Dunn men, I presume?'

'Any men who happen to be here. There are usually two or three.'

His calm statement of fact set the final spark to her anger. 'If you think I am going to make myself available to a half dozen men you can think again.'

181

'You won't be given any choice in the matter.'

'I'll shoot any man who tries to force himself on me.'

Lucas cast her a disdainfully disbelieving look. 'I doubt any man would ever need to use force with you, my sweet. Anyway, you don't have a gun.'

She moved so quickly she took Lucas by surprise, lifting his rifle from its holster before he realised what she was about. 'I have now,' she declared, resting the butt against her hip to steady the barrel at his heart. In that moment she hated him enough to pull the trigger.

He became very still, eyes narrowed to assess her mood. 'You won't use it, Bridie, even if you think you will. Give it back to me. Before the damned thing goes off.'

Sensing he was going to lunge for the rifle, Bridie jerked back, her finger unintentionally depressing the trigger. Her horse reared in fright at the report and she was thrown to the ground, the rifle flying from her hand. She landed with a thud on her back to lie winded and gasping, wondering if the bullet had hit Lucas.

Within moments she discovered it had not. He loomed over her, his face tight with cold rage. 'You damned near shot me.'

'I'm sorry,' Bridie mumbled, cowering back into the ground away from his fury.

'You'll be a damned sight more sorry.'

He yanked the trousers she was wearing halfway down to her knees, roughly jerked her legs up and pushed her knees back against her chest. The bunched trousers prevented her from seeing but she knew he was poised above her. Then he was plunging deeply, his shaft intended as an instrument of punishment.

Despite the brutality with which he was taking her, Bridie's body responded immediately to provide the lubrication which allowed him to slide easily within her, and rendered his deliberate, forceful thrusts more enjoyable for both.

His chuckle was savagely malicious. 'You can't help yourself, can you, Bridie?'

With an inward groan she admitted it was true. Though there was no lessening of the punishing force with which he was taking her and her mind said she wanted no more of him, her flesh swelled and responded. Bridie gave herself up to the inevitability of her orgasm.

There were shouts, loud demands to know what was going on. Aghast at the nearness of the voices, Bridie attempted to push Lucas away. The weight of his shoulders against her legs kept her imprisoned beneath his body. Nor did he break the forceful evenness of his thrusts even though she knew he, too, had climaxed. He was claiming mastery. 'You won't defy me again, Bridie Flannagan. You will do exactly as I say.'

There was a delighted chortle from somewhere near at hand. 'That's right. Show her who's boss.'

Bridie's face flamed. When Lucas finally lifted free she rolled on her side away from the direction of the laugh to pull her trousers back over her hips, glad that her hair had fallen over her face. Through the strands she found herself looking at another pair of boots. Expensive boots. While she wriggled the trousers into place, her gaze travelled in curiosity up a pair of moleskin-clad legs to reach the unmistakable evidence of the man's interest in what he had seen.

Just then Lucas reached down to haul her to her feet and as her hair fell back from her face she heard an astonished gasp followed by a startled exclamation.

'Bridie!'

Bridie swung round to find herself staring into the astonished face of the Honourable Harold Beechmont.

Just which of them was the more startled was difficult to say. While they stared in silent astonishment at each other, Lucas demanded an explanation of their acquaintance.

The Honourable Harry smiled with all the suave charm Bridie remembered. 'We were just starting to become acquainted when I was compelled to leave Melbourne in a hurry.' His eyes, resting on her face, gleamed with appreciation. 'I'm glad we have met again, Bridie, though I never expected it to be here.'

'Neither,' said Bridie shortly, gathering her composure around her with hauteur, 'did I.'

The return of an obviously angry Jack Dunn prevented any further exchange. 'Who the devil fired that shot?' he demanded to know.

Lucas shrugged. 'The rifle went off accidentally. I don't believe she was really trying to shoot me.'

The man's distrustful glare fixed on Bridie before returning to Lucas. 'You said she'd be no trouble. She looks like big trouble to me. Even in them trousers I can see she's no common whore. Why did you bring her?'

The cruel smile Bridie knew well curled across Lucas's lips. 'She was my ticket to freedom and she also happens to be of interest to Nat Durrant.'

At that Jack Dunn gave a harsh bark which passed for a laugh. 'You still trying to pay him back? OK. You keep her in line and make sure there's no more shooting.'

One of the other men gave a lewd hoot of laughter. 'There'll be plenty of shooting, Jack, but it won't be from rifles.'

Bridie's quick temper flared afresh. She glared at the man, her fists clenched and lips compressed to prevent herself from saying something she might well be made to regret. If she was to be sport for them all, she doubted there was much she could do. She would get no help from Lucas nor possibly even from Harry.

Resigning herself to the inevitable, she almost sagged with relief when Lucas challenged them all with his cold stare. 'Don't act like a pack of rutting animals. You only get her if she's willing. Understood?'

They understood even if Bridie didn't. Lucas Martin was far too complex a man for her to ever figure out. She could only be thankful not one of the men seemed prepared to challenge his authority. For reasons of his own he had given her a reprieve and, while she knew he would soon enough be urging her to various acts of sex, she was grateful. She slid a glance at Harry, wondering if he could be persuaded to help her get away before Lucas changed his mind. While she knew herself to be a very sexual woman she liked her lovers to be civilised in manner and physically pleasing to the eye. The dark-skinned man seemed passable enough. The appearances of the others filled her with distaste.

All of them were walking towards the huts, with Lucas slightly ahead of Bridie and Harry, leading the horses. Speaking in low tones she asked Harry if she could possibly see him alone.

'Eager?' he whispered back. 'I can't wait. I'm also immensely curious about him.' He nodded towards Lucas who had glanced back with a knowing look. Jack Dunn also looked back, his eyes suspicious.

Eyeing him warily, Bridie lowered her voice even more. 'He makes me shiver. I don't trust him any more than I like him.'

'You are wise not to. He is a real nasty piece of work. He doesn't like women, either.'

'Is that supposed to make me feel safer or not?'

'He won't be seeking your favours.'

Bridie's relief was enormous. She hoped Harry was right. 'What about the others?'

'They're normal men, Bridie. You will find they are not so bad. That's Mick Dunn with the brown hair. Just as dangerous as his brother but easier to get on with. Most of the time he's OK. The fair one is Jed Hayden and the other is Johnny Ramirez.' He smiled slightly at the surprised lift of Bridie's brows. 'His skin might be almost black but there is a mixture of races in his blood. Spanish, islander, Negro, even a bit of Irish. He's a bit of a charming scoundrel.'

'Like yourself?' Bridie quipped.

Harry flashed her an appreciative smile. 'We came here

185

together. He was a professional gambler. Perhaps you should try your luck.'

Conversation ceased on their arrival at the hut. Lucas, Harry and Bridie followed Jack Dunn inside, the others moving away to continue whatever had been interrupted when the rifle discharged. Bridie glanced with interest around the interior of the hut, which had no partitions. There was a fireplace, near which hung several blackened pots and pans. Crude shelves made from bush timber held a variety of foods and eating utensils. The middle of the hut was dominated by a roughly hewn table flanked by two benches.

Jack Dunn watched Bridie look around. 'Anyone who comes here pulls their weight. Now do your women's work and get us some coffee and food.'

Though her temper came close to boiling point and her eyes flashed blue sparks, Bridie clamped her mouth shut and set about making coffee from the kettle that boiled over the fire. She found bread, cheese and cold meat to put on the table.

Lucas and Jack Dunn talked while they ate, about people, places and events which held no interest for Bridie. Nor Harry either, apparently. After sitting for some time without contributing he took advantage of a brief pause to ask Jack Dunn if he could take Bridie outside to show her around.

'That all?' growled Dunn.

'Well, we do have a lot of catching up to do.'

'Huh. As long as Lucas don't object I guess it's all right.'

'I don't,' said Lucas, his lips twisting in a half smile. 'But you don't have to leave if all you want to do is renew your acquaintance. We won't take any notice.'

He was taunting Bridie and she knew it. She silently seethed while Harry flashed him a disbelieving look. 'I think you would take a lot of notice and Jack wouldn't be too impressed. We'll go for a walk.'

They did not walk very far. Only to a small store hut

filled with assorted boxes and stacks of supplies. Scant light found its way through the high-set window and when the door was shut Bridie could barely see Harry's face. Not that it was important, for she knew the expression he would have in his eyes. She held him away when he tried to draw her into his arms.

'You must satisfy my curiosity first, Harry. I want to know what you are doing here and you must surely be wondering the same about me.'

'Martin has already explained, hasn't he? Unless there is more? I'll admit I was stunned when I recognised you, especially meeting again under those particular circumstances.' He reached to fondle her breast through the material of her shirt. 'As for me, I owed too many people too much money. I needed to get out of Melbourne and by chance met up with Johnny, who was in much the same boat. I needed somewhere to give me a breathing space until the heat dies down. Johnny had done Mick a favour one time, in case you are wondering how he fits in with the Dunns. They are a bit too uncouth for my liking. I am planning to leave soon and make my way overland to Sydney.'

'How soon?' Bridie's question was breathless, the manner of Harry's fondling making it difficult for her to keep her mind entirely on gleaning the information she wanted to know.

'Not so soon now that you are here. I had thought to go today or tomorrow.'

'Today?' asked Bridie, her voice breathless with eagerness. 'Would you be willing to leave right now, Harry, and to take me with you?'

Harry ceased fondling her breast to ponder her request. The lasciviousness in his eyes faded in disbelief. 'You're serious. Is it because of the men?'

'Partly. I want to get away from Lucas.'

'Are you really his hostage?'

'The answer to that is both yes and no. He is not an easy man to deny.'

187

'So it is sex that keeps you together.'

'Yes. He will not let me go until he tires of me.'

'And you?'

'He only has to look at me and I want him. I have no will to resist. He has a hold over me which I must break.'

'Yet he knew I was planning to have sex with you. Why didn't he object to your coming with me? In fact, he suggested we stay in the hut.' Harry was puzzled.

'That must tell you what manner of man he is.'

'Then he will not object to you having sex with any of the men?'

'He would not object to me having sex with all of the men together,' Bridie retorted with some heat. 'That is why I want to leave right away.'

Harry did not reply immediately and Bridie sensed he was considering her statement. He continued to fondle her breast, making her nipples harden to responsive peaks. 'I have thought about you a lot, Bridie. I always regretted not being able to call on you again. You don't know how many womanless nights have been made bearable by reliving our visit to that moonlit pavilion. I need only picture you, semi-naked and clutching the post while I fucked you, to be able to forget it was my hand around my cock and imagine it was your delicious cunt. I want you like that now, Bridie. I want you to bend over while I take you from behind.' He gave a despairing groan. 'Take those goddamned trousers off, Bridie, before I rip them off.'

Bridie, who was now as eager as Harry to relive that experience, hastily undid the fastenings and slid the trousers down her hips. So quickly had his words aroused her to a wet eagerness she wondered briefly what it was about her that made her always so ready for sex and men hot with desire for her body.

The trousers were barely past her hips when Harry's impatient hands turned her around and tilted her forward. She clasped the edge of a box to steady herself against the rhythmic thrusts. Harry wasted no more time in entering her than Lucas had done so short a time earlier. However, his rod did not strive to punish. It slid slowly, steadily, Harry's long drawn 'Aaah' evidence of his savouring of every additional degree of union.

When he was fully embedded he simply held himself, body slightly tensed, as if to move would be to spoil the pleasure he was experiencing. Even his voice held a tense huskiness.

'This is how I have remembered the feel of you. Smooth, silky, and moist. Ah, yes. Clench me like that, Bridie, grip me tightly.'

The initial contraction of her internal muscles had been unconsidered, a spontaneous physical response to the evocative erotism of his words. Now she clenched him consciously, contracting and releasing her sex muscles without pause between each action. She was controlling the sex, delighting in Harry's shuddering groans and revelling in her own body's response.

The degree to which she was arousing herself demanded a higher level of activity. She began to circle her hips, sliding smoothly around Harry's shaft, working it deeper into her body. Within moments she was gasping at the deliciousness of the sensations she aroused within her. The delight was too great to be contained. Bridie's action became urgent with the need to bring herself to a climax.

An expletive cry left Harry's lips. He gripped her and he began to pump while swivelling his hips to complement her own action. There was not a single cell within Bridie's being that was not becoming stimulated, not a nerve ending that was not responding. The gasps of both were becoming louder and louder, hips moving faster, then bodies climaxing.

'Yes!' shouted Harry. 'Yes, yes, yes!'

Lucas's mocking laugh echoed in the tiny hut. 'Don't use all your strength, Bridie, you will need plenty tonight. And when Harry decides to part himself from your body –' for Harry was continuing with slow thrusts in apparent total unconcern of the other man's presence '– you can come and cook everyone's dinner. You will make yourself useful in more ways than one while we are here and don't try to tell me you don't know how to cook on an open fire because I know that you do.'

He strolled away, and when Harry finally pulled his softening shaft free, Bridie reached down to wearily pull the trousers back in place. Her back remained to Harry, her head down, her voice low. 'I won't stay here, Harry. You must help me to get away.'

'I can't, Bridie. I'm sorry. The pass is the only way out. We would be seen and brought back. No one leaves this place without Jack Dunn's consent. I've also seen enough of Lucas Martin to know he is not a man to be crossed. He won't let you go.'

'You're a coward,' Bridie hissed, turning to face him. 'You are only concerned for your own skin.'

'I happen to like my skin. Yours, too,' he added with a lopsided smile which begged forgiveness. 'You enjoy sex, Bridie. Surely it won't be so bad?'

'Ooh.' Bridie fumed. Harry did not know Lucas had declared his intention of sharing her again with another man. She had told Harry that Lucas would raise no objection to her having sex with all of the men together. How could she confess he would very likely be the one to instigate the event? Bridie was certain Lucas's sexual aims were the reasons he had chosen to bring her to this place. Well, if Harry was not going to help there was not a great deal she could do about her situation but, she vowed, by all the saints in Ireland, they would none of them make her do anything against her will.

The men all came into the kitchen hut at various times while she was engaged in preparing the meal. She prepared a mutton stew, boiled potatoes and made damper, determined to produce a meal which would be well appreciated. While she could not have cared less if all they had to eat was beef jerky, she was determined to

190

make them regard her as a person, not simply an available female body.

Therefore she spoke a little to each of them, her manner pleasant, friendly, unprovocative. Only with Jack Dunn did she remain silent. His glowering observation of everything she did had her making a silent, fervent prayer that Harry had spoken the truth in declaring Jack Dunn had no liking in any way for women.

All six men sat at the table drinking rum while they waited for her to dish stew and potatoes on to metal plates and to cut the damper into thick slabs. Interested eyes watched her, some more assessing than others. Bridie smiled when she placed a full plate in front of each man and wondered privately how much rum they intended to drink. If they became too intoxicated they might lose interest in sex. On the other hand, they might just become drunk enough to be brutal in their demands. That unpleasant prospect was shed with relief when they all set aside the rum to demand she brew coffee after the meal.

When the coffee had been poured and cigarettes lit she gave the dark-skinned Johnny Ramirez her brightest smile. 'I believe you are a gambler, Ramirez. I enjoy a game of poker myself. What about it, gentlemen?' She glanced around the table. 'Winner takes all?'

Jack Dunn's surly, 'I don't like gambling' had Bridie wondering if there was anything that unpleasant man did like. He heaved himself to his feet. 'I'll leave you lot to do whatever you want,' he said.

None of the men appeared concerned by his departure. Cards were produced and the remaining five men and Bridie arranged themselves around the table.

'What are you going to use for a stake, Bridie?' asked Lucas at his most sardonic. 'You don't have any money.'

Bridie smiled sweetly back. 'Not yet.'

'You need something to start,' declared Ramirez.

With her lips and her eyes holding a challenge, Bridie looked at him. 'I have something you all want. That is my stake.' Her unflinching gaze then went to the face of each man. 'Any one of you could choose to take me by force and I would be powerless to prevent you. To do so would undoubtedly afford you physical satisfaction. I promise you it would not give you any great enjoyment. Both Lucas and Harry know how ardent a lover I can be. I am sure each of you would rather enjoy my talents than have me lie tense and unresponsive. Shall we make things more interesting by pitting your gambling skills against mine? Are you prepared to take a chance? If I win you all lose.'

'And if you lose?' Lucas asked quietly.

'Then I will do whatever the winner asks of me.'

She was already gambling, even while she spoke, relieved when the appreciative gleam in Ramirez' eyes became reflected in the eyes of the others and the cards were dealt. Tonight she would need all her wits about her; need every ounce of her gambling skill to keep the game going until one by one the men were forced to drop out. There would be a winner other than herself. Bridie was shrewd enough to realise she would lose her precarious control of the situation otherwise. The winner would be the man of her choice – Johnny Ramirez.

During the afternoon she had made her own quiet assessment of them all while she formulated her plan. By their former acquaintance with her, neither Lucas nor Harry could be considered, and of the others Ramirez was the one whose dark-skinned good looks captured her interest. He also seemed to possess more gentlemanly traits. Mick Dunn, who had passed all the lewd remarks earlier in the day, carried a perpetual leer on his face. Jed Hayden she summed up as a man who would be obedient to the word of the Dunns. Johnny Ramirez was definitely her safest bet.

Within an hour she knew she had gained his admiration and the grudging respect of Mick Dunn. Forced to withdraw, Jed Hayden shook his head in amazement. 'Not only cooks well, she plays poker like a professional.

That's some woman you've got there, Martin. If she does everything else as well, I'm surprised you aren't keeping her all to yourself.'

Lucas's pale eyes stared directly at Bridie. 'We have an understanding, don't we, Bridie? I made her a promise I will have to keep.' At Bridie's glare, a smile twisted his mouth and his voice lowered with the suggestive cadence that stirred her sexually. 'Only when you are ready for it to be kept.'

Another hour later the game reached the conclusion Bridie had planned. Ramirez' smile was brilliantly white against the near blackness of his skin. 'So. Do I collect payment now?'

'Naturally,' said Bridie.

'And we get to watch,' Mick Dunn declared with lewd delight. 'Then we get our turn.'

'You are mistaken there.' Ramirez voice was so dangerously quiet Mick Dunn flashed him a startled look before resuming his belligerent lechery.

'Yeah? We all sleep in the same hut or have you forgotten?'

Bridie had not considered the sleeping arrangements either. Feeling the growing tension between the two men, she began to wonder if all her deviousness had been for naught. Lucas was simply watching, awaiting with interest the outcome. From the flush on Harry's face she gained the distinct notion he had no objection to becoming a voyeur either.

Jed Hayden surprised Bridie by being the one to speak up. 'Leave it, Mick. We set the rules when we started. Johnny won her fair and square. We can all stretch our legs in the moonlight for a while.

Johnny Ramirez chuckled. 'I would hate to deprive all of a night's sleep. We'll make do here.'

Chapter Twelve

*A*fter the men departed, Mick Dunn continuing to grumble and Lucas exhorting Bridie to enjoy herself, Ramirez swung round to lean his back against the table and lit another cigarette. Seated at the opposite end of the same bench, Bridie awaited his first move. He appeared in no hurry to claim the prize he had won. Dark eyes smiling, an amused quirk at the corner of his mouth, he regarded her quizzically.

'You intrigue me,' he said. 'You dress like a man, speak like a lady, can cook over an open fire and play poker as shrewdly as any professional gambler. You come here as one man's woman and do not blink an eye at the prospect of becoming mine. Harry vouches for your charms yet you are not some loose-living whore. Who are you?'

'I am an ordinary woman.'

'Ah no. That I refute. There is not a single thing about you that is ordinary. You are very beautiful. I have always admired that peculiarly Irish combination of black hair, blue eyes, flawless skin and well-defined bone structure. Oh I know you are Irish,' he added when she showed her surprise. 'You speak in a cultured voice but you cannot disguise your genetic features.'

Bridie could not help smiling. 'One could not say the same of you. Harry told me your ancestry is quite mixed.'

'It is. I have been fortunate in inheriting the best features of every one of my ancestors. Even my colour is an advantage. Most women seem fascinated by the idea of taking a dark-skinned lover.'

His gaze challenged her and again Bridie smiled. His colour had definitely been one of the things which had made him her choice.

'I would love to see you dressed as a woman. I would like to have you draped in finery and draped on my arm in some exclusive gambling club.' He paused, his gaze sweeping over the masculine garb. 'I would like even more to see you naked.'

First pulling off her boots and the woollen socks, Bridie stood without speaking. Facing Ramirez, her gaze holding his, she stripped off her shirt and his sharp intake of breath when her breasts were exposed gave her a thrill of pleasure.

'So full, so firm,' he murmured. 'They are truly beautiful. Is the rest of you as lovely?'

Bridie undid the trousers and allowed them to fall to her ankles. She lifted one foot free then the other.

Ramirez, eyes gleaming, breathing more heavily, ground out his cigarette on the table. 'Turn around. Very slowly.'

Almost able to feel his gaze touching her body, Bridie did as she was bid. When she had turned full circle he stretched out his hand. 'Come here.'

Bridie walked slowly to stand in front of him. He pulled her down to sit astride his lap, her knees bent, lower legs on the bench on either side of his thighs. Her sex was pressed against his groin, able to feel the bulk of what stirred beneath his trousers. His hands pulled the pins from her hair and when it cascaded down he buried his fingers in it to pull her head back and arch her breasts to his seeking mouth.

His tongue circled the areola of each before it was

enclosed by his lips. He sucked lightly then drew the nipple gently through bared teeth, repeating the action again and again to maximise her shuddering response. With her head held back so firmly Bridie was unable to look at him. Instead, she could only feel what he was doing; feel the material-covered hardness against which her sex rested. To absorb every nuance of those feelings Bridie closed her eyes and enjoyed Ramirez' hungry mouth. He seemed not to be able to get enough of her breasts – licking, sucking, teasing – until her nipples were hard tips of desire on pleasure-swollen peaks.

Eventually he lifted her aside. In the same way that she had done, he removed his boots and socks then stood to take off his shirt. This time it was Bridie who admired the view. His upper torso was perfectly sculptured, the muscles of his arms indefectibly defined. His skin was without visible hair and glistened like polished mahogany. When he removed his trousers she gasped, her awe-filled eyes lifting from his magnificent penis to his face.

White teeth flared in a smile. 'I told you I had inherited the best attributes of all my ancestors.'

Bridie swallowed and looked back at his massive swollen phallus again. If she analogised his skin to polished timber, this was surely the magnificent curving branch of a tree. Her voice was soft with awe. 'I did not know any man could be so big.'

'Are you worried by my size?'

'No.' Bridie knew her denial was uncertain. Ramirez' organ was so very big she was wondering how it was possible for any woman to take him without causing herself some internal damage. At the same time her body was preparing itself by precipitating a greater flow than normal of anticipatory fluid.

'I won't hurt you,' he promised. 'I became accustomed to my size at an early age and only give a woman as much as she can comfortably take. I derive no pleasure from a woman's discomfort or pain.' He smiled down at Bridie. 'Your eyes tell me you want to touch.' One step sideways brought him directly in front of her. 'Touch me however you will. I won't instruct you what to do.'

Feeling almost mesmerised, Bridie reached out to curl her right hand lightly around his shaft. How tiny and white her hand was against the dark-skinned column. She ran her finger tips wonderingly up and down its length and around the velvet-soft glans. Almost without volition her head moved forward, her tongue eager to duplicate the path of her fingers.

So great an organ could never be taken fully into her mouth but she wanted to taste him; to feel the softness of his glans against the softer inner flesh of her lips. Her right hand continued to run lightly up and down the column while she sucked the tip and she used her left to gently feel the weight of the heavy sacs below.

Acting with the instinct of desire, Bridie slid from the bench to kneel on the floor. Her tongue trailed down the curve of his organ as she sank lower and lower, until she was at the right height to suck on those sacs and roll the inner balls in her mouth.

Ramirez gave a shuddering cry and within moments he was demanding she cease. When she did, he took a pace back and reached down to draw her to her feet. 'You are too good.' His voice was husky with wonderment. 'If I was intrigued by you before I am fascinated now. A woman who can give a man so much pleasure should receive her own. I must taste you too, explore all your secrets with my tongue.'

He lifted her to seat her on the table then stepped across the bench to sit between her thighs. Firm hands guided her legs wider and gentle fingers parted her labial folds. 'It is the loveliest quim I have seen,' he murmured. His tongue swept along the crease. 'And the sweetest I have ever tasted.'

He tasted her well, running his tongue over every fold and crease of her sex to thrill her with its touch. So very experienced was that tongue in imparting delight Bridie took a moment from her responsive pleasure to be thank-

197

ful Ramirez was the one she had chosen. Mick Dunn would most certainly not have bothered to consider her enjoyment.

All too soon Ramirez decided she had been pleasured enough by his tongue. He knelt on the seat, his hand around his cock guiding it to her opening. Panting slightly, Bridie tried to relax her sexual muscles in preparation for his entry. Instead of penetrating her he began to tease her with it, rubbing the head along her crease and over her yearning nub.

The sight of his great dark organ against her fair skin was even more arousing than had been the sight of his black-haired head between her milky white thighs. Not satisfied with reducing her to a trembling mass of awakened nerves with his teasing, he began to slap his cock against her quim. The first light blow made her suck in her breath at the unexpectedness of the action, the second had her shuddering with her response to this new, highly erotic method of arousal. By alternately teasing her trembling flesh then slapping it he brought her to the point where the quivering of her body was uncontrollable.

'Are you ready for it now?' Ramirez stroked the head of his shaft down her crease one last time before pressing it between her inner folds.

'Yes, oh yes,' Bridie gasped, lifting herself forward to take in more.

A groan greeted her action. 'I could become so carried away by the delicious feel of you I might hurt you. You must control the degree to which I penetrate.'

Once again he turned and sat with his back resting against the table, his great phallus rigidly erect. This time Bridie stood on the bench, a foot either side of his legs. Ramirez' hands on her hips steadied her as she bent her knees and slowly lowered herself until her eagerly moist sex was again encasing his tip.

With her hands on his shoulders to give her greater control and his hands still steadying her hips Bridie began to slide slowly down over the column. Conscious

198

of the size of him, Bridie took her time, lowering, lifting up, lowering again a little further, lifting up, lowering to embrace more.

He was nearly all in, his length filling her to her womb. She was gasping, lifting and pressing down again. 'Take it easy,' he cautioned. 'You might not be able to take all of me.'

'I want to.' She pushed harder, tears smarting her eyes. Never had she been penetrated so deeply. Never had she experienced this ache in the very centre of her body. Even so she knew he was not yet fully encased. Eyes screwed tightly shut, teeth biting her lower lip, she pressed herself all the way down. It was painful; orgastically painful. Bridie cried out. Her fingers dug into his shoulders and the tears streamed down her cheeks while the waves of orgasm seeped from her body.

Through it all she knew Ramirez was studying the play of rapturous emotions across her face and, when the searing flow ceased, he lifted her free, the separation of his organ from her creating the same gasping awareness as their union.

He made her lie on her back along the bench, legs hanging on either side. Straddling the bench himself he slid his hands beneath her buttocks to lift her slightly. Knees flexed, torso angled slightly forward, he placed the tip of his cock accurately against her opening once more. In the same manner she had used, he entered her, carefully sliding in, withdrawing then pushing a little further. All the while he exhorted her to tell him if it began to hurt.

Bridie managed to gasp an assurance. 'No. It's all right.'

Ramirez was very deep now and it was beginning to hurt. But it was a wholly sexual pain, a salacious discomfort, and Bridie wanted him filling her to his maximum so very much.

'By God, you are magnificent,' he declared, his breathing ragged. 'You have taken all of me.'

He then began to pump more quickly, though still cautiously, until he was driven beyond the point of self-control. Bridie was crying again. Partly from the hard pounding of that mighty organ and partly from the magnitude of her body's response. Her orgasm started on a wrenching sob and she was near to swooning when he finally lowered her hips, bending over to kiss her mouth.

So deeply and firmly was he bedded inside, Bridie thought she might remain joined to him for all time. They certainly did not come apart when Ramirez wrapped her legs around his hips and straightened with her clinging to him like a monkey. He stepped back across the bench and sank to his knees on the floor, then back on to his heels. Bridie's arms and legs remained wrapped around his torso and his penis tightly fitted within.

Gentle hands cupped her face and he kissed her with lingering gratitude. 'I wish you were mine. I would allow no other man to share you if you were. I am honoured you chose me tonight.' The white flash of his smile mocked her surprise. 'I am a professional gambler, Bridie. I watched the way you played and soon knew what you were about. You were very clever. We could do extremely well together. Would you leave Martin to come with me? I promise you would only ever need to be mine.'

Deeply touched by his declaration, Bridie was almost swayed by the sheer strength of him. She touched her lips to his. 'I will think about it,' she promised. Perhaps she would be wise to forget about seeking Harry's help and use Ramirez to take her away from this place.

The stone floor of the kitchen hut did not give Bridie the most comfortable sleep she had ever had. Not that Ramirez allowed her much opportunity for sleep. He only left her at daybreak, when it was almost time for her to set about replenishing the fire to brew the morning coffee and prepare the men's breakfast.

Before she could begin, Lucas came into the hut. His arrival, so promptly after Ramirez' departure, made Bridie wonder if he had been waiting for the moment she was alone.

'I congratulate you, Bridie. You were very clever last night to turn a situation you did not like into one you could control. I would ask you if you enjoyed yourself with Ramirez except the question would be superfluous. You look as though you had little sleep.'

Because she knew he was mocking her, Bridie would not deign to answer when he paused in study of her face. 'The trouble is,' he continued, 'I did not get much sleep either. I lay awake thinking about the two of you in here and wishing I could join you.'

'I am surprised you didn't,' Bridie retorted.

'Would you have welcomed me if I had?'

'No.'

'There you have your answer. But before we leave here I will have what I want, Bridie. I want to see you in abandoned enjoyment of the attentions of all these men.' He pressed a firm finger against her mouth when she opened it to object. 'After a few days, after you have become accustomed to each of the men, and they to you, I believe you will be willing to accommodate the demands of any one of us. Right now you must accommodate me. I deserve something for allowing you Harry and your night with Ramirez.'

Lucas took her on her back on the floor in the age-old position, the swift coupling making her feel like an unawakened woman dutifully submitting to conjugal rights.

Despite her expectation of being subjected to numerous salacious remarks, not one of the men treated her any differently from the night before. Except Mick Dunn, who sauntered into the hut later than everyone else. Leering at Bridie, he gave voice to a crudely lewd comment which Bridie and the other men all ignored.

When, their breakfast finished, they had all drifted away again, Bridie detained Lucas to tell him of her need for a bath. 'I must at least wash even if I cannot bathe properly.'

'There is a wash basin on a bench in the lean-to behind the sleeping hut.'

Bridie gave Lucas a scathing look. 'I need somewhere considerably more private. The lean-to has no sides and I have no desire of an audience.'

'Perhaps you are right,' Lucas agreed, though Bridie knew he was envisaging her providing the men with erotic entertainment. 'Why not in here? I will bring you the wash basin, soap and towel.'

'Thank you,' said Bridie.

With the basin on the bench seat nearest the fireplace, Bridie tipped in hot water and added only sufficient cold water to reduce the temperature to a degree that was bearable. While she would have given anything to have been able to immerse herself in a full-sized bath tub she intended to make the best of what was available. She striped naked to enable her to thoroughly wash her entire body.

Lucas had also brought her a flannel. She wet and soaped it and, careful not to splash too much water on the floor, she rubbed it down her arms, across her shoulders and over her breasts. Rinsing the flannel, she wiped away the soapiness, the heat of the water feeling so very good. By the time her whole body had been scrubbed and rinsed Bridie was considerably refreshed.

There remained only her genital area to be cleaned. Bridie placed her right foot on the bench beside the basin and re-wet the flannel. Head down, she concentrated on washing thoroughly and carefully the creases and folds of her sex. She did not hear the door being opened quietly. Nor would she have thought Mick Dunn could move so silently until she heard his horrid, lecherous chuckle.

'I'll do that for you, beauty. Except it'll be my fingers pushing up your hole and then my cock.'

Looking into his leering face, Bridie knew she would never want, nor allow, this hateful man to touch her body. With calm movements that belied the nervous beating of her heart she lowered her foot, took up the towel which lay on the table and wrapped it securely around her body. She used her most cultured tone of voice in an endeavour to put him in his place.

'I am afraid it won't be either, Mr Dunn. We set the rules last night. You have to beat me at poker first.'

'Hah. That was last night, you snooty lush. You only got away with it then 'cause Martin was there. Well, he ain't here now and I am. You didn't make that toffee-nosed Harry Whoever-he-is win you at cards, either. I knew he was up you almost as soon as you got here. Well, it's my turn now and there ain't anyone going to stop me.'

He lunged towards Bridie, who had anticipated his move. She picked up the wash basin and threw it with all her strength. It hit Mick Dunn in the chest, drenching him and sending him staggering back. He swore viciously, his face contorted with fury. Bridie realised then just how dangerous a man he was. Step by step she began to back away from his determined advance, wondering if she could possibly reach the opposite side of the table to make a dash for the door.

There was the malicious gleam of the predator in the man's eyes. Mick Dunn would show her no mercy now. He was enjoying the fear she could no longer hide. From the corner of her eye Bridie saw the cast-iron frying pan where she had left it on the table. She grabbed it, threw it and made a wild scramble across the table in an attempt to reach the door.

She heard the pan thud against the wall and the man's blasphemous oaths. Then a rough hand was gripping her ankle and she was being hauled back over the table. Her leg was twisted painfully to flip her on her back. Staring up at Mick Dunn's lust-contorted face, Bridie kicked out with her free leg, somehow managing to catch him a glancing blow on the side of his face. The viciousness of his expression made her quail.

'You want it rough, eh, beauty? Well, I like a bit of rough stuff myself. Reckon it makes a woman real horny to be shown who's boss.'

He backhanded her savagely across the cheek to knock her head sideways. Bridie cried out at the pain then again at the brutality of his fingers thrusting between her thighs. She kicked him again in the stomach only to be rewarded with another slap.

'Keep that up, beauty, and you won't be too pretty by the time I've finished with you.'

'You've finished with her now.' Lucas stood in the doorway, his expression threatening, his eyes ice chips of anger.

'Oh yeah?' snarled Dunn, not moving away. 'You wouldn't want to stop her from enjoying herself with me.'

Lucas glanced pointedly at the tears in Bridie's eyes and the darkening bruise on her cheek. 'She doesn't look like she is enjoying herself.'

'Oh she is,' jeered Dunn, thrusting his finger so savagely back into Bridie she cried out again. 'You should feel how wet it is in here.'

'Let her go, Dunn.' Lucas's voice was dangerously quiet.

'Gonna make me?'

'If that's what you want.'

Lucas moved quickly. So did Mick Dunn but he was not quick enough to evade the punch aimed at his chin. A second sent him reeling back against the wall. He recovered to come at Lucas with a knife in his hand.

Crouched on the table, the towel gathered protectively around her body, Bridie saw the knife and screamed. There was a brief fierce struggle then Mick Dunn was staggering back against the wall again, the knife embedded in his side. There was a shot and Lucas fell too, clutching his shoulder.

Jack Dunn stood in the doorway with a smoking revolver in his hand. Harry, Ramirez and Jed Hayden crowded behind. Bridie sobbed quietly, the acrid smell of the gunpowder stinging her nostrils, her face aching. Jack Dunn glared at her with pure hatred.

'Help Mick,' he ordered over his shoulder to Jed, who pushed past to hurry to the man who had now slipped semi-conscious to the floor. Lucas, a hand pressed to a bleeding wound in his shoulder, was slowly getting to his feet.

'I told you I wanted no trouble,' Jack Dunn snarled. 'Take her and get out of here before I put another bullet in you and one in her, too.'

Lucas was pale with the pain of his wound but his eyes when he looked at Jack Dunn were hard with hatred. 'We would have been going anyway after what Mick tried. I think we can agree that from now on we are enemies.'

Bridie bound Lucas's shoulder to the best of her ability. Tears continued to stream down her cheeks. Having started to cry, she did not seem able to stop. Lucas reached his good hand to lay it gently against her bruised face.

'Are you crying for me or because of what that scoundrel did to you?'

'I don't know. Perhaps both.' The flow of tears increased. She sniffed them back and knew she was crying for a great many things.

His shoulder bandaged, Lucas curved his good arm around her shoulders to draw her against his chest. 'I am so very sorry, Bridie. I never intended for anything like that to happen.'

'Yet you brought me here, knowing what the Dunn men are like.'

'I thought it the safest place for us to go.'

205

'You also thought you could have your sexual fantasy.'

'Not originally.' Bridie lifted her head to look at him in surprise. 'I really only expected the Dunn brothers to be here. I knew Jack would not want to touch you and I thought I could handle Mick.'

'But, the others, the things you said you wanted me to do?'

'I would still like to do them. One day. Bridie, you weren't slow to renew your acquaintance with Harry and I could tell you were interested in Ramirez. It seemed like I had found the ideal opportunity to stretch you to the limits of your sexuality. I simply misjudged Mick Dunn.' He gave a deep sigh. 'Come on. We had better get going before Jack does decide to put those bullets in us both.'

Chapter Thirteen

Ramirez and Harry left with them. They were a sombre group who guided their horses back down the treacherous slope to the lower country. There they parted company – Harry and Ramirez to go in one direction, Bridie and Lucas in the other. Ramirez gave Bridie a long, searching look before he turned away. Inexplicable though it was, Bridie knew that, even given the chance to leave, she would choose to stay with Lucas.

Mid-afternoon they came to an isolated prospector's hut. There was no sign of the owner even though there were various evidences of its occupancy.

'We will stay here,' declared Lucas.

'What about the owner? Might not he object?'

'He might, but that is a chance I'll have to take. I cannot ride farther today.' He shrugged awkwardly out of his coat and opened his shirt to show her that his wound continued to bleed.

'I will change the dressing,' Bridie said quickly. 'There must be something I can use.'

She found a relatively clean sheet from which she tore long strips. Lucas nodded towards a whisky bottle on a shelf.

'It is an age-old remedy. Some of that might help

207

prevent infection and what you don't pour over the wound I can drink. Either way it's bound to help.'

He took several swigs from the bottle while Bridie redressed his shoulder, his eyes speculative on her face. 'Ramirez wanted you to go with him. Why didn't you?'

A frown drew Bridie's brows together. 'You were hurt. I did not want to leave you on your own.'

'Do you care about me, then?'

'I don't know.' She squatted back on her heels to look up at him. 'You confuse me, Lucas. You have made me fear you, at times to even hate you. You say things to me that I do not like. You are content to let other men have sex with me yet risk your life to save me from Mick Dunn.'

'I promised you I would never allow you to be hurt.'

'Yet you would do other things to me – with me. Like the night with Seamus.'

'Why does that bother you so much, Bridie? Because you enjoyed it more than you want to admit?'

Bridie lowered her eyes. 'It bothers me because I could not say no to what you wanted. If we had stayed at the Dunns' I would also have done what you wanted, as well you know.' She raised her eyes again to search his face. 'You have some kind of sexual power over me, Lucas, from which I cannot break.'

'Why do you want to? Is there any reason why we cannot stay together?'

Once again, even though she did not answer, her too expressive face gave her away.

'Who is he, Bridie? Nat Durrant?'

She felt her anguish tighten her face. 'Yes.'

'Does he love you?'

'He wants me. He wanted to set me up as his mistress.'

'But not make you his wife.'

'No.'

'What would you say if I asked you to become my wife?'

Startled, Bridie simply stared at Lucas. He reached

208

down with his good hand to pull her on to the bunk and lay down with her held against his body. 'You cannot dislike me too much, Bridie, or you would have gone with Ramirez and Harry. I would not have stopped you if you had made that choice. All I can say is that I am very pleased you didn't. This morning, when I saw what Mick Dunn was doing to you, I realised how much you have come to mean to me. Now what is the matter?'

Bridie was crying again. 'Everything you do, everything you say, only confuses me more. I will never understand you.'

'Then do not try. Let your body tell you what is right. I want you now, Bridie, but I am not going to move in case I start my shoulder bleeding again. If I lie quietly will you show me how much sexual control I have over you?'

Bridie helped him undress before shedding the shirt and trousers she was beginning to hate. Then, because her emotions were in tatters and because the things Lucas had said had created a confused ache in her heart, she made love to him.

She kissed him first, a softly sensual movement of her lips which tested the firmness of his. Lucas had a beautiful mouth; a mouth that was soon kissing her back. He was arching his head up in an endeavour to deepen the kiss, his tongue seeking entry to her mouth.

Bridie lifted slightly away. 'Lie still,' she ordered quietly. Her mouth followed the passage of her hands over the muscular contours of his chest. She traced the brown male nipples with her tongue and heard him suck in his breath. Lower down she teased around his navel then moved down to his shaft.

That rigid column she treated with adoration, her actions still gentle, drawing her fingers from tip to base then back again. Her tongue circled the definition of his glans, slid across the velvety skin and teased the tiny eye. She took his extremity in her mouth, sucking softly in the way which pleased him most.

Only when he cried out for her to stop did she kneel across him to lower herself down until he was fully encased. She rode him slowly, revelling in the enjoyment she was giving him. When, driven to the need for release, Lucas tried to thrust up, Bridie again ordered him to lie still.

Knowing he was on the brink of his climax, she ground down against his pelvis and began to circle her sex around his stationary shaft. First one way, then the other, until he was gasping and pulsing within her and her own hot juices were flowing out to dampen his pubic hair. Bridie leant forward then to lie against his chest, careful to avoid his injured shoulder. His other arm encircled her to hold her tightly. It was the most loving embrace they had shared.

Lucas slept after that, the loss of blood from his wound taking its toll. For a while Bridie sat watching him before going outside to walk around the hut and to think. Near the edge of the clearing in which the hut stood she saw a fallen tree and went to sit on the trunk. Elbows on knees, chin in hands, she pondered the enigma that was Lucas Martin.

The last thing Bridie had ever expected was that Lucas Martin should ask her to be his wife. She could not even be certain whether or not he had been serious. In the time that had followed, when she had made love to him, she had experienced an incredible tenderness, had really cared for this hard, complex man.

But now, sitting quietly with her thoughts, she knew he would never change. Bridie doubted she could ever really be certain whether he cared for her or not. Remembering the enmity between Lucas and Nat, she could not help wondering if Lucas was using her as a weapon in his vendetta against Nat. After all, she had virtually admitted it was Nat whom she loved. She just wished she knew how deep were Nat's feelings for her. She wished he had told her he cared for her too much to consider marrying Lisette.

Not so very far away Nat Durrant sat on a similar log, also deep in thought. Legs outstretched, he stared at the small flickering fire of twigs on which he had brewed the tea he now drank. A mist was settling and, if he did not find shelter soon, he would be spending another damp, uncomfortable night in the open.

Which was one reason he was deep in thought. Why Bridie Flannagan was so important to him that he followed their trail day after day was another. There was the near despair he experienced with each nightfall when he had failed to catch his quarry. That despair was exacerbated by the knowledge that while he lay alone Bridie was somewhere in the arms of Lucas Martin.

Not that Nat feared for Bridie's safety. She had told him in no uncertain terms of her intimacy with his sworn enemy. Nat had discovered he could not bear the thought of any man other than himself enjoying the passionate surrender of her body. That last twenty-four hours they had spent together had shown him just how much she had changed from the raw Irish lass he had first known.

Bridie dressed elegantly, carried herself with confidence, could hold an intelligent conversation, was well informed on many subjects and could deport herself with credit in any company. But underneath she was the same passionate Bridie, the woman he had considered beneath his station in life and had only wanted beneath his body. Nat had started her sexual education and he regretted now that he had not been the one to nurture her and watch her blossom and grow.

He recalled too that in the days since he had ridden away from Lisette he had given his betrothed scant thought. Even when he did think of her, Bridie's dark Irish beauty soon superimposed on Lisette's delicate fairness. Nat was beginning to realise that when – if – he got Bridie back he was not going to be able to let her go.

211

Hoofbeats, soft on the turfy ground, intruded into his thoughts. His awareness of them had him tensing, alert to the possibility he might be about to meet up with his quarry. But the rider who materialised through the dripping mist was an older man, grizzled of beard and gaunt of face.

'Can you spare a cup?' he asked, his gaze on the quartpot on the fire.

'Help yourself.' Nat poured another mug of tea for himself while the man dismounted.

Shrugging his coat around his shoulders, the newcomer rubbed his hands together. 'It'll be a cold one tonight. I'll be glad to get home.'

'Where is home?' asked Nat, the enquiry made for more than casual interest.

'A few miles further on. Got a small selection though I don't farm much. Spend most of my time scouting around the hills. Reckon there's got to be gold around here if only someone can find it.'

'Well, you may get lucky. You haven't seen anything of a man and a woman while you've been scouting around, have you?'

'Nope. Who are they? They lost or something?'

That unlikelihood had Nat's mouth shifting to a downward curl. 'I doubt it. I was following them for a few days then lost the trail yesterday when the mist came down. I haven't been able to pick it up again. I am beginning to wonder if they went up into the high country.'

'Might have. Why are you looking for them, if you don't mind me asking?'

'She's my woman. I want her back.'

The old man spat at the fire. 'Bah! Women. More trouble than they're worth. Never allowed one to tie me down and I never will. Where you staying tonight?'

'Could I beg your hospitality? I was envisaging a pretty cold night out.'

'You might've come across my place anyway if you're

heading north. It's only small and I ain't got much but I don't turn away anyone that needs food or shelter.'

'I have food. The shelter will be fine, thanks.'

By the time they were nearing the hut the mist had closed in. Trees which were no more than a few yards away were merely ghostly ill-defined shapes. The hut was itself no more than a solid mass in the mist, the horses which were tied outside barely visible.

'Must have visitors.' The prospector pulled his horse up with Nat reining in alongside. 'Them horses weren't there this morning.'

He went to ride on and Nat raised a cautionary hand. 'Wait. Two horses means two people.'

The old man gave him a sharp look. 'You mean the couple you are looking for?'

'Possibly. The man is almost certainly armed and he is not a person to be approached without caution.'

Shaggy brows rose in indignation. 'You never said anything about that. He must be the one that police patrol was looking for. Didn't mention it afore, did I? I met up with them not long before I come across you. They were looking for a man who might be with a woman.'

This time it was Nat who gave his companion an intent look. 'Why didn't you tell me?'

'Reckon you had your reasons for trying to find them on your own and they ain't no concern of mine.'

Nat was thinking quickly. 'I have a gut feeling they are your visitors. You must ride back and fetch the patrol.'

'Jeez, I dunno about that. I'd find my way back to the police sure enough but I don't reckon we'd be coming back tonight.'

'There is a fifty pounds reward for Lucas Martin's capture. Bring back the police and it's yours. I believe I can detain him until morning.'

When the prospector turned back through the mist, Nat dismounted, tethered his horse, and made his way cautiously towards the hut. Pressed near the wall to the side of the door, he paused to listen to the sounds from within. He heard Bridie's voice and the deeper man's voice answer. While the actual words were indistinguishable, he could tell from their tone neither person knew he was outside. Gun in hand, Nat turned to face the door and kicked it open.

Bridie jumped up with a startled gasp. Lucas, half propped on the bed, jerked his head around. Both stared at Nat who was rapidly noting that Lucas Martin was wounded, there was no firearm within easy reach, and Bridie was standing almost protectively by the bed.

'No welcome, Bridie?' he jibed. 'The last time I rescued you, you ran into my arms.'

Torn between pleasure at seeing Nat, curiosity as to how he came to be there, and concern for Lucas, Bridie remained silent.

Lucas drawled, 'So you found us, Durrant. You are probably the only man who could. I didn't know you cared enough to try.'

At that, Bridie tore her anguished gaze from Nat's face to look down at Lucas. Her eyes confirmed the deliberate challenge and she waited, a curling ache in her gut, for Nat's reply.

'I would care about the welfare of any woman who fell into your clutches.' He looked at Bridie again, the expression in his eyes hardening. Bridie remembered the bruise on her cheek. 'Did he do that to you? Because if he did –'

'No.' Bridie interrupted quickly. 'It wasn't Lucas. He saved me.'

'From what? Trouble he got you into?'

When she did not answer he turned back to Lucas. 'I find you wounded and Bridie with a bruised face. Perhaps you might tell me what the devil has been going on?'

'I might, if I knew whether you had come for Bridie or for me.'

'What difference does it make?'

'A great deal. You see, I happen to care for Bridie even if you don't. There is something else you should know. Bridie could have left me this morning. She chose to stay.'

'Why?' Nat barked the question at Bridie.

'He has lost a lot of blood. I was concerned for him.'

'You really care about him?' Nat was perplexed.

'I do.'

'More than you care for me?'

When Bridie remained silent, Lucas prompted her to answer. 'Tell him.'

Unable to look Nat in the eye, Bridie stared at the floor. 'I do not love Lucas.'

Nat was still, intent. 'Does that mean that you love me?'

'Yes.'

'Well then, you've got a damned peculiar way of showing it.'

'And you, Nat?' Bridie did stare into his eyes now. 'What have you ever shown me except lust?'

'I did not track you all this way for lust.'

'So,' drawled Lucas, who had watched them both with interest. 'What happens now? Are you going to shoot me, Durrant?'

'I am not in the habit of shooting people.'

'Nor,' declared Lucas in a hard-edged voice, 'am I. Unless there is a very good reason.'

The two men stared at each other, pale cold eyes holding hard brown ones in challenge. There was tension now in the room, so tangible it accelerated the beat of Bridie's heart. No longer their concern, she understood the bitterness of the vendetta that had torn these friends apart.

'Enough,' she cried. 'That's over long ago. Oh yes, Nat. I know the story and I understand why Lucas sought

215

revenge. I even understand why you are so bitter. But carrying it on to use me as a pawn between you I will not have. I will come with you, Nat. You can take me back home. I only ask that you let Lucas go.'

Nat shifted his gaze first. 'We are none of us going anywhere tonight, the mist outside is too thick. Give me his gun, Bridie. I don't want to be shot in the back.'

Lucas sneered. 'You won't be able to stay awake all night.'

'If I need to I will.'

Sometime in the early hours of the morning Bridie stirred. She had fallen asleep on the narrow bed after Lucas had rolled out a swag on the floor. Nat had settled in a chair beside the door. By the light from the glowing fire she saw that Nat had fallen asleep in the chair and that Lucas bent beside him to carefully retrieve his gun. She realised then that it had been Lucas's mouth brushing over hers that had brought her awake.

With the gun in his possession he glanced back and across the firelit room, their gazes held. Lucas raised a finger to his lips, mouthed the words, 'I'm coming back for you one day,' and cautiously opened the door. As he slipped through into darkness, and before the door was softly closed, Bridie saw that the mist had lifted and starlight bathed the night. Smiling to herself she rolled over and went back to sleep.

A hand shaking her shoulder woke her again to broad daylight. 'Wake up, we've got company. The police have arrived.'

Jerking to full wakefulness, Bridie sat up. 'You knew they were coming.' Then, fearfully. 'Lucas? Have they got him?'

'Not yet, but I have no doubt they soon will. I will go out and talk to them.' He gave her a hard look. 'If you are lucky they won't want to question you but if they do you had better make your story good.'

Whatever Nat said to the police was apparently convincing enough to send them away on the trail of Lucas. The old prospector brushed aside Bridie's apologies for presuming on his hospitality and then Nat and she were also on their way, riding silently through the dew-wet bush.

Perhaps Nat had a lot on his mind. Bridie certainly did. 'If you knew the police were coming why did you allow Lucas to get away? You knew he would if you fell asleep.'

'Isn't that what you wanted? I thought I would give him a chance, seeing as you appear to have become extremely fond of the man.'

'He asked me to marry him.'

'What?' Nat expressed disbelief. 'I don't believe it.'

'Why? Because you have never considered me worth marrying?'

Nat ignored her jibe. 'You would not have been happy with him.'

'I know. Otherwise I would have been with him now.'

'Then you would be arrested, too.'

'Lucas always boasted the police could never catch him and if they did he would get away.'

'So far that has been true. However, I think his luck might just have run out.'

While Lucas's luck might have run out, his mind had lost none of its cunning. He might be a wanted man. There might be a price on his head. There was double the amount on Jack Dunn's and an equal bounty on Mick's. Lucas Martin was small fry compared with the Dunn brothers. Following a brief persuasive discussion, Lucas was leading the police up to the high country to show them the pass that led to the Dunns' stronghold. The ubiquitous mist was again closing in and, while the police carefully guided their horse through the treacherous terrain, Lucas took advantage of the damp concealing veil to ride back down the valley to freedom.

* * *

Late afternoon Nat and Bridie reached a small settlement, one she recalled passing through with Lucas. Nat took rooms at the inn and left her on her own, telling her he would buy her some decent clothes.

'I could buy my own,' Bridie objected.

'Have you any idea of the sight you present? No. You will stay here until I come back.'

He returned some time later with a reasonably attractive dark-blue dress and undergarments. Bridie's thanks were effusive. In his absence she had seen in the mirror just how questionable a sight she did present, clad in the now filthy male garments, with her hair uncombed and the great bruise on her cheek.

By the time she had washed, brushed her hair and dressed, Bridie felt more like the elegant Bridie Flannagan of Rosalie. There was not much she could do about the bruise except hope that no one would be interested enough in her to take any notice; even though the gown flattered her figure and the colour enhanced the blueness of her eyes.

There were few customers in the inn's dining room, Nat having decreed they dine early. None took much notice of the man and woman who sat silently throughout their meal.

Bridie was beginning to wonder if Lucas or Nat was the most difficult man to understand. Not once, since that initial taut conversation in the hut, had he given any indication he wanted to be other than her escort back to Melbourne.

On Bridie's part each hour in his company increased the ache of her own longing. Nat was exhibiting none, his withdrawn manner making Bridie regret her confession of love. After all, she still did not know the true degree of Nat's feelings. When she considered the feud between him and Lucas, his cryptic statement in the hut about lust having no bearing on his pursuit of them might not have been connected with his feelings towards her at all.

218

'I need to go outside for a while,' Nat stated when they had finished their meal. 'Do you want to go to your room or wait for me here?'

'I will wait here. I can see the sunset from this window.'

Bridie had been watching the intensifying brilliance of the sunset for some minutes when a shadow fell across the table. Expecting it to be Nat, she turned to find herself looking up at the smiling dark face of Johnny Ramirez.

'So we meet again,' he said, sliding into the chair opposite. 'Where is Martin?'

'I don't know. We parted company.'

'Aah. Then I am even more pleased we have met again. You look quite different. I always wanted to see you in a dress. I would still like to see how beautiful you would be done up in finery. Not that you aren't beautiful when you are completely natural.' He regarded her with a sexually reminiscent smile. 'I am all alone, Bridie. Would you keep me company tonight?'

'I am not alone.'

Ramirez' face showed his disappointment. 'Have you found another man already?'

'He found me. He followed Lucas and me from Melbourne.'

'So now he has laid claim to you. You are a very popular woman, Bridie. All men seem to want you, I no less than any other. Lucas was good enough to share you. Who is this man who claims you? Would he be willing to share you, too?'

'I am that man.' Nat loomed over the table glowering at them both. 'And I do not share her with any other.'

Ramirez pushed back the chair to stand, lifting his hands in a deprecating gesture. Nat's attitude suggested any man who tried for Bridie's favours would find himself on the receiving end of an iron-fisted punch. 'No offence. I respect your claim. I told her myself that if she was mine I wouldn't be letting any other man near.' He gave Bridie another of his flashing smiles. 'I will cherish my memories.'

Silence followed his departure, Bridie not knowing what to say, Nat apparently choosing not to say anything until he tersely suggested they retire for the night.

'I want to get back to Barkers Ridge by tomorrow night. It will be a long ride and we must make an early start.'

At the door of her room he would have left her if Bridie had not put a detaining hand on his arm. 'Nat?' Her voice held a plea. 'Aren't you going to sleep with me tonight?'

He lifted his arm to shrug her hand away and looked her slowly, almost insultingly, up and down. When his gaze returned to her face she saw the indifference had gone from his eyes. In them blazed a turbulence of emotions, the only recognisable one of which was anger. His voice was tight with suppression of that anger.

'I am not going to touch you until every trace of every other man has been scrubbed from your body.'

Chapter Fourteen

*F*or a second time Bridie stepped into scented water in Nat's big copper bathtub. The first time it had been a new, almost decadent, experience. Such luxury was taken for granted now. However, having been deprived of it for so many days, Bridie lowered her body into the water with an enjoyment equivalent to that experienced the first time.

The only disappointing difference was that she bathed alone. After the long, hard day's ride Bridie was happy simply to lie back and allow the hot water to ease the aches from her body. The ride might not have seemed so bad if Nat had not maintained his taut, angry silence. He spoke only when it was absolutely necessary, answering her attempts to draw him into conversation with a brevity which soon discouraged her from trying to break through the barrier he had erected. Even after their arrival at the homestead he had spoken little.

Bridie leisurely soaped her body and, with some difficulty, managed the washing of her hair. She was tipping water over her head to rinse away the soap when Nat entered the room. Once again he was clad only in a robe and from the clean smell of him Bridie realised he had bathed elsewhere. He took the dipper from her hand. 'I will do that.'

When her hair was rinsed he took up the flannel, soaped it, and began to scrub her nearest arm. 'I have finished washing,' Bridie told him, only to be subjected to an implacable stare.

'I want to make certain every trace of every other man is washed away.'

Nat scrubbed Bridie's body with a vigour he might have used if he had been scrubbing away the grime from a coal mine. There was not an inch of her body that was not scrubbed so hard her skin stung.

Satisfied at last, Nat pulled her to her feet and when she stepped out of the bath he dried her with the same roughness. The towel was tossed aside and she was scooped in his arms to be carried through to the bed. He set her down, shrugged off his robe, parted her legs and climbed over her.

His shaft came swiftly at her opening, paused momentarily at the entrance to be assured of her readiness, and drove straight in. Bridie exhaled on a soft gasp, her eyes wide, searching Nat's. She saw the suppressed anger which flickered for a moment before becoming transferred to his rod. Almost savagely he thrust and pounded, to the delight of Bridie's inner flesh.

'Nat, Nat,' she cried, arching up to meet him thrust for thrust, his savage need of her igniting her own wild response. For all the sex she had enjoyed since last they were together, her body was acting like it was starved for this one man. Her climax when it came was as tumultuous as their coupling.

Then Nat's mouth was devouring hers in hungry possession, his pelvis jerking with the slower thrusts of his release. Bridie lifted her legs around his waist and wound her arms around his neck. Her breasts were crushed beneath his chest, her mouth mobile in response to the turbulent kiss, their bodies locked together in passion.

Forever it seemed, they remained in that position,

Nat's kiss devouring, his shaft pressed within. Eventually he lifted his head and raised his torso to take the weight off her breasts. Propped on his hands he made a few perfunctory strokes within her.

'I had to take you like that. You have been driving me to the limit of self-control with my need of you.'

Bridie, contented now, clenched her muscles wickedly around his softening cock. 'Is your need fully satisfied?'

'I have only taken the edge off my appetite. There is another hunger which has yet to be appeased. We will dine first, before you make up to me for all the torment you put me through.'

'You are forgetting my torment.'

Nat's expression was puzzled. 'Are you referring to Martin?'

'To you. You have tormented me by never telling me how much I really mean to you.'

'You must know that by now, if indeed you ever had cause to doubt.'

'I have never been completely certain.'

'So I have things to make up to you, too.'

'Most definitely,' declared Bridie.

Nat's lips were instruments of torturous pleasure. By her own choice Bridie lay on the sheepskin in front of the fire, wanting to enjoy the sensual feel of the fibres against her skin. At first Nat had stretched out beside her, propped on an elbow to gaze at her face while his hand toyed lazily with her far breast.

Wanting him so very much she had stretched sensuously, her gaze beguiling. She saw the half-amused expression in Nat's eyes change and his hand stilled on her breast. His features went tight while his eyes flamed.

'What is it?' she asked. 'What is the matter?'

'You. When you stretch your beautiful body like that, offering it to me, inviting me to take you as I choose, I remember that you have done that for other men. I find it very hard to control my anger when I think of the others who have had you. Especially after we had been so ardently together again.'

Annoyed that he should remind her of those things, Bridie spoke more sharply than she intended. 'Then do not think.'

'How can I help it when you took delight in taunting me with your lovers?' Nat retaliated.

Bridie held his eyes with a steady gaze. 'I believe you know the reason why,' she said softly.

Nat resumed his casual caress of her breast. 'If you planned to make me suffer you certainly succeeded.'

'I planned to make you beg. I was not going to allow you to have sex with me again until you went down on your knees to beg my favours.'

'Why did you relent?'

'I wanted you. I also realised it would take a great deal to make Nat Durrant go down on his knees for any woman.'

Nat moved to kneel. 'I am on my knees for you now, Bridie, except I won't be using words to beg. I can think of better ways to coax you to surrender your lovely body to mine.'

His lips were the instrument he employed. Starting on her face he kissed her closed eyelids, the tip of her nose, the corners of her mouth. Erotic lips moved around beneath her chin then back to her mouth again to coax her lips apart in a softly seductive kiss.

Floating on a cloud of bliss, Bridie allowed herself to pretend they had returned to that faraway night when Nat had taken her unawakened body along a path of sensual discovery. Somewhere during that journey she had discovered love. On reaching its end she knew she had developed into a sexually confident woman. That in itself would have been sufficient to make her eternally grateful to Nat if her heart had not gotten in the way.

With remembered thoroughness Nat was again awakening her body to desire. Kisses touched the undersides of her breasts and the valley between. Nat kissed the

224

peak of each breast, the nipple enclosed in lips that pressed on the areola.

Lower they moved, touching every inch of skin, even the sides of her waist, and lingering at her navel before skating over the flat plane of her abdomen to reach the edge of softly curled dark hair.

As before he moved to her toes to work with tantalising slowness up her leg to her inner thigh, his lips stopping just short of the wanton flesh which quivered for his touch. And again he did the same with her other leg but, when he would have rolled her to continue the caress of her back, Bridie cried out.

'No. Don't make me wait, Nat. I could not bear it.'

He leant over her, eyes gleaming. 'Who is begging now?'

'I am.'

'What are you begging for?'

'Don't tease.' The plea was close to a groan, so fiercely was her sex tingling. 'I want your mouth on me.' When still he did not move she added, 'I want you tasting me, licking me. Please.'

Nat kissed her gently on her mouth. 'You plead so beautifully. How can I refuse? I will remain on my knees to beg this time the sweetness of your essence.'

He lifted Bridie's thighs and sat back on his heels between them. Very gently he drew her towards him, her buttocks sliding over his thighs and up his torso until her pulsing sex had been brought within easy reach of his mouth. To Bridie's continuing frustration and delight Nat continued to tease by kissing the highest extremities of each of her inner thighs. When his lips did touch the centre of her sex he simply held them there in a passive kiss which had her flesh pulsing for more.

'Such lovely sweet lips beneath mine,' he murmured, raising his head slightly before lowering it again to nuzzle her. Mobile lips moved folds, to find creases, then the peak of all sensation, to suck on it and send Bridie into a continuum of moaning approval.

Nat's tongue replaced his lips, the tip sliding along her central crease from base to tip again and again. In inverted shivering pleasure Bridie's body convulsed each time that marvellous tongue ran across her nub. From a teasing, licking instrument his tongue was turned into a probe which pushed into her. The lingual probe made several stabbing actions, each of which raised the level of Bridie's delight. Erotic sensation shivered along heated veins, nerve endings pulsed and all of the most wonderful pleasures in the world were there between her thighs.

Stabbing became licking, then a feathering that teased her peak to ecstasy. Liquid fire pooled in her core then burst upward in volcanic response. Nat's mouth sucked hard on her sex, drawing up her flow, tongue stabbing and flicking to coax more. Mouth sucking again until her body was spent.

Carefully moving out from beneath her, Nat lowered her to the floor. He turned her immediately on to her hands and knees and came into her swiftly from behind. Bridie's sheath welcomed the filling of the climactic void. Holding her hips with firm hands, Nat pumped into her with force. He paused, bent over her back to reach under her body. One arm curved across her breasts. A finger of his other hand located her still highly sensitised nub.

In orgasm once more, Bridie cried out. Nat was grinding into her, circling his pelvis, stroking every part of her sex-salved canal to maximise her pleasure. His hands shifted to her shoulders to massage them. Strong fingers moved across her scalp and through the long strands of her hair. Those strands were twisted in his fingers, her head drawn up while he thrust with renewed vigour.

Bridie felt the power of his climax, her body pulsing in response. Nat shifted back to sit on his heels, pulling her upright and back against his body. With one hand kneading her breast, the other massaging her nub and his lips

226

passionate on the side of her neck, he renewed her orgasm while his own throbbed deep within her body.

The next day, Nat left her. For all Bridie's insistence she go home to Rosalie, Nat was adamant she remain at Barkers Ridge.

'The police were not entirely convinced of your innocence. They suspected you of being Lucas Martin's accomplice. For your own safety you would be wise to remain here. I have influence in high places. A few words to the right people, perhaps even a bribe or two, will ensure you are not bothered when you do return.'

'When will that be?'

'Never, if I had my way. From the very first I wanted you with me always. My feelings have not changed.'

'Nor your offer, either?' Bridie asked quietly.

Nat's expression became sombre. 'I am not in a position to change that, Bridie. I cannot ask you to marry me while I am betrothed to Lisette.'

'Ah yes,' said Bridie, 'Lisette. The eminently suitable fiancée who has everything Nat Durrant perceives as important in a bride. Except, perhaps, the one thing he expects.'

'Is that jealousy speaking, Bridie, or do you know something I do not?' Nat's eyes narrowed in suspicion. 'Just what are you hinting at?'

'That,' stated Bridie carefully, 'is for you to find out.'

That fateful afternoon when Lisette had gone to meet Seamus had been a revelation to the girl in more ways than one. The first had been Bridie's admission of being Nat's lover. The last had been the expression in Nat's eyes when he declared his intention of going after Bridie. In between there had been the wildly improbable, carnally sublime experience with Seamus and the policemen.

By the end of that afternoon Lisette had resolved her quandary. Once for such a magnificent sexual encounter could never be enough. Lisette knew she was addicted to the narcissistic pleasure of surrendering her body to the salacious attentions of men. One man, no matter how virile, would never be able to satisfy her sexual ego.

No matter for the hurt and embarrassment it would cause her parents, for the anger and humiliation it would cause Nat Durrant, Lisette was going to run away to Paris with her dear Mr Graham. She faced the truth of how stifled she would be as a grazier's wife, both artistically and sexually. With Mr Graham as her champion the horizons of both her passions would be wide.

Her decision having been taken, their plans were made swiftly. Sally, the maid, was the only one Lisette trusted. Her silence and loyalty would be well rewarded. Lisette's bags were packed and hidden in the wardrobe, the arrangements in place for an early morning flight. If the weather was favourable their ship would be well out of the harbour before anyone realised they were gone. There was only one person to whom Lisette wished to say goodbye.

Sally took the message to Seamus, asking him to meet Lisette in the deserted house. This time Lisette had Mr Graham accompany her. Seamus was waiting and it was with trembling excitement Lisette led the two men inside. They went to the dining room, the scene, Lisette considered, of her greatest sexual triumph.

While she was not able to re-enact it, Lisette knew what she wanted – to do absolutely nothing. The men were to do everything to her. Theirs was the choice. Hers would be the pleasure. Her only demand was that they take off their clothing first. Lisette fancied the idea of being undressed by two naked men.

Having used his influence to make certain Bridie was no longer under suspicion by the police, Nat set off for the Cunninghams' to speak with Lisette. He hoped she would be understanding and accept that it was no insult to her that he wanted to marry Bridie. Nat was basically a man of honour and if Lisette was to be too distressed by the cancellation of their engagement then he would have to go through with the marriage. Even though the certain loss of Bridie would tear him apart.

If that happened he would only have himself to blame for not securing her when she was his alone. Whatever happened with Lisette, Nat intended to keep Bridie at Barkers Ridge for as long as she would stay. Perhaps if he loved her well enough they could reach a compromise. After all, Nat would not be the first man to love his mistress more than his wife.

Because his entire future depended on his talk with his betrothed, Nat was chagrined to learn she was not at home. No one was able to tell him where she had gone except it was somewhere with her painting master to paint. The time of her return was uncertain. All Nat could be told was that she had been gone over an hour.

Not particularly keen on the frustration of having to cool his heels in the genteel atmosphere of the Cunninghams' house, Nat decided to fill the time in going out to Rosalie. He wanted to assure Bridie's servants she was safe and have her maid pack whatever clothing she thought her mistress might need. Nat also wanted a word with Seamus O'Flynn. Regardless of the outcome of his interview with Lisette, he wanted every one of Bridie's former lovers out of her life.

At Rosalie Nat spoke with Rogers, left instructions for Bridie's maid and, on asking where the young Irishman could be found, was informed he had been seen walking down the path to the neighbouring property.

Several things came rushing into Nat's mind. He remembered Lisette and Seamus had come from there the afternoon Bridie was taken. There was a mental image of the painting of an old pavilion which Lisette had shown him with justifiable pride. Most vividly he recalled Bridie's innuendo of there being something about Lisette which he did not know. The faint suspicion she had raised in his mind he had dismissed as feminine pique. Now, as he strode the path through the bush, Nat

229

acknowledged that Bridie was not a person to indulge in malicious spite. When he saw the horses outside the house he was almost certain what he would find inside.

When Lisette was naked she was lifted to the table. There she was tied on her back with bonds Mr Graham had brought for that purpose. Cushions were found to push beneath her buttocks, the raising of her pelvis seemingly opening her wider. Her avaricious flesh pulsed in anticipation and she wondered which man would touch her first. They had devised a special pleasure. Twin tongues began to flick at that flesh to coax her body to moist and eager response. Lisette felt herself bound in delight.

Those tongues touched her everywhere, together and in different places. While one man licked her sex the other would suck her breasts. Seamus did so gently. Mr Graham dragged each nipple through his teeth to make her gasp with pain and her sex tingle with heightened awareness of Seamus's tongue thrusting like a tiny penis.

Mr Graham was the one who made her come. He licked, teased and sucked her quim while Seamus knelt astride her body thrusting his organ between her breasts. This for Lisette was a new experience and she revelled in the feel of him sliding against her breastbone. Seamus's hands pushed her breasts together to make a sheath for his cock. His thumbs rubbed her nipples, the long strokes of his rod taking it up to hit against her chin.

Lisette thought he would come all over her. His thrusts seemed to become more urgent when Mr Graham's mouth took her to the edge of the climactic precipice and tipped her over. Panting her pleasure, she arched against her bonds, hands clenched, body tensed to ongoing delight.

Both men maintained their control. They knelt either side of her chest, their organs held down towards her mouth. Aroused by their subtle differences, Lisette turned her head from side to side. Her tongue licked first at one then the other.

Seamus had the weaker self-control. He pulled away with a panting declaration of his need to bury himself inside her. Mr Graham wanted Lisette to take him in her mouth. They untied her and carried her into the adjoining parlour. There Mr Graham sat on a sofa with Lisette on her knees in front of him. Without hesitation she curved her hand around his shaft to take it in her mouth. Positioned behind her, also on his knees, Seamus slid his rod deep into her moist canal. The harder he thrust the more avidly Lisette sucked on Mr Graham's shaft.

Not one of the three saw Nat pause outside the window then quickly step away.

Though he was deeply shocked Nat was not totally surprised. With every step that had brought him closer to the deserted house, and the certainty of that being where he would find Lisette, Nat recalled a multitude of incidents, of guarded expressions, of nuances of voice that had seemed, each in its own, unremarkable at the time. Gathered together they gave substance to what Bridie had suggested.

While Nat had skirted the empty house with every expectation of finding Lisette with a lover, he had certainly never expected to find her in so carnal a situation with not one man but two. He could barely begin to imagine what else she might have done. Nor did he wish to find out.

Silently moving away, Nat found his shock being replaced by anger, a scathing self-anger that he could have allowed himself to have been so deceived. The bitterest gall was that it might very well have cost him Bridie. There was something else he realised which showed him the true state of his heart.

Apart from his natural anger at her deceit Nat found himself unconcerned by what his betrothed was doing. There had been no sickening clench of his gut at the sight of her with one man's cock in her mouth and another between her thighs. Yet when Bridie had taunted him with having done similar he had been driven to a near-murderous rage. He knew if it had been Bridie in that room instead of Lisette he would not be walking calmly away.

On their first afternoon in that house Seamus had quickly learnt all of Lisette's desires. He moistened his thumb to push it into her anal opening. Lisette would have cried out her delight if her mouth had not been so full of Mr Graham. She was taking him deep in her throat knowing he would be able to withhold his climax for as long as he chose. That was his special skill, his ability to refrain from orgasm and give her several before he allowed his own. Seamus did not have the same control. Lisette felt him jerk inside her sex, which clenched and moistened in exultant response.

When he shifted free, Mr Graham urged her to turn and sit over him so that his spear could drive into the opening prepared by Seamus's thumb. Lisette sucked in her breath as she lowered herself on to the thin rigid pole then exhaled in delight. Body arched back, hand on the sofa for support, guided by Mr Graham's hands on her hips, Lisette flexed up and down. Soon she was panting from the long-enjoyed pleasure of having that thin spear of manhood driving in her bottom-hole.

Standing nearby, Seamus clasped his cock in his hand to bring himself to hardness again. He was watching Lisette, eagerness in his eyes. When he stepped forward to touch her moist slit with his free hand Lisette gasped.

'Do it,' she ordered. 'I want you both.'

Seamus straddled them both. A knee resting against the sofa on one side and a foot flat on the other, he guided the head of his shaft to Lisette's front opening. Mr Graham held her steady. Seamus pushed. Lisette gasped. With her bottom already filled by one organ the entry of the other was rendered incredibly tight. By the time Seamus had pushed all the way to his depth Lisette was in orgasm again. Seamus was the only one able to move, to make slow careful thrusts. Mr Graham used the tensing of his buttocks to work his cock. Lisette near swooned from the incredible sensation of having two shafts moving within her body. Sandwiched between her lovers in orgasmic bliss, Lisette cried loudly her carnal delight at having two men come in her at once.

Nat had decided not to wait for Lisette and her lovers to emerge from the house. He found himself reluctant to face her when the scent of sex would be so heavy on her body. Instead he left as soon as he had arrived and called on her that evening. He noted she seemed disturbed to see him, asking quickly after Bridie.

'She is safe. For the moment she is staying at Barkers Ridge.'

'I am relieved. I really like Bridie. You like her too, don't you, Nat?'

'Why do you ask?'

'Because she –.' Lisette's courage failed her.

'Because Bridie will make me a better wife?' Nat asked quietly. Lisette had the grace to drop her gaze. 'I came here intending to beg you to release me from our engagement. Instead I discover I have every entitlement to call it off.'

When Lisette's gaze shot up in fearful query, Nat's lip curled. 'I was looking for O'Flynn and was told he had gone to the old house. You were clever in your deceit, Lisette. I thought you an innocent virgin.'

Lisette's main reaction was relief at Nat's apparent lack of anger. She tossed her head in defiance. 'Well, I am not, nor have I been for some time. But if it appeases your pride, I had no intention of going through with our marriage anyway. My bags are already packed. Tomorrow Mr Graham and I sail for Europe. We are going to Paris where I will study art. My parents,' she added, 'do not know.'

Nat slowly nodded his head. 'I see. Then perhaps things have worked out for the best after all. I have

233

always been aware you have great artistic talent, Lisette. I wish you well.'

Left on her own at Barkers Ridge, Bridie soon became bored. On the third day, from a combination of restlessness and curiosity, she asked Jim to saddle her a horse and rode back down the valley to her former home. She found it to be in surprisingly good condition and remembered Nat saying it was useful for housing itinerant workers.

There were so many memories which came rushing back. Bridie walked to her father's grave and stood looking at the sturdy cross Seamus had made. The man who had planted his seed in her mother's womb had also been responsible for the more recent dramatic changes in her life.

Because of Flannagan's dishonest activities she had been brought to the attention of both Nat Durrant and Lucas Martin. Two powerful men, both sexually dominant. One she loved, the other she lusted for even while she feared. By a quirk of fate they were the bitterest of enemies. Bridie could not rid herself of the notion she had now become a part of the feud between the two.

Back in the hut she was staring at the cold empty fireplace when she heard the sound of the approaching horse. The door was flung open and Nat loomed within its frame. Except for the absence of a rifle in his hand there was a strong sense of *déjà vu*.

'So,' he declared, eyes gleaming. 'I find Flannagan's delectable daughter alone. Undress. I want to see you naked.'

With hands which trembled and with the moist thrill of anticipation in her sex, Bridie did as she was bid. This time she knew what to expect. Nat stood watching each garment being peeled away.

'As beautiful as I remember,' he murmured. 'I wonder if you will still feel so silky and wonderful encasing my cock. Bend over the table.'

Enjoying the charade, Bridie turned to lay her upper torso on the table, her buttocks raised towards Nat. She heard him fumbling with his trousers then fingers probed her wetness to find her ready. Hard male muscle displaced the fingers to slide deliciously deep. Bridie sighed and Nat chuckled.

'You don't know how much I am looking forward to having you always ready for me like this.' He began to move his hips, his shaft sliding back and forth. 'You must promise you will be. It is a wife's duty to obey.'

Perhaps it was not the most romantic of proposals but happiness swelled Bridie's heart and sent a glow throughout her body. When it came to sex, she knew there would never be any question of disobeying.

If only she could forget Lucas's silently mouthed promise. 'I'll come back for you, one day.'

BLACK LACE NEW BOOKS

Published in October

SEARCHING FOR VENUS
Ella Broussard
£5.99

Art history student Louise decides to travel to rural France to track down a lost painting – the sensuous *Venus of Collioure* – whose disappearance is one of the mysteries of the art world. She is about to embark on another quest: one which will bring her sexual fulfilment with a number of dashing Frenchmen!

ISBN 0 352 33284 0

UNDERCOVER SECRETS
Zoe le Verdier
£5.99

Anna Caplin is a TV reporter. When her boss offers her the chance to infiltrate a secret medical institute, she grabs the opportunity – not realising the institute specialises in human sexual response. It isn't long before Anna finds herself involved in some highly unorthodox situations with Doctor Galloway – the institute's director.

ISBN 0 352 33285 9

Published in November

FORBIDDEN FRUIT
Susie Raymond
£5.99

Beth is thirty-eight. Jonathan is sixteen. An affair between them is unthinkable. Or is it? To Jonathan, Beth is much more exciting than girls his own age. She's a real woman: sexy, sophisticated and experienced. And Beth can't get the image of his fit young body out of her mind. Although she knows she shouldn't encourage him, the temptation is irresistible. What will happen when they have tasted the forbidden fruit?

ISBN 0 352 33306 5

HOSTAGE TO FANTASY
Louisa Francis
£5.99

Bridie Flannagan is a spirited young Irish woman living a harsh life in outback Australia at the turn of the century. A reversal of fortune enables her to travel to the thriving city of Melbourne and become a lady. But rugged bushranger Lucas Martin is in pursuit of her; he wants her money and she wants his body. Can they reach a civilised agreement?

ISBN 0 352 33305 7

To be published in December

A SECRET PLACE
Ella Broussard
£5.99

Maddie is a locations scout for a film company. When a big-budget Hollywood movie is made in rural UK in the summer, she is delighted to be working on-set. Maddie loves working outdoors – and with a hunky good-looking crew of technicians and actors around her, there are plenty of opportunities for her to show off her talents.

ISBN 0 352 33307 3

A PRIVATE VIEW
Crystalle Valentino
£5.99

Successful catwalk model Jemma has everything she needs. Then a dare from a colleague to pose for a series of erotic photographs intrigues her. Jemma finds that the photographer, Dominic, and his jet-setting friends, have interesting sexual tastes. She finds their charms irresistible but what will happen to her career if she gives in to her desires?

ISBN 0 352 33308 1

SUGAR AND SPICE 2
A short-story collection
£6.99

Sugar and Spice anthologies mean Black Lace short stories. And erotic short stories are extremely popular. The book contains 20 diverse and seductive tales guaranteed to ignite and excite. This second compendium pushes the boundaries to bring you stories which go beyond romance and explore the no-holds barred products of the female erotic imagination. Only the best and most arousing stories make it into a Black Lace anthology.

ISBN 0 352 33309 X

If you would like a complete list of plot summaries of Black Lace titles, please fill out the questionnaire overleaf or send a stamped addressed envelope to:

Black Lace, Thames Wharf Studios, Rainville Road, London W6 9HT

BLACK LACE BOOKLIST

All books are priced £4.99 unless another price is given.

Black Lace books with a contemporary setting

ODALISQUE	Fleur Reynolds ISBN 0 352 32887 8	☐
VIRTUOSO	Katrina Vincenzi ISBN 0 352 32907 6	☐
THE SILKEN CAGE	Sophie Danson ISBN 0 352 32928 9	☐
RIVER OF SECRETS	Saskia Hope & Georgia Angelis ISBN 0 352 32925 4	☐
SUMMER OF ENLIGHTENMENT	Cheryl Mildenhall ISBN 0 352 32937 8	☐
MOON OF DESIRE	Sophie Danson ISBN 0 352 32911 4	☐
A BOUQUET OF BLACK ORCHIDS	Roxanne Carr ISBN 0 352 32939 4	☐
THE TUTOR	Portia Da Costa ISBN 0 352 32946 7	☐
THE HOUSE IN NEW ORLEANS	Fleur Reynolds ISBN 0 352 32951 3	☐
WICKED WORK	Pamela Kyle ISBN 0 352 32958 0	☐
DREAM LOVER	Katrina Vincenzi ISBN 0 352 32956 4	☐
UNFINISHED BUSINESS	Sarah Hope-Walker ISBN 0 352 32983 1	☐
THE DEVIL INSIDE	Portia Da Costa ISBN 0 352 32993 9	☐
HEALING PASSION	Sylvie Ouellette ISBN 0 352 32998 X	☐
THE STALLION	Georgina Brown ISBN 0 352 33005 8	☐

Black Lace books with an historical setting

PLEASURE'S DAUGHTER £5.99	Sedalia Johnson ISBN 0 352 33237 9	☐
SAVAGE SURRENDER £5.99	Deanna Ashford ISBN 0 352 33253 0	☐
CIRCO EROTICA £5.99	Mercedes Kelly ISBN 0 352 33257 3	☐
BARBARIAN GEISHA £5.99	Charlotte Royal ISBN 0 352 33267 0	☐
DARKER THAN LOVE £5.99	Kristina Lloyd ISBN 0 352 33279 4	☐

Black Lace anthologies

PAST PASSIONS £6.99	ISBN 0 352 33159 3	☐
PANDORA'S BOX 2 £4.99	ISBN 0 352 33151 8	☐
PANDORA'S BOX 3 £5.99	ISBN 0 352 33274 3	☐
SUGAR AND SPICE £7.99	ISBN 0 352 33227 1	☐

Black Lace non-fiction

WOMAN, SEX AND ASTROLOGY £5.99	Sarah Bartlett ISBN 0 352 33262 X	☐

------×------------------

Please send me the books I have ticked above.

Name   ....

Address   ....

            ....

            ....

            .... Post Code ....

Send to: **Cash Sales, Black Lace Books, Thames Wharf Studios, Rainville Road, London W6 9HT.**

US customers: for prices and details of how to order books for delivery by mail, call 1-800-805-1083.

Please enclose a cheque or postal order, made payable to **Virgin Publishing Ltd**, to the value of the books you have ordered plus postage and packing costs as follows:

UK and BFPO – £1.00 for the first book, 50p for each subsequent book.

Overseas (including Republic of Ireland) – £2.00 for the first book, £1.00 each subsequent book.

If you would prefer to pay by VISA or ACCESS/MASTERCARD, please write your card number and expiry date here:

....

Please allow up to 28 days for delivery.

Signature ....

------×------------------

B L A C K
lace

WE NEED YOUR HELP ...
to plan the future of women's erotic fiction –

– and no stamp required!

Yours are the only opinions that matter.

Black Lace is the first series of books devoted to erotic fiction by women for women.

We intend to keep providing the best-written, sexiest books you can buy. And we'd appreciate your help and valued opinion of the books so far. Tell us what you want to read.

THE BLACK LACE QUESTIONNAIRE

SECTION ONE: ABOUT YOU

1.1 Sex (*we presume you are female, but so as not to discriminate*)
Are you?
Male	☐
Female	☐

1.2 Age
under 21	☐	21–30	☐
31–40	☐	41–50	☐
51–60	☐	over 60	☐

1.3 At what age did you leave full-time education?
still in education	☐	16 or younger	☐
17–19	☐	20 or older	☐

1.4 Occupation _____

1.5 Annual household income _____

1.6 We are perfectly happy for you to remain anonymous;
     but if you would like to receive information on other
     publications available, please insert your name and
     address

     _____

     _____

     _____

     _____

SECTION TWO: ABOUT BUYING BLACK LACE BOOKS

2.1 Where did you get this copy of *Hostage to Fantasy*?
     Bought at chain book shop   ☐
     Bought at independent book shop   ☐
     Bought at supermarket   ☐
     Bought at book exchange or used book shop   ☐
     I borrowed it/found it   ☐
     My partner bought it   ☐

2.2 How did you find out about Black Lace books?
     I saw them in a shop   ☐
     I saw them advertised in a magazine   ☐
     I read about them in _____
     Other _____

2.3 Please tick the following statements you agree with:
     I would be less embarrassed about buying Black
     Lace books if the cover pictures were less explicit   ☐
     I think that in general the pictures on Black
     Lace books are about right   ☐
     I think Black Lace cover pictures should be as
     explicit as possible   ☐

2.4 Would you read a Black Lace book in a public place – on
     a train for instance?
     Yes   ☐   No   ☐

SECTION THREE: ABOUT THIS BLACK LACE BOOK

3.1 Do you think the sex content in this book is:
    Too much ☐ About right ☐
    Not enough ☐

3.2 Do you think the writing style in this book is:
    Too unreal/escapist ☐ About right ☐
    Too down to earth ☐

3.3 Do you think the story in this book is:
    Too complicated ☐ About right ☐
    Too boring/simple ☐

3.4 Do you think the cover of this book is:
    Too explicit ☐ About right ☐
    Not explicit enough ☐

Here's a space for any other comments:

SECTION FOUR: ABOUT OTHER BLACK LACE BOOKS

4.1 How many Black Lace books have you read? ☐

4.2 If more than one, which one did you prefer?

4.3 Why?

SECTION FIVE: ABOUT YOUR IDEAL EROTIC NOVEL

We want to publish the books you want to read – so this is your chance to tell us exactly what your ideal erotic novel would be like.

5.1 Using a scale of 1 to 5 (1 = no interest at all, 5 = your ideal), please rate the following possible settings for an erotic novel:

Medieval/barbarian/sword 'n' sorcery ☐
Renaissance/Elizabethan/Restoration ☐
Victorian/Edwardian ☐
1920s & 1930s – the Jazz Age ☐
Present day ☐
Future/Science Fiction ☐

5.2 Using the same scale of 1 to 5, please rate the following themes you may find in an erotic novel:

Submissive male/dominant female ☐
Submissive female/dominant male ☐
Lesbianism ☐
Bondage/fetishism ☐
Romantic love ☐
Experimental sex e.g. anal/watersports/sex toys ☐
Gay male sex ☐
Group sex ☐

5.3 Using the same scale of 1 to 5, please rate the following styles in which an erotic novel could be written:

Realistic, down to earth, set in real life ☐
Escapist fantasy, but just about believable ☐
Completely unreal, impressionistic, dreamlike ☐

5.4 Would you prefer your ideal erotic novel to be written from the viewpoint of the main male characters or the main female characters?

Male ☐ Female ☐
Both ☐

5.5 What would your ideal Black Lace heroine be like? Tick as many as you like:

Dominant	☐	Glamorous	☐
Extroverted	☐	Contemporary	☐
Independent	☐	Bisexual	☐
Adventurous	☐	Naive	☐
Intellectual	☐	Introverted	☐
Professional	☐	Kinky	☐
Submissive	☐	Anything else?	☐
Ordinary	☐		

5.6 What would your ideal male lead character be like? Again, tick as many as you like:

Rugged	☐		
Athletic	☐	Caring	☐
Sophisticated	☐	Cruel	☐
Retiring	☐	Debonair	☐
Outdoor-type	☐	Naive	☐
Executive-type	☐	Intellectual	☐
Ordinary	☐	Professional	☐
Kinky	☐	Romantic	☐
Hunky	☐		
Sexually dominant	☐	Anything else?	☐
Sexually submissive	☐		

5.7 Is there one particular setting or subject matter that your ideal erotic novel would contain?

_____

SECTION SIX: LAST WORDS

6.1 What do you like best about Black Lace books?

_____

6.2 What do you most dislike about Black Lace books?

_____

6.3 In what way, if any, would you like to change Black Lace covers?

_____

6.4 Here's a space for any other comments:

_____

_____

_____

_____

Thank you for completing this questionnaire. Now tear it out of the book – carefully! – put it in an envelope and send it to:

Black Lace
FREEPOST PAM 6899
London
W6 9BR

No stamp is required if you are resident in the U.K.